NOT UNDER THE LAW

Yes, he knew he was a transgressor of the law. He had broken the law of the land. Everybody else was doing it, some doing it bunglingly, and not getting away with it. He despised them. He had gone into it more for the game than the money. He had known he could do it without discovery.

But he had not gotten away with it. He had been discovered. And by that girl! Not only that, but by the girl he most honored in all the earth!

Suddenly, he knew that he loved her. He had loved her all along. That was why he was going after her. She was lost and he was finding her. And somehow it was beginning to dawn upon his soul that he would not find her until he had set this thing right which was wrong with himself. . . .

Bantam Books by Grace Livingston Hill
Ask your bookseller for the books you have missed

Not Under the Law

Grace Livingston Hill

BANTAM BOOKS
TORONTO · NEW YORK · LONDON · SYDNEY · AUCKLAND

NOT UNDER THE LAW
*A Bantam Book / published by arrangement with
Harper & Row Publishers*
Bantam edition / May 1986

ISBN 0-553-25733-1

Published simultaneously in the United States and Canada

PRINTED IN THE UNITED STATES OF AMERICA

H   0 9 8 7 6 5 4 3 2 1

Chapter 1

The kitchen door stood open wide, and the breath from the meadow blew freshly across Joyce Radway's hot cheeks and forehead as she passed hurriedly back and forth from the kitchen stove to the dining room table preparing the evening meal.

It had been a long, hard day and she was very tired. The tears seemed to have been scorching her eyelids since early morning, and because her spirit would not let them out they seemed to have been flowing back into her heart till its beating was almost stopped by the deluge. Somehow it had been the hardest day in all the two weeks since her aunt died; the culmination of all the hard times since Aunt Mary had been taken sick and her son Eugene Massey brought his wife and two children home to live.

To begin with, at the breakfast table Eugene had snarled at Joyce for keeping her light burning so long the night before. He told her he couldn't afford to pay electric bills for her to sit up and read novels. This was most unjust since he knew that Joyce never had any novels to read, but that she was studying for an examination which would finish her last year of normal school work and fit her for a teacher. But then her cousin was seldom just. He took especial delight in tormenting her. Sometimes it seemed incredible that he could possibly be Aunt Mary's son, he was so utterly unlike her in every way. But he resembled markedly the framed picture of his father, Hiram Massey, which hung in the parlor, whom Joyce could but dimly remember as an uncle who never smiled at her.

She had controlled the tears then that sprang to her eyes and tried to answer in a steady voice:

"I'm sorry, Gene, I was studying, I wasn't reading a novel. You know last night was the last chance I had to study. The examination is today. Maybe when I get a school I'll be able to pay those electric light bills and some other things too."

"Bosh!" said Eugene discourteously. "You'll pay them a big lot, won't you? That's all poppycock, your trying to get a school, after a whole year out of school yourself. Much chance

1

you'll stand! And you may as well understand right now that I'm not going to undertake the expense of you lying around here idling and pretending to go to school for another whole year, so you better begin to make other plans."

Joyce swallowed hard and tried to smile:

"Well," she said pleasantly, "wait till after the examinations. I may pass and then there won't be any more trouble about it. The mathematics test is this morning. If I pass that I'm not in the least afraid of the rest. It is all clear sailing."

"What's that?" broke in Nannette's voice sharply. "Are you expecting to go off this morning? Because if you are you've missed your calculation. I have an appointment with the dressmaker in town this morning, and I don't intend to miss it. She's promised to get my new dress done by the day after tomorrow, and you'll have to stay home and see that the children get their lunch and get back to school. Besides, it's time the cellar was cleaned and you'd better get right at it. I thought I heard a rat down there last night."

Joyce looked up aghast:

"But, Nan! You've known all along I must go to the schoolhouse this morning early!"

"You needn't 'but, Nan' me, young lady, you're not in a position to say 'must' to anyone in this house. If Mother chose to let you act the independent lady that was her affair, but she's not here now, and you're a dependent. It's time you realized that. I say I'm going to town this morning, and you'll have to stay at home."

Nannette had sailed off upstairs with the parting words and Eugene went on reading his paper as if he had not heard the altercation. For a moment Joyce contemplated an appeal to him but one glance at the forbidding eyebrows over the top of the morning paper made her change her mind. There was little hope to be had from an appeal to him. He had never liked her, and she had never liked him. It dated back to the time when she caught him deceiving his mother and he dared her to tell on him. She had not told, it had not seemed a matter that made it necessary, but he hated her for knowing he was not all that his mother thought him. Besides, he was much older than she, and had a bullying nature. Her clear, young eyes annoyed him. She represented conscience in the concrete, his personal part of which he had long ago throttled. He did not like to be reminded of conscience, and too, he had always been jealous of his mother's love for Joyce.

Joyce glanced with troubled eyes at the clock.

She was due at the schoolhouse at nine-thirty. Gene would take the 8:19 train to town, and Nan would likely go with him. There would be time after they left to put up a lunch for the children if she hurried. Nan didn't like them to take their lunch, but Nan would have to stand it this time, for she meant to take that examination. She shut her lips tightly and began to remove the breakfast things from the table swiftly and quietly, leaving a plate for Junior who would be sure to be down late.

Her mind was stinging with the insults that had been flung at her. She had always known that she and her cousins were not compatible but such open words of affront had never been given her before, although the last few days since the funeral there had been glances and tones of contempt that hurt her. She had tried to be patient, hoping soon to be in a position where she would no longer be dependent upon her relatives.

There was something wrangling between Junior and his sister before Nan and Gene left for the train, and Joyce had been obliged to leave her work to settle the dispute; and again after they were gone she had to stop spreading the bread for the lunches and hunt for Junior's cap and Dorothea's arithmetic. It was a breathless time at the end, getting the lunches packed and the children off to school. She met with no opposition from them about taking their lunches for they loved to do it, but they insisted on two slices apiece of jelly roll which so reduced the amount left in the cake box that Joyce added "jelly roll" to the numerous things she must do when she got back from her examination.

But at last she saw them run off together down the street and she was free to rush to her room, smooth her hair, and slip into her dark blue serge. It remained to be seen how much time there would be left for the cellar when she got home. But whatever came she must get those examinations done.

When she was halfway downstairs she ran back and picked up a few little treasured trinkets from her upper bureau drawer sweeping them into her bag, some things that Aunt Mary had given her, a bit of real lace, some Christmas handkerchiefs, one or two pieces of jewelry, things that she prized and did not want handled over. Both Dorothea and her mother seemed to consider they had a perfect right to rummage in her bureau drawers and the day before Joyce had come upon Nan just emerging from her clothespress door as if she had been looking things over there.

It was not that the girl had anything of much value, but there were a few little things that seemed sacred to her because of their association, and she could not bear to have them handled over contemptuously by her cousin. Nan might return sooner than she expected and would be sure to come to her room to look for her. It would only anger her if she found the door locked, and anyhow the spare room key fitted her lock also. There was no privacy to be had in the house since Aunt Mary's death.

Joyce closed and locked the house carefully, placing the key in its usual place of hiding at the top of the porch pillar under the honeysuckle vine, and hurried down the street toward the school building. She registered a deep hope that she might get home in time to do a good deal of work in the cellar before Nan arrived, but she meant to try to forget cellar and Nan and everything till her examinations were over.

At the schoolhouse she found to her dismay that the schedule had been changed and that three of her tests came successively that day. There would be no chance of getting through before half past three, perhaps later. Nan would be angry, but it could not be helped for this once. She would try and forget her until she was through and then hurry home. She resolved not to answer back nor get angry that night if anything mean was said to her, and perhaps things would calm down. So she put her mind on logarithms, Latin conjugations, and English poetry. These examinations offered the only way she knew to independence, and it must be taken.

Late in the afternoon she hurried home, tired, faint, worried lest she had not answered some of the questions aright, palpitating with anxiety lest Nan had preceded her, or the children were running riot.

Breathlessly she came in sight of the house, and saw the front door open wide and the doctor's car standing in the drive. She ran up the steps in fright and apprehension.

Nan was very much home indeed, and was furious! She met Joyce in the hall and greeted her with a tirade.

Junior had been hurt playing baseball and had been brought home with a bandaged head and arm, weeping loudly.

Dorothea lolled on the stairs blandly eating the remainder of the jelly roll and eyeing her cousin with contempt and wicked exultation. She had already lighted the fuse by saying that she and Junior hadn't wanted to take their lunch, but Cousin Joyce had insisted, and had given them *all* the jelly roll. The light in her mother's eye had been such as to make Dorothea linger near at the right time. Dorothea loved being on the virtuous outside of a fight. If one showed signs of dying she knew how to ask the right question or say the innocent word to revive it once more. Dorothea contemplated Joyce now with deep satisfaction.

The doctor's car was scarcely out of the gate and down the road before the storm broke once more upon Joyce's tired head.

Joyce did not wait to go upstairs to her room and change her dress. She took off her hat on the way to the kitchen and put it and her bag and books and papers on the little bench outside the kitchen door where no one would be likely to notice them. She enveloped herself in a big kitchen apron and went to work, preparing the vegetables for dinner and getting out materials for jelly roll. Then Nan entered, blue blazes in her eyes.

Nan had not taken off her hat yet and around her neck she was wearing Joyce's pretty gray fox neckpiece, Aunt Mary's last Christmas gift, which Joyce had supposed was safely put away in camphor on her closet shelf. Joyce had not noticed it in the darkness of the hall, but now the indignity struck her in the face like a blow as Nan stood out in the open doorway smartly gowned and powdered and rouged just a bit, her face angry and haughty, her air imperious:

"You ungrateful, wicked girl!" broke forth Nan. "You might just as well have been a murderer! Suppose Junior had been brought home dying and no one to open the house?"

"I'm sorry, Nan," began Joyce, "I did not expect to be gone so long. I was told there would be only one examination today."

"Examinations! Don't talk to me about examinations! That's all you care about! It's nothing to you that the little child who has lived under the same roof with you for three years is seriously hurt. It's nothing to you even if he had been killed. And he might have been killed, *easily*! Yes, he might, you wicked girl! It was at noon he was playing ball when he got hit, and you knew I didn't want him to stay at school at noontime just for that reason. The bad boys tried to hurt him," so she raved on. "It was your fault. Entirely your fault!"

There was absolutely no use in trying to say anything in reply. Nannette would not let her. Whenever she opened her lips to say she was sorry her cousin screamed the louder, till Joyce finally closed her lips and went about her work with white, set face, wishing somehow she might get away from this awful earth for a little while, wondering what would be the outcome of all this when Gene got home. Gene was not very careful himself about Junior. He spoiled him horribly, but he was very keen about defending him always. As she went about her kitchen work she tried to think what she could say or do that would still the tempest. It seemed to her that her heart was bursting with the trouble. Maybe she ought to have given up the examination after all. Maybe she should have stayed at home. But that would have meant everlasting dependence upon those to whom she was not closely bound. And Junior had already recovered sufficiently to be out in his bandages swinging on the gate. He could not be seriously injured. Oh, why could she not have died instead of Aunt Mary! Why did people have to bring children into the world and then leave them to fend for themselves where they were not wanted? What was life all for anyway?

Dorothea hovered around like a hissing wasp, filching the apples as they were peeled and quartered for the applesauce, sticking a much soiled finger into the cake batter, licking it, and applying it again to the batter several times, in spite of Joyce's protests. She seemed to know that her mother would not reprove her for anything she did to annoy Joyce tonight.

Gene came in while Joyce was taking up the dinner, and Joyce could hear his wife telling him in a high suppressed key all the wrongs of the day, with her own garbled account of Junior's accident and Joyce's disregard of orders. So the tears stung into her eyes and her hot cheeks flushed warmer and the only thing in the world that gave her any comfort was the sweet spring breath from the meadow coming in the kitchen door as she passed and repassed, carrying dishes of potatoes and cabbage and fried pork chops. Their mingled hot odors smothered her as they steamed up into her face, and then would come that sweet, cool breeze, blowing them aside, laying a cool hand on her wet brow like the hand of a gentle mother. How she longed to fly away into the coolness and sweetness and leave it all behind. How many times during the last two hard weeks had she looked out that kitchen door across the meadows and longed to be walking across them into the world away from it all forever.

Gene came into the dining room just as she set the hot coffeepot down on the table, and he looked at her with his cold blue eyes, a look that was like a long, thin blade of steel piercing to her very soul. She thought she had never before seen

such a look of contempt and hate. She felt as if it were something tangible that he had inserted into her soul which she
would never be able to get out again.

"Well, you're a pretty one, aren't you? Mother was always
boasting about how dependable you were. I wonder what she
would think of you now! I always knew you had it in you. You're
just like your contemptible father! Get an idea in your head
and have to carry it out. Bullheaded. That's what you are.
That's what he was. I remember hearing all about it. He
wanted to study up some germ and make himself famous. Had
to go and get into some awful disease, subject himself to danger, and finally got the disease and died. Pretended he was
doing a great thing for humanity at large, but left his wife and
child for her poor sister to support and saddled us all with a girl
just like him to house and feed and clothe. Now, young lady, I
want you to understand from this time forth that we're done
with nonsense and whether you pass or whether you don't
pass, your place is *right here in this house doing the work and
taking the orders from my wife*! I've got you to look after and
I'll do it, but I don't intend to stand any more of your mon-
keyshines. Do you hear? *I won't have* anybody in my house
that doesn't obey me!"

Joyce looked at him in a kind of tired wonder. She knew
there were things being said that were dissecting her very
soul, and that by-and-by when she moved she would bleed,
perhaps her soul might bleed to death with the sharpness of it
all, but just now she had not the strength to resent, to say
anything to refute the awful half-truths he was speaking, to
shout out as she felt she ought, that he had no right to speak
that way about her dear, dead father whom she had not known
much, could scarcely remember, but had been taught by both
mother and aunt to love dearly. She could only stand and stare
at him as he talked. She was growing white to the lips. Her
knees were shaking under her, and the children stared at her
curiously, even Nannette eyed her strangely. She was sum-
moning all her strength for an effort:

"Cousin Eugene," she said clearly as if she were talking to
someone away off, and her voice steadied as she went on. "You
know I don't have to stay here if you feel this way. I will go!"

And then, like a bird that suddenly sees an opening in its
cage and sets its wings swiftly, she turned and walked out of
the room, across the kitchen, and out the kitchen door into the
evening sunlight and the sweet meadow breath.

On the bench beside the door lay her hat covering her little worn handbag and books and papers. She swept them all up as she passed, and held them in front of her as she walked steadily on down the pebbled path among the new grass toward the garage, the blinding tears now coming and blurring everything before her.

"Let her alone!" she heard Gene sneer loudly. "She'll go out to the garage and boohoo awhile and then she'll come back and behave herself. Dishes? I should say not! Don't you do a dish! Let her do 'em when she gets over her fit. It'll do her good. She'll be of some use to you after this."

Joyce swept away the tears with a quick hand and lifted her head. Why should she weep when she was walking away from this? She had wanted to go, had wondered and wished for an opening, and now it had come, why be sad? She was walking away into the beauty of the sunset. Smell the air! She drew a deep breath and went straight on past the garage, down through the garden to the fence, and stooping slipped between the bars and into the meadow.

There were violets blooming among the grass here, blue as the sky, and nodding to her, dazzling in their blueness. There was a dandelion. How bright its gold! The world was before her. The examination was not over. But what of that? She could not go back to take her diploma anyway, but she was free, and God would take care of her somewhere, somehow.

A sense of buoyancy bore her up. Her feet touched the grass of the meadow as if it had been full of springs. She lost the consciousness of her great weariness. Her soul had found wings. She was walking into a crimson path of the sunset, and April was in her lungs. How good to be away from the smell of pork chops and hot cabbage, the steam of potatoes and Gene Massey's voice. Never, never would she go back. Not for all the things she had left behind. They were few. She was glad she had her few little trinkets. They were all that mattered anyway. Except for the fur neckpiece. It went hard to lose that. The last thing Aunt Mary bought her. Of course it would have been wiser to wait to pack. There were her two good gingham dresses, and two others that were faded, but she would need things to work in, and there was the little pink georgette that Aunt Mary bought her last summer! She hated to lose that. But Aunt Mary, if she could see would quite understand, and if she could not see it could all be explained in heaven someday.

There would be no use sending to Nannette or Gene for anything. They would never send her a rag that belonged to her. There would be inconveniences of course, her hairbrush, her toothbrush—but what were they?

And then, quite suddenly as she climbed the fence, and stood in a long, white road winding away over a hill, the sun which had been slipping, slipping down lower and lower, went out of sight and left only a ruby light behind, and all about the world looked gray. The sweet smells were there, and the wonderful cool air to touch her brow lightly like that hand of her mother so long ago, just as it touched and called her in the kitchen a few minutes before, but the bright world was growing quiet at the approaching night, and suddenly Joyce began to wonder where she was going.

Automobiles were coming and going hurriedly as if the people in them were going home to dinner, and they smiled and talked joyously as they passed her, and looked at her casually, a girl walking alone in the twilight with her hat in her hand.

Joyce came to herself and put on her hat, she put her papers together in a book, and the books under her arm, and slipped the strap of her handbag over her wrist. She went on walking down the road toward the pink and gold of the sunset and wondered where she was going, and then, as she lifted her eyes she saw a star slip faintly out in the clear space between the ruby and rose, as if to remind her that One above was watching and had not forgotten her.

Chapter 2

Back in the kitchen she had left silence reigned, and all the pans and kettles and bowls which had been used in preparing the hurried evening meal seemed to fill the place with desolation. It was not a room that Nannette cared to contemplate as she came out to get the coffeepot for Eugene's second cup which he insisted be kept hot. She frowned at the jelly roll all powdered with sugar and lying neatly on a small platter awaiting desert time. It was incredible that Joyce had managed to make it in so short a time with all the rest she had to do, but she needn't think she could make up for negligence and diso-bedience by her smartness.

"Gene, I think you better go down to the garage and talk to her," said Nannette coming back with coffee. "The kitchen's in an awful mess and she ought to get at it at once. I certainly don't feel like doing her work for her when I've been in the city all day, and then this shock about Junior on top of it all."

"Let her good and alone," said Gene sourly. "She's nothing to kick about. If I go out there and pet her up she'll expect it every time. That's the way Mother spoiled her, let her do ev-erything she took a notion to, and she has to learn at the start that things are different. What made her mad anyhow? She's never had a habit of flying up. I didn't think she had the nerve to walk off like that, she's always been so meek and self-righ-teous."

"Well, I suppose she didn't like it because I wore that pre-cious fox scarf of hers to the city. She's terribly afraid her things will get hurt, and she pretends to think a lot of it because mother gave it to her last Christmas."

"Did you wear her fur?"

"Why, certainly. Why shouldn't I? It's no kind of a thing for a young girl like her to have, especially in her position. She ought to be glad she has something I can use that will make up for what we do for her."

"Better let her things alone, Nan. It might make trouble for us if she gets up the nerve to fight. You can't tell how Mother left things, you know, till Judge Peterson gets well and we hear the will read."

"What do you mean? Didn't your mother leave everything to you, I should like to know?"

"Well, I can't be sure about it yet. I suppose she did, but it's just as well to know where we stand exactly before we make any offensive moves. You know Mother said something that last night about Joyce always having a right to stay here, that it was her home. I didn't think much of it at the time of course, and told her we would consider it our duty to look out for Joyce till she got married of course, but I've been thinking since, you can't just tell, Mother might have been trying to prepare me for some surprise the will is going to spring on us. You know Mother had an overdeveloped conscience, and there was something about a trifling sum of money that Joyce's father left that Mother put into this house to make a small payment, I think. I can't just remember what it was but that would be just enough to make Mother think she ought to give everything she owned to Joyce. I shan't be surprised at almost anything after the way she made a fool of that girl. But anyhow, you let her alone till she gets good and ready to come in. She won't dare stay out all night."

"She might go to the neighbors and make a lot of talk about us," suggested Nan. "She knows she'd have us in a hole if she did that."

"She won't go to the neighbors, not if I know her at all. She wouldn't think it was right. She has that kind of a conscience too. It's lucky for us."

"Well, suppose she doesn't come in and wash the dishes tonight?"

"Let 'em go then till tomorrow. You've got dishes enough for breakfast haven't you? Well, just leave everything where it is. Don't even clear off the table. Just let her see that she'll have it all to do when she gets over her tantrums, and you won't find her cutting up again very soon."

"I suppose she'll have to come back tonight," speculated Nan. "She has another examination tomorrow morning I think, and it would take an earthquake or something like that to keep her away from that."

"Well, we'll order an earthquake then. I don't mean to have her finish that examination. If she happens to pass—and she likely would for those Radways have brains they say, that's the trouble with them—she'll make us all kinds of trouble wanting to teach instead of doing the work for you, and then we'd be up against it right away. It costs like the dickens to get a servant these days and there's no sense in having an outsider around stealing your food and wearing your clothes. Don't you worry about Joyce. Let her alone till she comes in. Lock the kitchen door so she'll have to knock. Then I'll let her in and give her such a dressing down as she'll remember for a few years. Come on. Let's turn out this dining room light and go into the living room. Then she'll know we're not going to wash those dishes, and she'll come in all the sooner."

Nannette slapped Dorothea for breaking off another piece from the jelly roll, and turned out the light quickly. It occurred to her that there would be nobody to make another jelly roll when this one was gone unless Joyce came speedily back. She hated cooking.

But although she intentionally neglected to lock the kitchen door, hoping the girl would slip in quietly when they were gone from the dining room and get the work done, Joyce did not return. Dorothea and Junior were allowed to sit up far beyond their usual bedtime, and after they were at last quiet upstairs, Eugene and Nannette continued to sit and read, loth to leave until their young victim should return repentant and they could tell her just what they thought of her for her base ingratitude. When you know you have done wrong yourself there is nothing so soothing as to be able to scold someone else.

When Nannette finally went upstairs to bed she took the borrowed fox fur and flung it across Joyce's bed, with its tail dragging on the floor.

"I'm sure I don't know why we can't have that will read without waiting for the old mummy to get well," she said discontentedly. "It's awfully awkward waiting this way and not knowing what is ours. Why can't someone else read it if Judge Peterson isn't able to?"

"Why, no one knows just where it is. His valuable papers are all locked in his safe, and the doctor won't let him be asked a thing about business till he gets able to be around. He says it might throw him all back to have to think about anything now. Of course it's all nonsense, but I don't see what we can do."

"Suppose he should die?"

"Why, then of course, they would open his safe and examine all his papers, but his wife won't hear to anything being touched till he gets out of danger, so we just have to wait."

"Well, I'm not going to worry about it," said Nannette with a toss of her head. "If the will isn't right we'll just break it, that's all. I'm not going to let that girl get in the way of my happiness. There's more than one way of going about things, and, as you say, she has that kind of a conscience. If that's her weak point we'll work her through that. If she thinks her beloved Aunt Mary is going to be proved in the court as not of sound mind, she'll give up the hair on her head. I know her. Smug-faced little fanatic! How on earth did she ever get wished on your mother for life anyway? You've never told me."

"Oh, her mother was Mother's youngest sister, and idol. Mother was perfectly insane about her. Then she married this Radway, and everybody said it was a great match, brilliant young doctor and all that. But the brilliant young doctor showed he hadn't a grain of sense in his head. He discovered some new germ or other and then he went to work experimenting on it, and two or three times was saved from death just by the skin of his teeth. Finally he let them inoculate him with the thing, just to observe its workings. He knew he was running a great risk when he did it, and yet he was fool enough to go ahead. When he died they sold the house and a good deal of the furnishings. Mother had some of the things up in the attic a long time. I don't know what became of them. Sold I suppose, perhaps to get that fox fur. Mother was just daffy on that girl. She always wanted a daughter you know. And after Aunt Helen died—she didn't live many months after her husband, just faded away you know—why Mother did everything for Joyce."

"Well, I think she did more than she had any right to do for just a niece," said Nannette scornfully. "It's time you had your innings. I think your mother should have thought of her own son and her grandchildren, and not lavished fox furs on a mere relation. She just spoiled Joyce. She thinks she has to live in luxury, and it's going to be very hard to break her into working for her living."

The clock was striking twelve before Nannette began to undress, and now and then she would cast an anxious eye out of the window and wonder how long the erring girl's nerve would hold out, or whether she had really dared to go to some neighbor's and stay all night. If she had what could they do?

Finally Gene got up from his reading chair and went downstairs to see if all the doors were locked, he said; but in reality he went softly out the kitchen door and walked down to the garage with slow, careful tread, stopping to listen, every minute or two. But no sound reached his ear save the dreamy notes of a tree toad. The little gray clouds drifting through the sky were hiding the moon and making the backyard quite dark. Somehow a vision of his mother's face came to him, that last day when she had called him to the bedside and reminded him that she left Joyce as a sacred trust to his care. She told him that of course he would understand the home was always hers and something like reproach came and stood before his self-centered, satisfied soul and gave him strange uneasiness.

He stepped quietly into the garage and looked around in the darkness. There was no car as yet, but he meant to purchase one the minute the estate was settled up. He felt sure there would be plenty of money to do a number of the things to the house that he had already planned. It was not really a garage, though he had called it that ever since he came home to live with his mother, it was only the old barn with a new door.

But there was no sign of Joyce inside the old barn, though he searched every corner and even opened the door of what used to be the harness closet.

He closed the door and went outside, puzzled, a trifle anxious, not for the safety of the girl whom he had driven from the only home she had by his unsympathetic words, but for the possibility of what she might have said to some neighbor with whom she might have taken refuge for the night. And yet he could not bring himself to believe that Joyce would be so disloyal to his mother's family as to let others know of a rupture between them.

He went outside and walked around, but there was no sign of anyone, and the dew glistened evenly on the new grass in the sudden light as the moon swept out from behind a cloud and poured down a moment's radiance. There were no marks of footprints on the tender grass anywhere near the building.

Standing in the shadow of the big maple halfway to the house he called: "Joyce!" once, sharply, curtly, in a tone that startled himself and shocked the tree toads into sudden brief silence, but the echo of the meadow came in sweet drifts of violet breath as his only answer. His voice sounded gruff even to himself and he realized that she would not come to a call like that. If she had strength of purpose enough to go at his harsh words she would not come at such a call. He tried again:

"Joyce!" and Joyce would have been astonished could she have heard his voice. He had never spoken to her with as much kindliness of tone in all his life, not even when he wanted to borrow money of her. Yes, he had really descended to asking her who had but a small allowance from the bounty of his mother, to loan it to him. And she had always been ready to lend graciously if it was not already promised for some necessity. He would soon have kept her in bankruptcy had not his mother discovered it and forbidden Joyce to lend any more, telling her son to come to her in any need.

He stood there some time calling into the darkness trying various tones and wondering at himself, growing more indignant with the girl for not answering, calling her stubborn, and finally growing alarmed, although he would not own it really to himself.

But at last he gave it up and went in, putting it aside carelessly as if it were but a trifle after all. The girl was stubborn but she would have to come back pretty soon, and the lesson would only do her good. As for the neighbors, they must prepare a story that would offset anything she might tell them. And what did the neighbors matter anyway? This wasn't the only place in the world. They could sell the house and move where Joyce had no friends, and there would be no trouble. Joyce would have to stick to them, for she had no way of earning money anywhere else. The idea of teaching school was fool nonsense. He wouldn't think of allowing it. She would always be taking on airs even if she paid board, and then they would get no work out of her, and she would not be pleasant to have around.

With this reflection he fell asleep, convinced that Joyce would be found safe and sound and sane on the doorstep in the morning.

About this time the new young superintendent of the high school who was taking the place of the regular superintendent while he was abroad for six months studying, settled down in his one comfortable chair in his boardinghouse room with a bundle of examination papers to look over. This was not his work, but the two teachers who would ordinarily have done it were both temporarily disabled, one down with the grippe and the other away at a funeral, and since the averages must be ready before commencement he had volunteered to mark these papers.

It was late and he was tired, for there had been a special meeting of the school board to deal with a matter connected with the new addition to the school building, and also to arrange to supply the place of a teacher who had suddenly decided to get married instead of continuing to teach. There had been much discussion about both matters and he had been greatly annoyed at the prospect of one young woman who had been suggested to fill the vacancy. She was of the so-called flapper variety and seemed to him to have no idea of serious work. She had been in his classes for the last six weeks, and he became more disgusted with her every time he saw her. The idea of her as a colleague was not pleasant. He settled to his papers with a frown that portended no good to the poor victims whose fate he was settling by the marks of his blue pencil.

He marched through the papers, paragraph after paragraph, question after question, marking them ruthlessly. Misspelled

words, how they got on his nerves! He drew sharp blue lines
like little swords through them, and wrote caustic footnotes on
the corners of the pages. The young aspirants for graduation
who received them in the morning would quiver when they
read them and gather in groups to cast anathemas at him.

But suddenly he came to a paper written in a clear, firm
hand as if the owner knew what she was talking about and
thought it really worth writing down. The first sentence caught
his interest because of the original way in which the statement
was made. Here was a young philosopher who had really
thought about life, and was taking the examination as something of interest in itself, rather than a terrible ordeal that must
be gone through with for future advantage. As he read a vision
of a clear smooth brow, calm eyes lifted now and then to the
blackboard, gradually came back to his memory. He was sure
this was the quiet young woman with the beautiful, sincere
unselfish face that he had noticed as he passed through the
study hall that morning. There had been half a dozen strangers
in from neighboring towns for examination. Only this one had
attracted him. He had paused in the doorway watching her a
moment while he waited for a book which the attending
teacher was finding for him, and had marked the quiet grace of
her demeanor, the earnest expression of her face, the pure regular features, the soft outline of the brown waves of hair, the
sweet, old-fashionedness of her, and wondered who she was.
He had not been long in the town and did not yet know all the
village maidens, yet it seemed as if she must be from another
place, for certainly he could not have been in the same town
with this girl and not have marked her sooner somewhere in
either church or shop or street.

The busy day had surged in and he had forgotten the face
and thought no more of the girl. But now it all came back with
conviction as he read on. He turned to the end of the paper for
the name "Joyce Radway." Somehow it seemed to fit her, and
he read on with new interest, noting how she gave interest to
the hackneyed themes that had become monotonous through
reading over and over the crude, young answers to the same
questions. How was it that this young girl was able to give a
turn to her sentences that seemed to make any subject a thrill-
ing, throbbing, vital thing? And she did not skim over the answers with the least possible information. She wrote as if she
liked to tell what she knew, as if her soul were *en rapport* with

her work, and as if she were writing it for the mere joy of imparting the fact and its thrill to another.

"Now, there's a girl that would make a teacher all right," he said aloud to himself as he finished the paper writing a clear blue "Excellent" upon it with his finest flourish, "I wonder who she is? If she's the one I saw I'll vote for her. I must inquire first thing in the morning. Joyce Radway. What a good name. It fits. She's the assistant I'd like if I have my way, unless I'm very much mistaken in a human face."

Chapter 3

Joyce had walked a long way on a long gray ribbon of a road before it wound uphill and she began to realize where her steps were turning. Up there on the top was the dark outline of the old Hill Church, its spire a black dart against the luminous night sky. A fitful moon gleamed palely and showed it for a moment, still and gray like a little lone dove asleep, and about it clustered the white stones of the graveyard on the side of the hill sloping down toward the valley. One tall shaft showed where lay the dust of the rich, old, good man who gave the land and built the church, and others less pretentious flocked close at hand, a little social clique of the select dead who had clung to the old church through the years of their life, who there had been christened, married, and buried.

With a catch in her breath like a sob Joyce hurried on, realizing that it was here her heart was longing to go, where she had left all that was mortal of her precious Aunt Mary.

It was not that she had any feeling that the spirit she loved was lingering there near its worn-out earthly habitation, it was only that the earth seemed so alien and she so alone that it did her good to creep away to the quiet mound that some kind neighbor had already made velvety with close-shaved turf.

She felt her way to the place, close beside the mound where her mother had been laid. They had always kept it neat and carefully tended when her aunt was alive, and now she sank down between the two graves, with her hands spread broodingly, anguishingly over the tender grass, and her face drooped down on its coolness.

How long she lay there she did not know. The hot tears flowed relievingly down her cheeks and fell into the cool grass, and overhead the quiet sky, with the single star in a clearing among the floating clouds, and now and then the serene, busy moon above it all, quite as if the world was going as it should even though hearts were being broken.

A sense of peace stole gradually upon her, and the ache drifted out of her weary limbs, and out of her lonely heart. It was almost as if some comfort had stolen upon her from the quiet grass, and the busy, serene heaven above. She did not feel afraid. She had no sense of the presence of her aunt, only a deep, sweet understanding that this little spot was sacred and here she might think entirely unmolested.

It might be that she slept for a space, for she was very weary and the day had been so hard, but she was not sure. Rather it was as if she were just resting, as she used to rest in her mother's arms and be rocked, long ago, the first thing she could remember. The sense of her troubles, and her terrible situation had slipped away from her. She was just resting, not thinking. When suddenly the sound of voices—voices quite near, broke upon her, as if they had suddenly rounded the hill and were close at hand, coming on. Cautious voices, albeit, with a carrying sibilant, and something familiar about one of them. She could not tell why they struck terror to her soul, nor at what instant she realized that they were not just foot travelers going on by, but were coming toward her. She found herself trembling from head to foot.

"Look out there, kid," said the familiar voice. "Don't skid over that poor stiff. Those headstones aren't easy to play with and we can't afford to lose any of this catch. It's worth its weight in gold you know, rare antique! We ought to make about four hundred bucks apiece out of this lot if we place it wisely."

The footsteps came on, and suddenly as the moon swept out from the clouds for an instant she saw five dark figures silhouetted against the lighter darkness of the road, stealing slowly into the cemetery among the graves carrying burdens between them, heavy, bulky, shrouded burdens. The hurrying clouds obliterated everything again, but she could hear the soft thud of their feet, as they slowly felt their way. An occasional dart of light from a pocket flash flickered fitfully on a headstone here and there as she watched with bated breath. They seemed to be coming straight toward her, and for an instant she thought of trying to flee, but a great weakness overcame her, so that she could hardly breathe, and it seemed impossible to rise. Then the flashlight jabbed into her very eyes, and she crouched against the sod and wished there were some way to get down beneath it out of sight.

"What was that, kid?" the voice whispered. The tiny flash fluttered here and there on the grass all about her as she crouched. In a moment they would be upon her. It seemed the culmination of all the terrible day. Her heart throbbed painfully, while she waited a long minute, hearing distinctly the oncoming feet swishing softly in the grass, the labored breathing of those who carried the heavy burden, the cautious whispers, and then, could it be? They were only two graves away. They were passing by. They were going toward the back part of the cemetery.

She lay absolutely motionless listening for what seemed hours. The soft thud of burdens laid down was followed by the sound of a spade plunged deep in the earth, and the ring of metal as it was drawn forth and hit against a stone.

By and by she gained courage to open her eyes and then to lift her head cautiously and glance about. Her frightened heart almost stifled her with its wild beating.

The sky was luminous off to the east and against it, the five dark figures were darkly visible, three with shovels, and one with a pick, the fifth watching, directing, occasionally flashing a spot of light on a particular place. On the ground a long line of something dark like a box or boxes. Had they murdered someone and come to bury him in the night, or were they grave robbers? She found herself shuddering in the darkness, and when she put a trembling hand to her brow it was cold and wet with perspiration.

She began to wonder if she dared to try and get away, and measured the distance with her eye. The men seemed so close when she considered making a move, especially the one with the flashlight! Its merciless eye would be sure to search her out if she attempted flight. Perhaps it would be safer to lie still till they went away and trust that they would go out by the same path they had entered and not discover her. Yet when she tried to relax and wait she was trembling so that it seemed as if the very cords that held her being together were loosed and she was slowly becoming useless like Dorothea's big bisque doll that lay on a trunk in the attic with its head and arms lolling at the end of emaciated rubber cords. She had a frightened feeling that if she lay still very long she would become unable ever to move again, the sensation that comes in nightmare.

Then into her frenzied mind came the thought of Eugene and Nannette and how triumphant they would be if they knew she was going through this agony. They would say it was good punishment for her behavior, a just reward for her headstrong actions. Had she been wrong in going away as she did? Had they been right to insist on her giving up the examinations? Somehow her conscience, hard-pressed as she was, could not see that they had a right to keep her from the only way she knew of earning her living. Somehow she could not feel that any law, either physical or moral, laid any obligation upon her to stay with the children when the mother had known for three weeks of her coming examinations, and when she often of her own accord let them take their lunch to school if it happened to suit her own convenience. Junior might have been hurt playing ball at recess as well as at noon, and he always played ball at recess. No, her conscience was clear on that score. She had a perfect right to put herself in the way of not being dependent upon them financially, and the school teaching was the only way she knew to do it. Still, of course it was all over now. She had gone away from any chance that might have come to her through those examinations, gone out into space alone without any goal or any plan. She might have done that in the first place of course if she had known they were going to act that way. Well, it couldn't be helped now. She had gone and nothing would induce her to go back. Perhaps when she found a home, if she found a home, she might send back to find out the result of her hard work. It might do her some good somewhere else. But she was too tired now, and too frightened to think about it.

She stole another glance toward the invaders. They seemed to be arguing in whispers about something, gesticulating, pointing. Perhaps she might manage to slip away while they were absorbed without their notice. She made a soft little move to sit up, and as she put out her arm to steady herself the metal chain of her handbag clinked just the faintest little bit against the iron pipe of the low fence that surrounded the neighboring grave. Instantly everything was silent among the group of men, the dark figures as if they had been but shadows crouched out of sight, only the alert head and shoulders of one showed dimly against the luminous spot in the sky. She could feel that their eyes were focused upon her as if they had been spotlights out of the darkness. She did not dare to move even to relax her fingers which had been stretched to grasp the iron rail. Her breath was suspended midway, and in the whole wide, peaceful acre the air seemed tense as though the very dead were waiting with her for the outcome.

"Oh, God!" she prayed. "Oh, God! Help me now!"

It was the first time since Aunt Mary's death that she felt herself to have really prayed. Somehow her heart had seemed stunned since the funeral, and when she said the words of prayer with her lips there had been such an empty ache in her heart that they had not seemed to mean anything. Now in her great need she had the distinct realization of crying out to a God upon whom she relied and whom her faith of the years had tested. And just as distinctly she felt the surety that He was there. He had answered.

It was as if that cry for help was a surrender, a committing of her way to Him. As if she had said, "Here am I. I am Yours. However right or wrong I may have been to have put myself into this situation I am here and helpless. If I am worth anything at all to You save me for I cannot save myself. I am giving my future into Your hands."

Of course there was no such logical sequence of thought or word in the swift flash of her appeal, but afterward she was aware it had been a commitment and a covenant.

As if an answer of assurance had come a calm came upon her. Her breath moved on, her heart beat naturally. The tensity of the air seemed gone. The dark shadows by the pile of dirt stirred. A low murmur passed among them. They moved and came upright again. Their eyes ceased to pierce her like spotlights. They moved with ease and took up their shovels. One even laughed in a low, half nervous tone. Only one still stood and watched, his attitude alert, not satisfied that the danger was passed. He murmured a low warning.

"Aw! What's eatin' ye?" another replied jocularly. "D'ye think the dead can walk? It's just a wild rabbit jumpin' amongst the gravel."

"Wild rabbits aren't metal shod," said the familiar voice seeming to come from a face looking her way, and she knew that one at least of the shadowy figures had not ceased to watch and listen.

It seemed hours that she lay there holding her breath, afraid to stir lest they come her way, yet feeling an impulse within her to get away. For at any moment they might come out and walk right in the path by her side. They could not fail to see her if they passed that way. Dear Aunt Mary lying so quietly beneath the sod! How good that she was not really there herself, that she could not know the peril she was in! Or was she perhaps near in spirit? Did God ever let those who had gone to live with Him come to guard and help those they had left behind? But at least she was not worried, for in heaven none could worry, being with the great God who knew all, and whose power was over all. God would not really let anything hurt her. She had cried for help and He would eventually bring her out of all this into safety.

The assurance that came with these swift thoughts made her calmer, and finally gave her courage to begin slowly to move a hand and foot out toward the path. There was a sound of soft thudding of the spade against the turf as if it were being replaced over the excavation and the men would soon be returning to the road. If she would escape unseen it must be done at once.

Slowly, cautiously, she put out her hand and firmly grasped the rail of the low fence surrounding the next little lot. The cold iron steadied her, and she next moved her foot with a motion so slow and cautious that there was absolutely no sound from it. But it was a work of time. Would the time hold out until she had removed herself entirely from the line of their possible route?

After the other foot had changed its place somewhat she was able to lift her whole body and move it over several inches into the path without perceiving any sign that she had been heard or seen. Pausing to take a deep breath, and holding her body steady a few inches above the ground she cautiously began to move forward. It reminded her of those moving pictures of divers and tennis players who by a slower manipulation of the machine are made to perform their tricks in measured rhythm so that every stage of the action can be observed. It meant perfect control of every muscle of the body. It meant deep breathing and a calm mind to perform the feat, and sometimes the wild beating of her frightened heart made her feel that she must just drop in the grass where she was and give it up. Besides, her whole body was trembling with weariness and excitement of the long, hard day, and her nerves were spent. Big tears welled into her eyes and dropped into the grass but she was unaware of them. Only her will kept her moving or held her back when she would have jumped to her feet and run screaming from the place; only her sense that God was near somewhere and would help her, kept her mind steady enough to direct her movements. And sometimes, as she moved inch by inch away from the direct line of the men it seemed so slow, so impossible that she could ever get away that she almost fell down.

She had crawled thus on hands and knees some twenty feet, and was just considering the wisdom of turning her course a little farther to the left before striking toward the road, when suddenly she heard a low murmur among the men and glancing back saw that they had shouldered their implements and were about to start away.

Fear overcame her and made her forget caution, and she lifted one hand with a sudden movement to hasten, grasping the handbag tightly and once more the tinkling chains, slipping from between her tired fingers, struck against a headstone and gave forth a weird little sound.

Instantly there was silence for the space of about a second, the five men froze into attention. Then stealthily, his body ducked low, one of them crouched and came forward. Almost silently he came, but she knew he was coming straight toward her. She was paralyzed with fear. She felt she could not move another fraction of an inch, could not any longer hold on to that cold, smooth stone she had grasped, could not draw herself out of sight behind a marble shaft that loomed benevolently close at hand. Then the realization that in a moment more he would be upon her gave strength to her weakness. Who knew what desperate criminals these might be? Grave robbers would not hesitate to dig a new grave and hide a victim in it where no one would ever suspect. Whatever they had been doing it was evident they did not wish it known, and it would go hard with anyone who might be feared as an eavesdropper. The thought gave wings to her feet as she stumbled up and flew away in the darkness among the shadowy gravestones, out toward the road.

It seemed miles she darted among those stones, as noiselessly as possible, but blindly, for it was dark, so dark, and the little spot of light chased her maddeningly, darting ahead of her and flickering into her eyes from the side unexpectedly, causing her to change her course. She was aware that the men had separated, and she seemed to be encompassed from all sides. Once she stumbled and fell across a grave with the myrtle brushing her face, and the scent of crushed rose geranium in the air. Strange that rose geranium should be identified in her mind at such a time as this. It seemed like a sweet thought reminding her of quiet home and love and peace. But she grasped the mossy stone over her and pulled herself up just in time to evade one of her pursuers; and lo, just at her left was the open field separated only by a scraggy hedge. She parted the shrubs and slipped between, thankful that her dress was dark, and sped away over the stubbly ground, only the impetus of her going keeping her from falling at almost every step. It was almost as if she were flying, as if she were upheld by unseen hands and guided. And the hedge grew taller as she approached the road, completely hiding her flight from those on the other side. She was conscious of confused noises behind her, but her own going was so rapid as to shut out any accurate sound. So at last she gained the fence, crept tremblingly beneath the lichen covered rails and tottered to her feet only to be confronted by a tall, dark figure looming in the road as if he had been waiting there for her a long time.

She caught her breath and turned to fly, but her hands were caught in a big, firm grasp like a vise, and a flashlight blazed into her frightened eyes for an instant. She closed the lids involuntarily and shrank away, with a dizzy feeling that for the first time in her life she must be going to faint.

Chapter 4

About half past seven the next morning, Nannette was going distractedly about the disheveled kitchen attempting to get a semblance of a breakfast for the irate Eugene and at the same time deal with her two unruly children who half dressed were contending about the cat.

The telephone suddenly rang out sharply and Eugene dropped the morning paper with a snap and sprang to take down the receiver, an arrogant frown appearing at once on his face and dominating the anxiety that had been there ever since the evening before:

"Hello!" he said insolently in the voice he meant to use for Joyce in case it was Joyce.

"Hello!" came back a voice equally insolent with the effect of having been the same word thrown back resentfully. A man's voice. Eugene was puzzled.

"Who are you?" he challenged with a heavy frown. Nannette paused in the kitchen doorway and listened and the children suspended operations on the cat and tried a bit of eavesdropping.

"Is Miss Joyce there?" The voice held authority, and denied any right to interference by a third party.

"Who *is* this?" demanded Eugene angrily.

"A friend of Miss Radway's" came the prompt dignified reply. "I wish to speak with Miss Radway." There was coldness in the tone. The voice had a carrying quality and could be heard distinctly across the room.

"There, I told you so!" cried Nannette hysterically. "The whole town will hear of it!"

Eugene made a violent gesture with his foot equivalent to telling her to go into the kitchen and shut the door, and Nannette retired out of sight with a listening ear.

"Joyce is busy," said her cousin in a lordly tone. "She can't be interrupted now. You can leave a message if you like that can be given her when she gets done her work."

"I see," said the calm voice after a moment of what seemed thoughtful silence, and there came a soft click.

"Who is this? Say! Who is this? Operator! Operator! You've cut us off. What's that? Who's calling? That's what I want to find out. You cut us off before the man told his name. Look that up and let me know at once where it came from. What's that? What number? Why that's your business. You ought to know where a call came from just two minutes ago. You'll look it up? All right. Get busy then. I have to make a train."

"Who was it?" demanded Nannette appearing wide-eyed with dishcloth in one hand and a piece of burnt toast in the other.

"Shut up!" said her husband rudely. "Don't you see I'm busy? I never saw such service as we have here in this town, can't find out who a call came from."

"Was it a man calling or a woman?"

"A man, of course. Isn't there always a man where a girl is concerned?"

"I never saw a man come to see Joyce," meditated Nannette wonderingly.

"Joyce was sly. Haven't you learned that yet? You women are all fools about each other anyway. This was a man, and a young one. I've heard his voice but I can't place it. Hello! Central! Central! Are you going to keep me waiting all day? What? You can't trace it? That's all bosh. Oh! You say it was a local pay station? Well, ring it up at once. What? You don't know the number—Aw! That don't go down with me. Give me the chief operator. Operator! Operator!

"Hang it all, she's hung up again! What time is it anyway! Gosh, hang it, I've missed my train. No, I don't want any coffee. Give me my hat; I must make that train. No, I can't stop to tell you anything! Where's my coat? It's strange you never can help me when I'm in a hurry. Get out of my way, Dorothea! Dang that cat, I believe I've broken my toe."

He was gone leaving an agitated family and a breathless cat emerging from the lilac bush where he had been savagely kicked.

"Well, anyhow, I bet I can find out who was on that wire," said Dorothea maturely. "I bet they'll know down to the drugstore. I bet I can get Dick Drew to tell me. Most everybody phones from the drugstore. They ain't but two or three local pay stations."

"Be still, Dorothea, you don't know what you're talking about," reprimanded her mother sharply. "Don't you go to talking or you'll make your father awfully angry. You go wash your hands and get off to school. You're going to be late. No, Junior isn't going to stay at home. He's perfectly able to go to school, and I'm not going to be bothered this morning. I've got too much to do to have either of you around."

The telephone rang again at this moment, and Nannette hastened to answer it.

It was a woman's voice this time:

"Is this you, Joyce? Oh! Is that Mrs. Massey? May I speak to Miss Radway?"

"Why, Joyce isn't here just now," answered Nannette sweetly. "Is there any message? Anything I can do for you?"

"Why, no, I guess not, thank you. How soon will Joyce be back?"

"Why, I'm not just sure," shifted Nannette uneasily. "Couldn't I give her a message?"

"Well, you might tell her Martha Bryan called up to know if she would take her Sunday school class next Sunday. I know it's a little hard on her to ask her to do it just now when she's been through trouble, but she isn't one to sit down and eat her heart out when there's work to be done, and I thought perhaps it would help her over a hard day to feel she was doing the Lord's work. She and her Aunt Mary always were ones you could rely on to help. And I wouldn't ask, only my daughter has been taken sick up at Watsonville, and she wants me. I do hate to go without seeing to my class, and I'm just sure Joyce'll take it. But I've got to leave by three o'clock. Joyce ain't going to be gone all day is she?"

"Oh, I think not," said Nannette nonchalantly. What if Joyce should stay all day! How dreadful!

"Well, you ask her to call me just as soon as she gets in. I want to relieve my mind of that class."

"I'll tell her," said Nannette ungraciously, "but she's got a lot to do at home. I doubt if she can manage it."

"Oh, but she promised me six weeks ago she would if I had to go."

"Well, I'll tell her." And Nannette hung up snappily. She didn't exactly relish everybody in town expecting that Joyce would go right on doing what she always had done, as if her circumstances in life were just as they had been. It was time people began to understand that Joyce was a dependent, and as such as not at the beck and call of every old woman and Sunday school class. She was tired and angry from loss of sleep last night, and it was high time Joyce came home and did her work. Of course she must be out there in the barn asleep somewhere. Probably she was waiting for somebody to come out and coax her in. Well, she would go out and find her. There was the harness closet and there was the hayloft. Probably Eugene didn't look very far. She would find her and teach her her duty once and for all, and there wouldn't be any question about it either.

Nannette marched out of the kitchen door with the air of a conquering hero and sailed into the garage, the very crackle of her step on the gravel foretelling what was in store for any luckless miscreant who might be found lurking in the hay.

But though she searched vigilantly, and thoroughly, there was no sign anywhere of Joyce. Out behind the barn a fluttering paper caught her eye and stopping to pick it up she found it was an examination paper with answers scribbled after each question in Joyce's fine script. Angrily she tore it in half and half again, and scattered it on the ground, scanned the meadow for an instant, and the distant road and then went

back into the house just in time to hear the telephone ringing
again.

It was a man's voice this time, a strange, dignified, young
voice, a voice that spoke as from authority:

"I would like to speak with Miss Joyce Radway."

The sense of panic returned to Nannette, but she summoned voice to demand sharply:

"Who is this?" At least she would not make Eugene's mistake
and let anyone get away without complete identification.

"This is J. S. Harrington, acting superintendent of the high
school. I wish to speak to Miss Radway with regard to her
examination paper. Is she there?"

"She is not," said Nannette with asperity.

"Perhaps you know if she is already on her way to school?"

Nannette wished she did.

"She'll not be able—" she began and then reflected that perhaps Joyce was on her way to school. No telling where she had
spent the night with this in view. At least she must not give
away the present situation to the whole village. Especially not
to this interesting stranger. He must be the man they were
talking about at the station last night, young and good-looking.
What could he want with Joyce?

"I'm not sure whether she is going over to the school today
or not," she equivocated. "Is there any message?"

"Just ask her to step into my office if she is coming to school.
If not I shall be glad to have her call me, as soon as she comes
in. Thank you. Good morning."

The click of the telephone was almost immediately followed
by a knock on the kitchen door, where stood a small boy with a
basket of luscious strawberries covered over with dewy leaves.
He was freckled and cross-eyed, with two upper teeth missing,
but he had a most engaging smile, and he wanted Joyce very
much. He seemed dubious about leaving the strawberries
when he heard she was not at home, and almost decided to sit
down and wait, but Nannette explained that it might be some
time and he surrendered the basket reluctantly with the message that "Ma" had "thent 'em for Joyth and wanted the rethipe
for her y'aunth's maple cake."

Nannette regarded the strawberries with a vindictive glare.
Why should Joyce have so many friends? Since Mother Massey
died everybody seemed so interested in doing things for Joyce
and nobody seemed to bother about her in the least, although
she was the son's wife. It certainly wasn't going to be pleasant

living in this town until she had made Joyce's position quite plain. But then, after everybody understood that Joyce couldn't go out as much as she used to, and wasn't wearing such fine clothes nor having leisure for picnics and Sunday school classes and the like, people would soon realize that Joyce was nothing.

The next call on the telephone came from the minister's wife. She wanted Joyce to come and take lunch with her. She thought it might take her mind off her sorrow a little and help her to get back into natural living again.

Nannette was furious, but she managed a vague reply. Joyce was away. She wasn't sure whether she would be back in time for lunch or not. No, she wasn't gone to visit friends. She went—well—on business.

The minister's wife was surprised but courteous. Later in the afternoon the minister called. He said he had been unusually busy since the funeral or he would have been there sooner. He said he wished to talk with Joyce about a little matter her aunt had been interested in, and had hoped to find that she had returned.

The new school superintendent called up again while the minister was there, and seemed quite upset that Joyce had not returned, and when she finally got rid of the minister and went out to the kitchen to consider the possibility of having to get dinner without Joyce's help, she was called back three times to the telephone. First, Susie Bassett wanted to know if Joyce couldn't come over and spend the night with her, she wanted to ask her advice about something. Then Mr. Elkins called from the store and said his wife was all alone and not feeling very well, and he would be so grateful if Joyce would run down and sit with her a little while till he could get away from the store. Then Patty Bryson from up in the country called to ask Joyce to come up and spend a week with her and the children while her husband was away, she thought it would be a nice little change for Joyce.

With flashing eyes and sullen mouth Nannette turned back to her kitchen only to find Mrs. Pierce her next-door neighbor standing on the doorstep just entering with a warning tap to borrow a cup of sugar—hers hadn't come yet—and ask if Joyce was sick, she hadn't seen her about all day.

Nannette was almost reduced to tears when she finally got rid of the woman who was a regular village gossip and had the real vulture smile on her face. But it was almost time for Eugene's train and he was not noted for being patient at meal-times. She flew around preparing what she could briefly, a can of soup, improvised salad out of odds and ends, a hastily concocted custard poured over some stale sponge cake she had hidden from the children a week ago and forgotten till necessity brought it to light. None of the articles were particular favorites of Eugene. He would miss Joyce's tasty cooking, but it could not be helped.

Meantime, where were the children? Six o'clock and they hadn't returned since schooltime! What would Eugene say if they were not here when he got home? She hastened to the telephone to call up their familiar spirits and get track of them, and almost every house she called either had some message for Joyce or wanted to know how she was bearing her trouble, and had some good word of sympathy for her. It was maddening to Nannette in her frantic haste, with one eye on the clock and the smell of the soup burning. Now she would have to open another can. There was only a vegetable can left and Eugene hated that.

Then just as she was looking up the number of the last place where she might hope to find her missing family, they trooped in.

"Ma, is Joyce here yet? Cause our teacher's coming down to see her right away. Say, Ma, can't I put on my new organdy dress? The superintendent's coming along with her. I heard them planning it when I was in the cloakroom. And say, Ma, that must have been him phoned Daddy this morning, 'cause I heard him say she had awful good exams. He said they were 'very clever' just like that. I'm going up to change my dress before they get here. I'm going to wear my new patent leathers too. And, oh, yes, Mrs. Bryan says for you to call her up *right away* and tell her what Joyce said about taking her Sunday school class. She's going to take the evening train, and she's *got* to know before she goes."

Dorothea's voice trailed off up the stairs as Junior stamped in angrily:

"Say, Ma, what did Joyce do with my baseball bat? I wisht she'd leave my things alone. Where is she anyhow? Steve Jenkins says he saw her walkin' along the state road last night with her hat in her hand. And the minister asked me when she was comin' back, and Miss Freedley told me to tell her she was comin' over after supper fer her to teach her how to knit her sweater sleeves. And say, Ma, ain't there any more jelly roll?

I'm hungrier'n a dozen wolves. You didn't have hardly anything fer lunch. I don't see why you let Joyce go away. There goes the telephone. I 'spect that's Ted Black. He wants to know if Joyce can help out on the country week picnic committee—"

His mother swept him out of the way and answered the phone just as Eugene entered with an angry frown:

"Where is Joyce?" he called out imperatively, just as a strange voice over the phone asked, "Has Miss Radway returned yet?"

Nannette, her nerves having reached the verge of control, snapped out an answer:

"No, she hasn't. I don't know when she's coming back. She's away on a visit," and hung up the phone with a click.

"Do you mean to tell me Joyce hasn't come back yet?" roared Eugene ominously as his wife turned to meet him.

"If you ask me that question again I'll *die!*" screamed Nannette, "I've had to answer it all day long. One would think Joyce Radway was the most important person in this town. I think it's ridiculous your mother letting her get into everything this way, a charity girl! Well, you needn't look so cross. She was, wasn't she, even if she was your cousin. Everybody in this whole town is wanting that snip of a girl for something. I told you you ought to go out last night and make her come back. She's as stubborn as a mule, and we've got a pretty mess on our hands. One would think she was a princess or something the way folks act. And the new superintendent is coming to see her tonight, and the minister wants—"

"There's something far more important than those trifles," glowered Eugene. "Judge Peterson has rallied and the doctor says he may read the will this evening. We've got to go over there exactly at seven and not keep him waiting. The doctor is awfully particular about exciting him. And I want to get this thing fixed up right away. They say the judge has heart trouble and might drop off at any time now and that would make no telling how much more delay. This is serious business for us and you needn't sit there and trifle about the village people! Joyce has got to be *found,* and *found right away.* Do you understand?"

"Well find her then!" retorted his wife. "You talk as if it was my fault she went away. Haven't I slaved all day doing her work? And I'm done now. I'm *just done!*" and Nannette burst into angry tears and ran upstairs to her room, slamming the door and locking it behind her.

Chapter 5

For three quarters of an hour Eugene made it lively for his family. He stalked upstairs, captured his pampered young son in the act of purloining one of his clean handkerchiefs, gave him a cuff on the ear, and ordered him in no gentle tones to go to one end of the village as fast as his legs could fly and find out if Joyce was at Auntie Summers or had been there, and demand her presence at home at once on important business. He jerked a library book away from his daughter and sent her to the other end of town to make the same inquiry at a home where Joyce had been a frequent visitor, and then he strode to his own door and shook it demanding entrance in such a tone that Nannette dared not ignore it. He gave his hysterical wife a rough shake and told her it was no time to indulge her temper, that action was necessary. She must get to work on the telephone at once and find Joyce. They must meet that appointment at Judge Peterson's on the hour or they might lose everything. The son had said that his father was very insistent about having Joyce present when he read the will. It would look very strange if Joyce didn't turn up in time.

He succeeded in frightening Nannette sufficiently so that she wiped her eyes and went to the telephone, calling up one and another of Joyce's friends, and in honeyed tones asking if she had stopped there on her way home and might she speak to her a minute, there was an errand she wanted done on the way back that couldn't wait. But one and all said that Joyce had not been there that day, and two women answered, "Why, I heard Joyce had gone away on a visit," so that Nannette turned from her fruitless task at last with a much disturbed face.

"She isn't in town," she said. "There isn't another place I can think of to call."

"Well, think of all the places out of town then, find out where she is, and I'll get an automobile and go after her. Little fool! She knew she was making me a lot of trouble. She did this on purpose, I'll wager. But she'll get paid back double for all she does. Just let her wait." Eugene was stamping up and down and suggesting places to call, while his wife with more and more agitated voice continued to call up numbers.

"I'm almost sure that operator is Jenny Lowe," she said with her hand over the mouthpiece of the telephone. "If it is she'll tell it everywhere that I've called all these numbers. She's probably listening in."

"Jenny Lowe be hanged!" said Eugene. "We've got to find Joyce! Look at the clock! It's half past six. Call Aunt Whinnie's."

Nannette called Aunt Whinnie's but got no answer, and while she was still trying to get it Dorothea came panting back saying that Joyce hadn't been heard of anywhere, and the teacher and the superintendent were just coming into the yard.

Eugene went frowning to the front door and disposed of the new superintendent in short order saying that his cousin had been suddenly called away and he was not sure how soon she would return. She might be gone several days. He intimated that she had gone to visit a sick relative, but when the young man got his pencil and notebook and asked for her address he replied vaguely that he was not quite sure whether she would remain more than a few hours where she had gone and she might make several visits before her return. But the young superintendent was not one who was easily baffled and asked for all the addresses, whereupon Eugene was put to the trouble of making up an address. It was rather hard on him for he had been brought up not to tell lies, and he always tried to avoid deliberate ones, but this time he felt he was in a bad corner and had to get out somehow. The hand of his watch said a quarter to seven, and he must get rid of these callers. What in Sam Hill did this young upstart want of Joyce anyway?

But the young upstart turned gravely away without imparting his business, and Eugene shut the door with unnecessary slamming, and went back to his wife:

"We'll just have to go over to the judge's and do the best we can. We'd better fix up some story about Joyce. Perhaps we can get around the old man. I'll tell you, we've had an offer for the house and we want to close with it right away. Man going to Europe and wants to get this property fixed up for a relative to live in. How'll that do? Then we can find a purchaser and get this house off our hands. I'd rather go back to Chicago anyway, wouldn't you, and get out of this rotten town where everybody's nose is in your business, and the minister thinks he owns the earth, and can boss it? I'd like to know what business of his it was to come after Joyce anyway? Doesn't he think we can take care of our own relatives without his intervention?"

At the door a small girl with tangled curls and big blue eyes presented a note which she said was to be given to Miss Joyce and "not to nobody else," and which she steadily refused to surrender even for a glimpse until Miss Joyce should be forthcoming. There was something strong-willed and characterful in the very swing of her little gingham petticoats as she swung sturdily down the front path and out the gate with the note still clasped to her bosom. Eugene called Dorothea to the front window to identify her, and Miss Dorothea lifted her nose contemptuously:

"Oh, that's Darcy Sherwood's niece, Lib Knox. She's a tomboy. She can throw mud just like the boys, and once she tied a string across the sidewalk and tripped our teacher and she fell flat, because our teacher told her she was too dirty to come in the schoolyard. She's only six but she's awful bad!"

Dorothea said it virtuously, and licked her lips to hide the jelly she had been eating out of a new tumbler she had just opened.

Darcy Sherwood! What had Darcy Sherwood to do with Joyce? Could that have been Darcy's voice over the phone that morning?

Eugene was silent and thoughtful during their walk to Judge Peterson's and strode so fast that Nannette could scarcely keep pace with him. As they waited after ringing the old-fashioned doorbell he looked down frowning and admonished his wife:

"Now, don't you be a fool and spill the beans."

They were ushered into the judge's room where he lay propped up by pillows in a great old sleigh bed, with his wife on one side fanning him gently, and his son sitting by the window with some papers in his hands, but as soon as they were seated the judge's eyes looked toward the door restlessly, and his big voice which had lost none of its brusqueness with his illness, although it quavered a little with weakness, asked:

"Where's Joyce? Didn't you bring the little girl?"

Nannette looked frightened and turned toward her husband to take the initiative and Eugene hastened to explain that Joyce hadn't been feeling well since the funeral and they had sent her away on a little trip to relatives to get rested after the shock of her aunt's death.

The kind, rugged old face looked disappointed, and his head sank back a little farther on the pillows:

"H'm! Then there's nothing doing," he said as if the matter were finished. "Dan, I thought I told you to tell 'em it was no use their coming without Joyce."

"I did, Father. I thought I made it plain."

"Yes, Judge, he told me, but I felt that if you understood the matter you would feel it wasn't necessary to wait for the formality of Joyce being here. She doesn't know much about business anyway and would naturally leave everything to me."

"H'm!"

The judge eyed the younger man thoughtfully, keenly, but said nothing more than that.

"You see," Eugene hurried on blandly, "it's about the house I'm especially in a hurry. We can't do anything till the business is settled up of course, but I've had an offer for the house, an unusually good offer. The man wants to pay cash and get possession right away. It's a man I met in the city in business relations, and he's going to Europe and wants to leave his family here all safely fixed before he has to leave. Every day counts with him, and he's especially anxious to get this house, and is willing to pay a good price if he can get the thing settled up at once. I thought perhaps you could put the matter through to-night for me so I could take advantage of this deal."

"H'm! Does Joyce want to sell?" questioned the old man from his pillows, "because if she does you better wire her to come on."

"I'm sure I don't know what Joyce has to do with it," fumed Eugene. "It was my mother's house wasn't it? Naturally I—"

But the old man's deep voice boomed out in stern and sudden interruption:

"Joyce has a great deal to do with it. The house belongs to Joyce."

Eugene arose excitedly, his face growing suddenly very red, his voice raised far beyond the sick room quality:

"I don't believe a word of it!" he shouted. "That's a rank lie! My mother—!"

But Dan Peterson stood suddenly beside him saying in a quiet voice:

"That will be all this evening, Mr. Massey. Step this way please," and Eugene found his arm grasped like a vise and himself propelled rapidly out of the room with Nannette in a frightened patter coming behind and someone inside the room shut the door. Afterward in remembering, it seemed that he had heard a sound something like a chuckle from the region of the bed. It made his blood boil hotly when he thought of it. Of course there had been nothing to laugh at and yet, he felt sure the old judge had laughed. There must be something—he must find Joyce at once.

They discussed it a long time after they got home and Eugene had got done scolding his wife for having been the cause of Joyce's leaving. Eugene wanted to get a detective at once and find Joyce. He was frantic. He couldn't stand the night through with this matter of the house facing him. He even had the telephone in his hand to call up a detective bureau in the city, but Nannette grappled with him for it, and pleaded with him to be reasonable for once.

"Just as soon as you get a detective the whole thing will be out, and everybody will be talking. You'll have the whole town arrayed against us, and then where will we be? Joyce may come back tomorrow, and then there won't be any need to tell anyone. And anyhow, you could have called her back when she first went if you had done what I told you, it was you that scolded her for burning the electric light so late last night you remember."

"It was you that wore her clothes to the city wasn't it? It was you that taunted her for being in a menial position and wouldn't hear to her going to those examinations that she set so much store by, wasn't it?"—responded he.

Into the midst of this loud altercation there came a tap on the side door close to which Eugene was sitting. It was so startling for anyone to come to that door at that time of night that Eugene jumped and sat up. Both were absolutely still for a quarter of a second. Nannette even turned a little white as she stared toward the door which had four latticed panes of glass and was lightly draped in open fishnet.

Nannette recovered first.

"There she is, I suppose," she said in a low whisper with lips that scarcely moved, for she was conscious that she must be under the eye of whoever was outside. "For pity's sake don't rave now and send her off again. And don't you give in either. She needs a lesson after acting like this."

She arose and gathered up her hat and wrap which were lying where she had thrown them when she came in from Judge Peterson's. Her action seemed to bring Eugene to his senses. He got up and went to the door, opening it but a few inches and looking out with an air of affront.

But Joyce was not outside, as he had half made up his mind she would be. A man stood there in the darkness, a stranger he seemed to be at first glimpse, tall, well built, of almost haughty bearing—a thing Eugene could never tolerate in any man but himself. For a moment they stood gazing at one another. It was almost as if the man outside were sizing up the man who stood against the light. Then Eugene remarked acridly:

"Well, what do you want?" giving the door the least bit of an impatient jerk as if he were about to close it. The visitor must speak quickly.

There was perfect courtesy in the voice that replied:

"Mr. Massey? Sherwood's my name. I'd like to have a few words with you?"

There was a grave assurance about the young man's tone that irritated Eugene. Then he reflected that the man might have some news concerning Joyce and it would be as well to hear him through.

"Well, if you don't take too long," he said curtly, stepping out to the porch and drawing the door to after him. "We were just about to retire. I suppose you're aware it's rather late for callers."

The young man lifted his hat with a grave smile that showed a row of irritatingly beautiful teeth, and gave him somehow the appearance of great advantage, but instead of telling his errand he put his hand out and pushed open the door saying pleasantly, and almost with an air of authority:

"We'll just go inside if you don't mind," and was in before Eugene could resent his action. This was most extraordinary behavior and Eugene, half ready to eject him for his presumption, was yet somehow compelled to follow him.

It was quite evident as they entered that the visitor had intended to come inside for a purpose, for he did not hide the fact that he was taking in the whole sitting room with a quick, keen glance, and even the hall and stairs and the living room beyond. He bowed deferentially to Nannette as she slid back into the room, curiosity in every line of her face.

Seen in the light of the room his face was extremely handsome, with an easy carelessness upon it that showed he made no merit of his comeliness, and cared little for impressions. Yet when he smiled even an enemy must needs listen:

"I came to see whether Joyce Radway has come home yet."

The tone demanded a straightforward answer, in fact it was

like a command, as of one who had the right to know. Eugene stiffened, resentfully:

"She has not," he answered. "I believe I told you that over the phone a little while ago."

"You did," said Sherwood. "I came to make sure." He gave a glance about that had a sense of listening in it.

"Indeed!" bristled Eugene.

"When did she go away, just what time?"

"What business of yours is that?"

"It isn't any of my business. I'm making it mine. What time?"

"Well, find out if you can. I don't answer impertinent questions." Eugene was white with anger. He would have liked to have put this intruder out, only the man was nearly twice his size.

"That's what I intend to do!" answered the visitor taking a step into the room where he could look well through the hall and living room without effort. There was a grim set look about his face that meant business, and yet he turned to Nannette with that winning smile he could flash forth suddenly like the sun coming out from behind a cloud:

"Mrs. Massey, I'm not a bandit, and I'm not as impertinent as your husband seems to think, although I may be a trifle unconventional, but it is necessary for me to find out when Joyce Radway left this house and I mean to do so. If you'll excuse me I'll just step upstairs and speak to your son a minute. Don't trouble yourself to lead the way. I'll find him all right—"

He took one swift stride into the hall before Eugene realized what he was doing and bustled irately to stop him. But the stranger did not need to go far, for Junior in bare feet and pajamas was hanging over the balustrade, his ears alert for the family scene.

"Hello, buddy," the young man said in a tone he might have used to an older pal.

Junior straightened up involuntarily and a gleam came into his eye. He threw one leg over the balustrade and balanced grinning, emitting a low, "'ello!" It was plain that he was both pleased and embarrassed.

"Still interested in that baseball bat of mine, are you, kid?"

"Sure!" responded Junior coming down to the steps again and sticking his tongue in his cheek expectantly.

"Well, how about that package you were to deliver? Did you deliver it last night?"

Junior hung his head, and wriggled on one bare toe.

"Couldn't," he murmured in a low voice. "She went away 'fore I had the chance. She didn't come back yet."

"That's all right, son," said the young man pleasantly. "That's all I want to know. May I trouble you for the package?"

"I got it hid."

"Get it, please!"

"Junior!" broke forth Nannette's indignant voice, "come here to me this instant."

But Junior's bare heels were flying up the stairs, and before his mother could pursue him he returned with a small indiscriminate bundle which he thrust over the balustrade where it disappeared inside the visitor's coat.

"All right, buddy, the bat is yours when you call for it tomorrow. At the old stand. You know."

"Aw'right!" answered Junior with delight in his eyes. It was plain that his mother was nowhere in his vision while this hero was in sight.

The young man turned and walked swiftly back through the sitting room past the angry father and mother and over to the door. With the doorknob firmly grasped in his hand he turned once more and faced his host:

"I happened to see Miss Radway alone on a lonely road quite late last night and was interested to know if she reached home in safety. I thought perhaps we might work together to find her if there was any necessity. But since you do not care to cooperate I will wish you good evening."

The young man flashed a distant smile and opening the door was gone before the man and woman realized what he was about to do.

For an instant they looked at each other speechless. Then Nannette broke forth:

"You ought to have asked him where he saw her! Go after him quick! Don't let him get away!"

Stung into action Eugene opened the door and called into the night:

"Oh, I say! Come here! Wait a minute!"

But his words seemed to float out on emptiness.

Eugene stood in the door for a moment listening, but there seemed to be no echo of footsteps. Yet it was scarcely a second since the visitor had stood inside the door. Where could he have gone? It was almost uncanny.

Nannette came and looked out the door, and Eugene hurried down the walk calling out again, but no answer came, and his own voice seemed to mock him. He looked up and down the street, but saw no one. He walked around the house, and back to the gate again. There was no sound of an automobile in the quiet moonlit street. Everyone had gone to bed and the lights were out. Strange! How could the man have disappeared?

"Junior! Who was that man?" screamed Nannette remembering and rushing back into the house. But Junior had a realizing sense of his disloyalty to his family, and had fled to his bed with the clothes tucked tightly around his ears, and his eyes screwed shut as if in deep slumber. When rudely shaken into being he yawned reprovingly and asked, "What man?"

Nannette brought him at last to a proper appreciation of the necessity and he nonchalantly replied, "Oh, him? He's our coach, Darce Sherwood. You just oughta see him pitch a ball. He's some crackerjack pitcher."

Questioned further concerning the package he said he guessed some old woman had sent it to Joyce. He guessed it was some seeds or "sumpin" to put on Grandma's grave.

The mother and father looked at one another completely puzzled.

"He certainly had no right to go away that way without telling me where he saw Joyce," declared Eugene angrily. "Now I suppose I shall have to go out and find him. The insolent sucker! He thought he had me in a hole. I *won't* go after him. Let him go to the dogs. Probably he never saw Joyce at all. What difference does it make if he did? Serves her right if she gets in trouble. I'm not going to hunt him up that's certain. I'll get a detective. What's he got to do with Joyce anyhow I'd like to know?"

"Then everybody'll find out—" wailed Nannette.

"What's the difference if they do? They'll find out if she doesn't come back at all, won't they? You haven't a brain cell working. You're just *like* a woman—!"

"But, Gene, why don't you see that this man is the only clue you have to where she was last seen?"

"Well, what if he is? Do you think I'm going crawling to a man that entered my house that way—? Say! That's an idea! I'll have him arrested for housebreaking. He came into my house against my express command. I told him we were retiring. I told him I would talk to him outside. But he just opened the door and walked in and said we would talk inside. I'll call up the police and have him arrested before he gets home, that's what I'll do. Then we'll tell him we'll release him when he tells where Joyce is. Perhaps he's got her kidnapped somewhere. Perhaps he knows more than he's willing to tell—!"

But while they were discussing it Darcy Sherwood was striding over the meadows and vaulting the fences back of their house, till he reached the public highway along which Joyce had walked the evening before.

Chapter 6

When Joyce felt her wrists clasped in that iron grip in the darkness, and felt the hot breath of a man on her face, she was more frightened than she had ever been in her life. All the stories of horrors in the night, of holdups and bandits and kidnappings came to her mind as she struggled vainly for a moment in that viselike grip. She tried to scream, though she knew she was too far away from houses to reach the ear of any people who lived about unless someone happened to be going along that road; and people did not go along that road at night unless they had to. It was lonely and desolate, and out of the way from the main highway, a quiet remote place for the dead. She had a quick feeling of thankfulness that Aunt Mary who had always been so careful for her safety, so anxious when she was out alone at night, was where she could not be alarmed; a quick wish that she could call to her. Then the thought of God came and her heart cried for help.

The flashlight sprung in her face sent her almost swooning. She was conscious that her senses were going from her, and that she must somehow prevent herself from going out this way in the dark, and then up through the billows of blackness that were surging to envelop her soul she heard her own name in startled, almost tender tones:

"Joyce!"

And back through the blackness she came again to earth and

consciousness and opened her eyes, straight into the eyes that searched her face; answering the call of that strangely familiar voice: "Oh—was it you?"

There was troubled relief in the voice as she said it, relief as if she would rather have had back the terror than to have found this one involved in the mystery. There was question, pain, almost reproach, in her tone; there was judgment held in suspense as if her soul rejected the witness of her eyes. Then, as if she could not bear the conclusion of her own judgment she cried out earnestly,

"Oh, *what* were you doing there?"

He dropped her hands as if they had been shot away from him and his head drooped, stooped perhaps would be better, as if a great burden had suddenly been let upon his shoulders. He tried to speak and his voice was husky, the words did not come from his lips. He half turned away with a motion as if he would hide his face.

Then a low stealthy whistle rasped between them and he started back toward her:

"Go!—" he said quickly. "Go! You must not be seen here! Joyce—little Joyce—" the last syllables were scarcely audible. She heard them in her soul afterward, like a long echo of a very fine whisper. A clear whistle close beside her, resonant, remembered from childhood, sounded just above her bowed head as she turned, and she knew he was signaling to the rest.

"Go! Straight down the road! Keep in the shadow. I'll come back after awhile and find you," he whispered. "Don't be afraid—" and in the same breath, louder:

"All right, kid, nothing but a scared rabbit. We'll go up the other way—"

He was striding away from her rapidly into the darkness and she stood almost petrified in the road where he left her, till she heard a rough laugh of one of his companions and fear lent strength to her feet once more and sped her down the road again.

Her heart was beating wildly, and her thoughts in a chaos. She could not think, nor analyze her own feelings. She could only fly along in the shadow, stumbling now and again over a rough bit of road, straining her ears to listen for sounds behind her, casting a fearful glance back.

But the darkness was reassuring. The dimmed lights of the automobile that had stood by the roadside were no long visible. The men had gone away in the other direction. She was alone on the road—with at least another mile to go before she could turn again into the highway, and she found an overwhelming tremble upon her. Her very spirit seemed to be quivering with it. The night which had been warm and balmy seemed turned to fearful cold and she shivered as she tried to hurry along. Now and then the moon swept out and threw her shadow along the way, and she glanced furtively behind her and shrank into the shadow of the elderberry bushes by the fence. Once a wild rabbit scuttled across the road and startled her so that she almost fell. She began to reproach herself for having gone away from home in this silly aimless way, losing her temper like a child and walking out from safety and protection without preparation. She wondered if God were angry with her for it. She wondered why she had done it and what she was going to do anyway, but most of all she wondered what those dark figures on the hillside had been doing, and why the shoulders of her friend had dropped as if with shame. Most of all this dragged upon her soul and kept her from fleetness. For how must the feet drag when the heart is weighed down!

She came at last into the highway and heard by the tolling of the clock on a distant barn that it was two o'clock. It gave her a strange sense of detachment from the world to be thus adrift at that dark, prowling time of the night.

The road was empty either way. Not even a light of a distant car was in sight. If she could only hope to find a place of shelter before another came. Surely it could not be much longer so empty on the highway. Someone would be going by. Someone would see her. They would think it strange. They would think ill of her if they saw her. There was no hope for help from any passing car. She would not dare accept it if it were offered.

Ahead she saw a strip of woods. Her brain began to function. That would be the grove just before you came to old Julia Hartshorn's house, and Julia Hartshorn lived just outside of Heatherdell. Heartherdell was a little town and she knew many of the people. She would not be lonely there. But where could she go? She must not be seen out at that time of night by anyone she knew unless she came to it and appealed for help. That would mean that she would have to tell the circumstances of her being out from home in the blackness of night. That would mean criticism for Eugene and Nannette, no matter how gently she might tell her tale, nor how much she took the blame upon herself. And that would have hurt Aunt Mary. For Aunt Mary's sake she must not let any talk go around. Aunt

Mary knew that Nannette was jealous of her, and that Eugene was sometimes hard on her, but Aunt Mary loved her son, even though she knew his faults, and Joyce would never willingly make any gossip that would reflect upon the family. Eugene was right. He knew Joyce's conscience. It was functioning right on true to type even now in her terror and perplexity.

If only she had not gone to that cemetery! If only she had not turned aside and allowed herself to give up and cry upon Aunt Mary's grave, and lose all that time. She might have been far away now, in a safe, quiet room somewhere that she had hired for the night. There would have been places where she could have found a room for a very little. She had some money, she didn't remember how much, with her—it didn't matter. There were a few dollars. Perhaps, too, she had put that gold piece in her handbag, she wasn't sure of that. The day had been so long and hard, so many things had been within its hours. She could not recall what she had picked up to carry with her that morning. She was too weary to care.

But she couldn't bear to go away without bidding goodbye to the spot where Aunt Mary and her mother lay, and perhaps too she had felt she could better think what to do, there in the quiet with the two graves.

Well, there was no use in excusing herself. She had gone. She shuddered at the horror of the last hour, and then that burden again to find out it was that one—and to wonder. What had he been doing? Was it then true, all the whispers that had come to her ears, of his life?

Around the bend ahead dashed a light. A car was coming at last. She remembered he had said he would come after her. She glanced back, but it was all darkness. Even if he did come would she want to meet him? Could she explain her presence out at night? He was now an almost stranger. He knew naught of her life. And perhaps it would be better if she did not know his.

She glanced fearfully ahead. The light was growing brighter, was almost blinding. She stepped out of its range and crept among some bushes till the glare and the swift passing car were gone, and watched the little red taillight blink and disappear. Then keeping quite close to the bank she slid along, fearful of another car so near to the bend of the road. It might come upon her unaware and if she were in the glare she would naturally be noticed by the driver. She trembled at the very thought, and hurried along, limbs sometimes stumbling and almost falling in the tall grass.

But presently she came in sight of Julia Hartshorn's cottage, a little quiet brown affair, with gingerbread fretwork on its porches and moss on its roof, set far back from the street in a grove of maples, like a tiny island off the mainland of the larger grove nearby.

A picket fence with scaling ancient paint, and a gate with a chain and weight guarded the quiet haven, and the fitful moonlight quavered out and showed the dim outline of a hammock slung between the maples close to the west porch. Joyce remembered a long, beautiful afternoon when she had lain in that hammock and read a book while Aunt Mary sat on the porch with Julia Hartshorn and sewed. How long ago and how beautiful that seemed. How like heaven in contrast with what she had been going through lately! Yes, here was a haven. She might go and knock at the door, and Julia's nightcapped old head would appear at the window above. She had only to tell who it was and that she was in trouble, and the door would be open wide for her. Neither would Julia Hartshorn ever tell.

But Julia Hartshorn was old, and she had a sharp-tongued niece who had come to live with her and go to school. It would never do. She must not venture that. The school in Heatherdell was too near to the school in Meadow Brook and too much gossip went back and forth. No, she must keep to her lonely way and go on. But there was no reason why she might not slip into that gate for a little while and lie in that hammock till daylight began to come. She could steal in so quietly no one would ever know, and get out again before the household was awake. She would be entirely safe outside a dwelling house of course, and need not fear to sleep for a few minutes under such protection.

Softly she lifted the latch of the old gate, lifting the gate as she swung it cautiously open lest it creak, and let herself in, closing it noiselessly behind her. Still as a creature of the woods she stole up the grass and tiptoed across the walk to the hammock, sliding gently into it, and slowly relaxing her tense muscles. It seemed as though she had suddenly been tossed up by a terrible and angry sea where her very soul had been racked from her body and laid upon a quiet stretch of sand, so wonderful it was to lie and rest.

She scarcely knew when her thoughts relaxed from their intense strain and rested with her body or when the night blurred into sleep and took her trouble all away. She only realized as she was drifting off, that her soul was crying, "Oh, God! Forgive me if I've done wrong. Take care of me, and show me what to do! For Jesus' sake—take care of me—show me."

Was that a dream or footsteps stealthily along the road, pausing at the gate, noiseless footsteps like those in the cemetery? He was coming back—but he must not. Oh, what was he doing out there in the dark! Something that he was ashamed of? He had drooped and had not answered! "Oh, God, show him!" Was there someone at the gate? Or was it fancy? Ah—now they seemed to be going on. How sweet the breeze on her forehead—like the breeze from the open kitchen door. "Oh, God. Save him! Help me! Show me what to do."

Chapter 7

The morning dawned with a luminous pink in the east and a sudden twitter of birds. April, and four o'clock in the morning; asleep in a hammock under a tree. What could be more perfect?

Joyce, half conscious of the wonder all about her, had come to life with the first bird, and a sense of peace upon her. The daylight was coming and God had kept her. She might go on her way now and be undisturbed. Then a stab of pain at the memory of the night before brought her further awake. A low flying bird almost brushed her cheek with its wing, and the petals of the apple blossoms drifted down in her face. Such exquisite perfume, such melody of many throats, would it be something like this when one wakened in heaven and heard the voices of the angel songs?

Beyond her sheltering tree the dim outlines of the old house loomed gently in the gray morning, such peace and safety all about. How good to be resting here.

But Julia Hartshorn's niece had picked out this special morning to get up early and do some housecleaning before going to school, and just as Joyce was allowing herself to drift off again into drowsiness Jane Hartshorn's alarm clock set up such a clang into the melody of the morning that Joyce came to herself in terror and sat up looking fearfully toward the house. Not for anything would she have them discover her there. She must get up and get out before the light. She must hasten now, for someone was evidently going to arise at once, and it was not safe to remain another second.

Hastily she felt for her handbag, realized that she had only one book instead of two, groped in the darkness for her hat which had fallen to the ground, and slid softly out of the hammock.

A glance toward the house showed a light in one of the upper windows and in a panic she stole breathlessly from bush to bush and from shadow to shadow till she reached the gate and the high road. Then a new fear overtook her. She would run the risk of meeting early milk carts, perhaps stray tramps if she walked along through the village. Someone might recognize her. It would not do at this early hour in the morning. Where could she hide until a respectable hour for a young woman to be out alone? How could she explain her presence there? For she was not one of the modern girls who go where they please and let people think what they like. She had been taught that there was a certain consideration for one's reputation that was right and perfectly consistent with independence. One of the precepts that Aunt Mary had ingrained into her nature had been that good old Bible verse, "Let not then your good be evil spoken of" and she had grown up with a sane and wholesome idea of values that helped immensely when she came to a crisis anywhere.

She hurried down the road which would presently merge into the village street, as noiselessly as possible, and cast about for a possible retreat. Then she came to a low rail fence skirting a pasture. The breath of the cows came sweetly in the gray dawn, mingled with the smell of earth and growing things. She could look across a wide expanse to wooded hills several miles away. There seemed to be no buildings to suggest the presence of humans, and cows were safe friends—at least most of them. She could keep close to the fence and climb if there happened to be a bull in the lot. With a hasty glance backward and each way she climbed the fence and dropped into the pasture, skirting along its edge, and down away from the street. It was still too dark for her to be visible from the road, and she would surely find somewhere to sit down and wait until a respectable hour.

She made her way safely through two pastures, stumbling

now and then over the clumps of violets, or little hillocks of grass, but the meadow was for the most part smooth with the cropping of the cows, and it was growing lighter all the time.

In the second pasture the ground dipped till it came to a little rivulet tinkling along over bright pebbles, and giving an absurdly miniature reflection of the dawn in pink and gold as it ran; and here, under a great old chestnut tree, she dropped down and looked about her.

Off to the right perhaps half a mile away there was a red barn, and house beyond it with smoke coming from the chimney. Farther away a village church spire rose among the trees. It was all so quiet and peaceful with the first tinge of red light from the sunrise putting a halo upon everything. Joyce never remembered having been out at this hour before, all alone with the spring. The fear of the night before had fled and it was as if she were sitting safe watching God make a new day. She wondered as the miracle of the sun began to appear in a great ruby light, what this day would bring forth for her. It hardly seemed real to her yet, what she had passed through since she left home. The experience in the cemetery was like an awful dream. She shuddered to think of it. Was it because an old friend had fallen from a high pedestal where she had placed him many years ago? Was it because a nameless fear hovered about her, and she could not bear to search out in her mind what he might have been doing? Whatever it was she realized that she must put it away until she had time and privacy. There were more important things to decide now and she must keep her poise and plan her day. It would soon be light enough for her to go upon her way and she must know where she was going and what she should try to do.

In the first place she must find out how much money she had with her. She had very little of her own anyway in change, and in her hurry she was afraid she might have left that behind. She opened her handbag and turned it carefully upside down in her lap, quickly sorting out its contents, the lace, the handkerchiefs and the little trinkets in one pile, the papers and letters in another, and oh, joy, she had brought her purse. She opened it quickly to assure herself of its contents. Yes, there was the gold piece that she had been saving so long, the precious gold piece that had been a present from her own mother when she was a tiny girl. Ten dollars had seemed a great sum when she was small and Aunt Mary had encouraged her to keep it and use it for something nice that she would like to keep always as a gift from her mother. That she would not use except as a last resort. She snapped the little inner pocket shut and turned to the next compartment, counting the pennies and dimes and half dollars and quarters carefully. There were three dollars and sixty-five cents, the change from the five-dollar bill with which she paid for her gloves to wear to the funeral. Last she opened the little strapped pocket that held her bills. She had been carefully hoarding her last month's allowance, and the few dollars saved from the months before to get a new coat and some things she would need for the winter in case she passed her examinations and got a school to teach. But she had been obliged to dip into her savings several times just before Aunt Mary died, and afterward to get things for Aunt Mary that Eugene did not think of or consider necessary, and now she was not sure just how much she had left. She counted, slowly, one ten-dollar bill, three fives, a two-dollar bill, nine ones, and two silver dollars. It looked a lot as she went over it again to make sure, thirty-eight dollars, and with the three sixty-five it it made forty-one dollars and sixty-five cents. Of course the ten-dollar gold piece made it fifty-one in all, but she was not counting fhat. That was to be saved at all hazards for the thing that she wanted most as a gift from her mother. Not unless life itself were endangered would she touch it, she resolved.

But forty-one dollars ought to keep her if she were careful until she could earn more. It didn't look a lot when one considered that she was starting in the world, but just suppose she hadn't anything. Girls had been in a predicament like that before. God was good to her. She would have to save every cent carefully, and get a job of some sort at once. She must not waste a day. Jobs were not easy to find, either, when one could give no references. She would not dare give references because somehow Eugene would make things unpleasant for her. No one must find out where she was. She realized that Eugene and Nannette felt that they had a good thing in her to do their work and look after the children, while they went around and had a good time, and that they would not easily let her go. They would not stop at talking a little against her if by so doing they could lose her a job and bring her back to take care of them. This conclusion had been forcing itself upon her for some time slowly, and had been fully revealed by their actions of the day before. She did not want to make any trouble, nor any talk in the town, but she was fully resolved not to go back to them. She felt that if Aunt Mary were here now, in the light of all the things that had been said to her since the funeral, she would not advise her to remain there. Indeed, there had been hints now and then before Aunt Mary was so sick, such as "If you should ever consider it advisable not to live with Gene and Nan, dear," or "You can't tell what may develop when you get to teaching. I know Nan isn't easy to get along with—" But these were only hints, and Aunt Mary had expected to get well. They all had expected her to, until the last three weeks of her illness. Joyce had shrunk from talking about the possibilities of death, and so it seemed had Aunt Mary. After all, it was her responsibility now, and she was doing what seemed the best for all. She could never live in Eugene's house. Her breath seemed stifled. How could she study and have her light watched every night? How could she be hampered in her comings and goings if she were to earn her own living? No, she had been right to come away. Perhaps the break might have been done more formally, not precipitated in such a headlong way, that was her greatest fault to jump headlong into a situation, but even so it would likely have been harder. She could hear even now the long arguments before she had brought the Masseys to her viewpoint. Indeed she doubted if she would ever have brought them there, or have been allowed to go away if they had really thought she meant it. She was half surprised at herself that she was really gone from home so easily, half expected to have Gene walk to her out of the dim of the morning and order her home. She remembered then for the first time that Gene had been fuming about the delay in the reading of the will and likely she ought to have remained until after that out of respect to her aunt, but after all, if Aunt Mary had been going to leave her something, some furniture or a little bit of money, while it would have been nice to have it, it would only have gendered more strife. Why not let Gene have it all? That would likely compensate for the loss of her service in the family, and it would have been hard to stay there and see Nan turn Aunt Mary's house upside down, perhaps sell or dispose of some of the dear old things that had grown precious through the years. It was just as well that she was gone before it came up at all. When she was settled in some nice place and everything fully assured she would write some letters to her old friends and to Gene and Nan and tell them where she was so that there would be no talk about her going. And she knew Nan well enough to be sure that until such time as they heard from her Nan would cover her going by some clever story of a visit to friends. She thought that it would not be more than a few days before she was in a position to write.

Having settled her finances she took up the pile of papers and letters, tied them in a neat packet and bestowed them in the pocket of her serge dress. She was like a bird let out of a cage. She could not go back, not while the sunshine of the new day was coming, not even if it grew dark and lowering. She would rather quiver in the heart of her own tree than be caged again for the pleasure of others and obliged to sing whether she felt like it or not.

As she reached this decision and put the little packet of letters firmly in her pocket a ray of sun reached out a warm finger and touched her hair, and she realized that the day was come and she must soon go on her way. Hastily she went through the other things in her lap. The trinkets and lace she folded into a handkerchief and pinned it inside her dress. Having thus lightened her handbag she set about making a meager toilet.

The brook was at hand, sparkling and clear, in which to wash her face, and she had a tiny mirror in her bag to tidy her hair. By way of breakfast until she could do better she folded one of the examination question papers into a cup and drank a long, sweet draught.

While she was setting her hat straight, far in the distance she heard a humming sound, and for the first time she noticed the poles and wires of a trolley line perhaps half a mile away over the fields. Sure enough! That was the new trolley line that had just been completed. She could ride on it as far as it went and then walk to another line perhaps. Somehow now that she was away she wanted to go far enough away from home to be really in a new atmosphere, where people would not find her and tell the Masseys about her. She must get at least a hundred miles away from home, perhaps more, or it would be no use going at all. Yet she dared not take much of a ride on the train, it would eat into her small hoard too much and leave her nothing to get started on when she found a new home. But a trolley! One could go a good many miles for five cents. She strained her eyes to watch for the car and soon spied it, a black speck moving from the east, growing momently larger and more distinct against the brightness of the morning. There would likely be another one going in the opposite direction soon. Could she make it across the fields before it came? They would probably run every half hour. If she missed this next one it would not be so long to wait for the next. Was it too early for a girl to board a car in the open country? She eyed the sun. It could not be more than five o'clock. She decided to try for it, and picking up her small effects was soon on her way across the fields.

Fortune favored her, and a car came along soon after she arrived at the highway. She boarded it and found a seat in the end next to a laborer with a pickax and muddy boots, who was fast asleep and did not even know when she sat down. Most of the men in the car were laborers and were nodding drowsily, scarcely looking at one another. She was the only woman in the car, but they paid no heed to her, and she dropped back into the seat as the car lurched on its way, thankful that her hasty glance revealed no acquaintance from Meadow Brook or Heatherdell. She put her head back against the window and closed her eyes and her senses seemed to swim away from her. She suddenly realized that she had had no supper the night before and no breakfast but spring water that morning. All the strain of the day before and the terrible night seemed to climax in that moment, and for an instant she felt as if she were losing her consciousness. Then her will came to the front and she set her lips and determined to pull through no matter how hard the ride or how long the fast. She was young and this was her testing. She must not, she would not faint.

The car stopped for a moment to let on some more tired looking men going to their work, and a whiff of spring blew in at her window fanning her brow. She thought again of the hand of her mother, and wondered if God were reminding her that He cared, and new strength seemed to come into her.

She was awakened from a half drowse at the next stop by the sound of a voice that sent terror through her heart. It was the same hoarse voice breaking out in raucous laughter that she had heard half subdued in the graveyard the night before, the one they had called "Kid."

Chapter 8

Joyce sat up startled and peered furtively from her window.

The man was outside waiting to board the car. He was big and red and ugly, with bold blue eyes and red hair. He had a weak mouth and a cruel jaw, and she couldn't help shrinking into her corner as she looked. Suppose he had been the one to catch her and hold her hands in a viselike grip last night! Her soul turned sick within her.

He came up the steps prating in a loud voice about women, called them "dames" and "skirts," and his laughter was an offense. Laughter is like smells, it can be fragrant as the morning or it can be foul as the breath of a gutter. This man's laughter was like a noxious gas.

Joyce would have fled if the aisle had not been blocked either way. Failing in that she shrank still further back in her seat, drew her hat over her eyes, and found herself trembling in every fiber. Why did such a man have to be on the earth, she wondered as she heard his voice going on in coarse remarks. And what possible companionship, even in business, could he have with the man she knew, whom she had always thought fine of soul?

The stab of that question came into her morning with renewed sharpness as she was compelled to sit and listen, as were all the rest of the passengers in the car, to this crude man's conversation.

There was nothing to fear of course, for it was broad daylight and there were plenty of men in the car whose faces told that they would defend her. They might be all common workingmen, but they had homes and mothers and wives and sisters and they respected them. There was a kind of nobleness in their faces that made one sure of that.

Joyce sat motionless and tried to still the trembling of her lips, tried to control the foolish desire to let the tears come into her eyes, tried to tell herself she was silly, and only needed her breakfast and there was no sense in her giving way to her feelings like this. This man did not know her. He had no idea that she had been the intruder at his midnight work. Oh, that work—that terrible work! What was it that bound these men together, the one so coarse, the other who had always seemed so fine? It haunted her with dark possibilities. Some money-making scheme of course it was. But—it must be something terrible! She could not forget the look, the droop of the man in the darkness, when she had asked him about it.

And this other one. He must live somewhere near where he had boarded the car. He was not anyone from Meadow Brook. The business was a partnership with strangers, yet the one she knew had been the captain, the head of it all. It was his voice that had given the orders, that had told them to go back and not come after her. Why should he be bound up in something that all too clearly was illicit—something of which he was ashamed? How she wished she had not had to know this about her onetime friend. Of course she had not seen him much since the old school days, but it had never seemed possible that anything gruesome, mysterious, *wrong,* could be connected with him. It would have been much pleasanter to have gone away from home carrying with her to the end of life the pleasant thoughts of those she left behind, those who were connected in a way with the dearness of the old days.

But this was no time to think of such things. The morning was full upon them in a flood of sunshine, and the car was coming to a halt at what seemed like some kind of a terminal. There was a platform, and a shedlike shelter, and the entire car arose as one man and crowded out on the platform. Joyce waited until they were gone and slipping out the other end went around the back of the car, crossed the tracks and walked rapidly up a side street, rejoicing to hear the hum of the cross line trolley for which the men seemed to be waiting. It would be good to know that that dreadful man was gone.

On the first corner was a small grocery whose door was just being unlocked by a sleepy looking lad, and Joyce went in and bought a box of crackers and some cheese. This would reinforce her and save time. She wanted to get well out of this region before people began to be about much. She did not care to run any risk of meeting anyone she knew who would go back home and talk about it.

So, munching her crackers and cheese, she walked briskly down the street, a new one evidently, filled with rows of neat two-story houses, some of which were not yet fully finished, for workmen were about and signs were up for rent and sale.

At a broader cross street she turned the corner and came full upon a band of men who were working away at a sewer that was being laid, and suddenly from out of the group arose the noxious laughter of the red-haired man of the trolley. She stopped as if she had been shot, and wheeled, back to the quieter street of the small houses. But not back in time to escape the mocking words that were flung after her:

"There she comes! That's my girlie! Isn't she a pippin? Oh, don't run away, darling! I won't let the naughty men hurt you!"

Words could not describe the taunting tone nor her horror, as if she had been desecrated. She was trembling and the tears were flowing down her cheeks as she fled, block after block without knowing whither she went. It seemed so degrading that she could not rally her usual common sense. She began to wonder if perhaps all this was to teach her that she ought not to have gone away from home? That she should have remained and borne all there was to bear and just waited until relief came. But at that her sound sense came to her rescue and she began to breathe more freely.

She had passed into quite another section of the city now, and trolleys were coming and going and plenty of people on the streets. She boarded one of the cars and rode until it came to a railroad station where she got off and went in. There was a restaurant here where she could get a glass of milk, and there was a rest room where she might tidy herself and sit down and get her bearings. She would study the timetables and find out where to go intelligently. This running away hit or miss might only lead her in a circle and bring her back home before night.

So she went in and asked some questions, finally buying a ticket to a small town about a hundred miles away. Half an hour later, she boarded the train, having added to her crackers and cheese, an orange and a couple of bananas for lunch.

It was a local train and slow, and Joyce curled up in her seat and had a good, long nap, then woke to eat her lunch and sleep again. She had thought to plan out a campaign for herself, make some definite outline in her mind of what she would do with the future so suddenly opened out before her, but sleep simply dropped down upon her and took possession. The strain under which she had been, the sudden sharp emotions following one upon the other had stretched her endurance almost to the breaking point and relaxation brought such utter weariness that she could not even think.

Something was the matter with the engine and they stayed on a side track for a long time while men rushed about shouting to one another and doing things to the engine and now and again seemingly to the machinery underneath the cars, but it all made no impression on Joyce. She slept on, curled into a slim little heap in her seat. After a long time a train came by from the other direction, bringing aid perhaps, for it halted, and then there were more poundings and shoutings, and at last the train went on and Joyce's train groaned and creaked and took up its limping way, lumbering slowly on like a person on crutches. About the middle of the afternoon, they came to a halt, and Joyce, sitting up suddenly warned by some inner consciousness, perceived she had arrived at the place she had aimed for, and got out quickly.

She had been told in the city that there would be an electric connection with another city, and sure enough, there stood a rickety old trolley in which she embarked, the only passenger for more than half the way.

Half an hour's ride brought her through a lovely rolling country, past country clubs, and estates, and into the real farming district again, then more country clubs, and scattering bungalows and cottages till it seemed evident that she was on the outskirts of a new suburb of the city that was just being developed.

It might have been the pretty little church, covered with vines and wearing the air of having been there before the bungalows came, that gave her the sudden impulse, or perhaps it was the well-kept hedges and the general atmosphere of hominess that pervaded the pleasant streets. She decided to get out and see the place. She was tired of travel in the stuffy, rickety old car, and at least she could get into another car after she had walked awhile if she found no place that seemed livable.

She got out and followed down a pleasant shaded street of homes, at first drinking in the beauty of the well-kept lawns and newly planted gardens and hedge rows, turning corners and admiring bits of stone dwellings, bungalows, all on one floor with charming variance of rough stone pillars and porches. Turning two or three corners thus, she came upon what seemed to be a large estate, an old stone house far back from the road almost hidden by wonderful trees and dense, clustering shrubbery. It had the air of having been a fine old house of a time past, probably the original estate from which the whole town had been divided, and down at the corner in a little V of land where three roads came together and divided, the land sloped from a high wall of hedge, with a tiny graveled path to the sidewalk, there stood the dearest little land office that ever a developing operation dared to build. It was not more than nine or ten feet long and six or seven feet wide, but it had five windows and a door, and the tiniest little front porch with a seat on each side as perfect and complete as any little house that ever was built. A vine had clambered over the portico and spread to cover one entire end, and there were window boxes in the front windows where flowers had grown the past year, though weeds were overrunning them now.

As she drew nearer Joyce perceived that it had a neglected air as if no one owned it or the owner was away and didn't care, and it seemed somehow so much like her own forlorn self, hunting a home and a place in life, that her heart went out to it wistfully.

Then strangest of all just as she was feeling that way she turned the sharp point of the corner and saw two men working about it at the back, and perceived one of them raise a heavy implement and deal a tremendous blow at the little dwelling sitting so cozily there on the little knoll, with such a smiling, inviting air, doing its best to urge people to buy lots and build in this pleasant town.

The little building shivered in all its timbers, and the sound with which it reacted to the blow seemed something between a groan and a sob. Joyce stood still with horror in her eyes, and then the man raised the heavy iron and swung it back for another blow.

But Joyce, without knowing what she was doing, was all at once by his side:

"Oh!" she cried putting out a detaining hand upon the exact spot where the iron must strike. "Oh! *Don't!*"

The man paused in his motion and looked at her in wonder, his iron on his shoulder:

"Ma'am," he said astonished, "did you speak?"

"Yes," said Joyce shyly. "Why are you doing that? You will ruin the little house."

"Them was the boss's orders, ma'am. Wreck it. That's what I'm here for."

"But—why? It's a perfectly good little house."

"He wants to clear this here corner, ma'am, and set the hedge out all the way around like the rest. He don't want no office here any more, he's bought the place. He said to get this out of the way the easiest way we knowed how. I'm obeyin' orders, ma'am!"

The man raised his arm for another blow and intimated by his glance that he would be pleased if the lady would move a little further away and give him more room to strike. But Joyce only stepped nearer in her earnestness:

"Wouldn't he, do you think he might—perhaps—*sell* it?" she asked eagerly.

The two men looked at one another amusedly. This was a queer, new kind of a girl. But they were dwellers near a great city and there were all kinds in a city. Their problem was to get rid of this one and go on with their work as soon as possible. The second man took the initiative:

"Lady," he said, stepping up with authority, "the boss is on his way to Europe an' we gotta git this here building out o' this piece of ground before we quit tonight. That's my contract, an' I generally manage to keep my contrac's. That's how I keep my reputashun—gettin' things done when I say I will."

Joyce drew her brows together thoughtfully:

"What are you going to do with this building?" she asked.

"Break her up an' cart her off. Got a man comin' in an hour to clean her up fer the kindlin' wood. We ain't got no time to waste, lady."

"Then the house is yours? To do as you please with?" Her eyes persisted, looking at the men earnestly.

"Wal, it amounts to that. Yas, it's ourn."

"Well, then, wouldn't you sell it?"

"But I tell you lady, the house has gotta git off'n this here piece o' ground before tomorra morning' 'r I lose my big contract on the rest o' this job."

"Couldn't it be moved?" persisted Joyce. "They move houses even bigger than that. I've seen them."

"Aw, yes, she could be moved. A course she could be moved ef you had a place to put her."

"I will get a place," said Joyce decidedly. "What will you sell the building for?"

The men looked at one another nonplussed;

"I guess we'd take five bucks apiece, wouldn't we, Tom?" said the older of the men winking slowly.

"Sure," said Tom. "But she's gotta get outta here this afternoon."

Joyce looked anxiously about her as if she hoped to find a bit of handy land close by:

"How much time have I?" she asked. "I'll have to hunt a

place. I'm sure there's one somewhere. Do you know where I could get a mover?"

The men grew interested. She really meant business. Well, five bucks was five bucks, of course, and if she really wanted the house, why they didn't mind earning double money and getting a bit of a rest in the bargain. They looked at each other again, a long meaningful glance:

"I guess Sam would fix her up, wouldn't he, Tom? I guess he wouldn't overcharge her for movin', would he? He's got the big jacks along today, ain't he? An' she ain't very big—"

"What do you think he would charge?" gasped Joyce awaiting the answer as if her very life depended upon it. It seemed as though she just couldn't bear to lose that little house. It seemed as though it had just been made for her need, and she found her heart praying, "Oh, heavenly Father, please make it possible, please make it possible!"

"Oh, he wouldn't charge you much ef you didn't go too fur. But I don't think you ken git enny land. It's all took up about here."

"How much time will you give me?" asked Joyce impatiently, anxiety growing in her face.

"Well, we oughtta be pullin' out o' here in about a nour," said the older man. "The truck don't leave fur a nour an' a quarter. We'll say a nour an' ten minutes. That oughtta give you time."

"Oh!" gasped Joyce and flew down the street looking about her on either side, and leaving the men gaping after her.

"Well, all I gotta say is," said Tom after gazing for some minutes, "she's some kind of a nut! Do you reckon to wait fer her to come back, er shall I go on bustin' her up?"

The older man dropped down comfortably on the grass and took out his pipe. "A bargain's a bargain, Tom," he said cupping his hands around the match. "I allus keeps my contrac's."

"H'm!" said Tom, dropping stiffly beside him. "But sposen she don't come back?"

"She'll come back," said the other.

"But sposen she can't find no land?"

"It's my opinion, Tom, that she's one o' them kind, that ef she can't find no land she'll *make* a little bit. I've seen 'em before, an' they can bamboozle the eyeteeth out of a tightwad ef they really try. She's really tryin' now. She wants this here cottage bad, an' I intend she'll have it."

Tom squinted his eyes and observed this chief thoughtfully remarking after a while:

"H'm!"

Pretty soon the chief arose, took up his implements of work and went up to the little house. He studied the foundation for a few moments and then he began with his pick to work about it, loosening the stones in which it was set. Tom arose and followed him, watching his movements a moment. Then he raised his eyes to the side of the little structure as if for the first time he observed it as a dwelling, a housing place for a human being.

"That's a purty vine," he observed. "Too bad it has to die."

"It ain't agoin' to die," said the chief. "We're agoin' to save it. Where's that there big lard kettle we hed around here? See ef it's inside the hedge."

Tom foraged behind the hedge and brought a battered tin can.

The chief dug carefully about the roots of the vine, in a good-sized circle, dug it deeply and neatly and together they lifted the roots of the vine with the earth firmly about it, and fitted it into the lard kettle.

"Now, we'll hev to work it so's this here don't git disturbed when we move her," said the chief.

Tom found a bit of board and some nails among their tools behind the hedge, and made a little shelf on the side of the building upon which they set the can, nailing it firmly to the house so that it would not be disturbed.

Then with deep satisfaction the two set about preparing the building for its removal.

Chapter 9

Joyce had walked for three blocks in frantic haste with sinking heart before she saw any land that looked at all promising. They were all smug dwellings with beautiful lawns about them, and she had sense enough to know that people who lived in houses of that kind wanted their lawns to themselves, and could not be persuaded to sell or rent even a foot for any such sum as she could offer. But the turn of the next block brought in sight a row of neat stores and just beyond an old-fashioned house set back from the street built of fieldstone that looked as if it had stood there years before the little new town had ever been heard of. It was neat and trim with a wide piazza the length of the front, and tall spruce and hemlock trees standing in a friendly group about it. There was a street running across between it and the stores, and on this side yard there was a bright garden of flowers and a grassy place with two maple trees just far enough apart to let her little house in, and here Joyce paused and looked with longing eyes. If only she could get permission to put her house here. If she could have it between those maples, with the right to use the side gate! And there was an outside faucet with a hose attached. They might let her get water there!

She stood for several minutes taking in the whole situation. It would be nice to have the protection of a house nearby provided nice people lived there. It would be around at the back of the house so the owners would not need to feel they were losing any of their own front yard, or privacy, and it was near enough to the street so that she would feel she had a spot of her own.

It was like Joyce not to hunt up any land agent and try to find a place in the conventional way but to just fasten her eyes upon the desirable spot and then go after it.

Timidly she opened the gate and went in, choosing the side gate instead of the front. It was unusual to have a gate. That was because it was an old-fashioned house. She was glad there was a gate. It made her feel as if she would be more secure in a little house all by herself to have a gate shutting her in. But this was too much like a fairy tale. She must not get up her hopes. Of course these people wouldn't hear to her request. They would think she was crazy perhaps to dare to ask.

There was someone in the dining room setting the table. The door was open on a side porch, and she could see as she went up the steps that the table was long, and spread with a white cloth, and there were flowers in the middle in a glass bowl, blue violets, quantities of them. The door beyond was open through an airy pantry to a kitchen, and there was a savory odor of broiling meat. She sniffed it hungrily as she put out a timid hand to knock, and thought anxiously that it must be getting late if someone was getting dinner ready so early.

A pleasant looking woman with her hair in crimping pins

over her forehead and a long, plain gingham apron covering her dress came to the door with a tea towel and a glass in her hand, polishing as she came. Joyce almost lost her voice at the thought of her own audacity while she looked into the pleasant gray eyes of the elderly woman. This was just the kind of woman she would have chosen if the fairy tale were real. But she remembered that ten minutes of her hour were already gone, and she must hurry.

"I've just stopped in to see if there is any possibility that I could rent, or perhaps buy, a few feet of your yard, here at the back. I have a little house, and I want to put it somewhere right away."

"A house!" said the woman astonished. "Why, no, we don't want to sell any land. This place has been in the family for four generations and it'll go on to my son when he comes of age. He's only in high school yet, but he's fond of the old place, and we don't want to give up any more land. We've just got about enough. My husband wouldn't think of selling any, not even a foot."

"Would you rent a little spot? It's a very little house. I could put it quite close to the fence if it was necessary, and away at the back."

"Mercy, no!" said the woman. "We like our privacy. We wouldn't want another house so close. It's bad enough to have all those stores across the street. My husband wouldn't have sold that land if he'd known they were going to build stores—Mercy! What's that?"

The woman had turned with a start of horror, for a flash of light had blazed up from the kitchen that flickered over the room like a sudden illumination, and a pungent odor of burning meat filled the air at the same instant. Strange what a short interval there is between cooking and actual burning, and what a sudden odor burnt meat can impart to a room. The place was filled with it.

Joyce was standing so that she could see straight into the kitchen range and she saw exactly what was the matter. There were flames bursting out from the cracks of the gas range oven, and flames lighting up the seams of the broiling oven. Having had the same thing happen to herself once when she was cooking she understood just what had occurred. Without more ceremony she threw the screen door open and walked in, straight through into the kitchen. While the owner of the calm eyes was hurrying distractedly about the kitchen seeking for the pie lifter and a holder, Joyce quickly turned out the gas under the oven, and threw open the lower door. It was as she supposed, there was grease and drippings from the broiling chops in the pan below the broiler and it had caught on fire and was blazing high. It was of no use to try to smother it out or to save the chops. They were burned to a crisp already and the kitchen was filling fast with a black, oozy soot that was fastening to every immaculate pot and pan and to the wall and ceiling.

The gray-eyed woman moaned, for the chops were many and expensive and she was preparing for a company dinner. Then her despair was changed to terror as she saw the flames shoot out into the room bringing dense, black smoke with them.

"I'd better call the fire company!" she gasped and turned toward the telephone.

"No! Wait!" gasped Joyce amid the smoke. "Give me that bread blanket! Quick!"

The woman seized the thick, soft woollen cloth that lay tucked snugly about three pans of biscuits on the table and Joyce swathed her hands in its folds and courageously gripping the broiling pan, broiler, chops and all, carried them flaming to the back door and flung them out into the grass.

It was all done in a second and the two stood in the doorway and watched the conquered fire flash up a few times and go out. Then the woman turned to the girl:

"You're wonderful!" she said earnestly. "I can't thank you enough. I don't know what I should have done if I'd been alone. I never could have carried that out all afire that way. I don't see how you did it. And you got burned! I'll bet you did! Yes, and there on your arm too. That's too bad! Now come over here and I'll do it up. I've got some sweet oil and linen."

The tears of pain were stinging into Joyce's eyes but she shook her head and tried to smile.

"No, thank you," she said. "I haven't time to wait. I'll just put it in cold water a minute to take the smart out, and then if you have some baking soda I'll cover it up and it'll be all right. It's not much of a burn anyway, and it was my fault your meat burned. If I hadn't hindered you, you wouldn't have forgotten it. I'm afraid you were going to have company too. I think I ought to pay for the meat."

"Oh, no, it wasn't your fault. I ought not to have left that grease in the pan. I knew it was there and I just forgot it. But I don't know what I'm going to do about the chops. It's Wednesday afternoon and all the stores are closed. My company comes on the five o'clock train, my cousins from New York on their way up from Florida, and they're only going to stop over till the nine o'clock train. I don't see them very often and I'd like to have a little something extra, and now I don't know what I am going to do. I shouldn't have broiled them so long beforehand only I wanted to get the smell out of the house before the folks came, and I knew I could keep them warm in the warming oven all right. Now what in time am I going to do for meat?"

"Haven't you got anything at all in the house?" asked Joyce turning from dusting her burns with soda.

"Nothing but some ham. Got plenty of that on hand, bought a whole one the other day, but one doesn't want to give New York City folks fried ham for dinner. That's kind of farm food. I wanted a little something nice."

"Do you ever bake it in milk?" asked Joyce, wishing she knew some way to help the woman for she understood her distress and felt that she was really to blame for having bothered her when she was busy.

"No, I never tried it. I've heard some say they cook it that way, but I don't know how. Do you? I don't see how that would be any different from stewed ham."

"Oh, but it is! It's delectable. If you can get the things quickly I'll fix it for you. You've just about time if you want dinner at five. It has to bake an hour. Have you plenty of milk? And mustard?"

"Loads of milk. We have a cow, and mustard too, but what do you want with mustard?"

"You'll see," said Joyce. "Cut the ham in thick slices, as much as you want. My! That's nice ham, nice and pink looking and good and big. How many people? Yes, I guess you need two slices. Can I use these two iron frying pans? I think it bakes best in iron. You light the oven, please, turn it on full power. Now, see, I take a handful of mustard and rub it into the meat, all over thickly, and put it into the pan. Then fill it up with milk till it almost covers the meat. Put it into the oven and bake it just an hour, a good hot oven, and it will be the sweetest, tenderest thing you ever put into your mouth. There, there's just room enough for both pans, and you needn't worry about meat. They'll like that I know. I found the recipe in an advertisement of ham in a magazine and tried it. Everybody loves it. Now I must go, but I just wish I could wait and help you to make up for spoiling those chops. You don't know anywhere I could go that they would rent me a piece of land, do you?"

"Well, no, I don't just know, but suppose you wait till tomorrow morning and my husband may know of something. He might be able to find you just the right thing. If you'd be willing to stay and help me here a little while I'd pay you well and I'd help you with all my heart."

Joyce smiled sorrowfully:

"That would be too late. I've got to have a place within a few minutes now or I'll lose the house. The man said they couldn't wait but an hour and ten minutes and I must have used up more than three-quarters of it now. I'd love to stay and help you, and if I can possibly get through what I have to do I'll come back and help you. Perhaps I could get here in time to wait on the table if you'd like me. I wouldn't want any pay. I feel as if I owed you something. But I just can't stay now. I must save this little house. It's the only place I could ever hope to have for a home that I could afford, and I've really bought it, so I *must* find a place to put it."

"For pity's sake! Bought a house and must have a place to put it right away. Why, I never heard of anything so unreasonable. Couldn't you buy the land it was on? Where is it?"

"No, the man wants to clear his land. When I came on them they were breaking it up into kindling wood, and it's the dearest little place, just big enough for one. It's about four blocks away from here on the edge of a big place."

"Oh! The land office. That *is* pretty. Yes, I heard someone had bought that old house and was going to fix it up. Why—but that's not a house. It's only a room. That wouldn't take up much room. I should think most anybody would be willing to let you have enough land for that. If that's all maybe Papa wouldn't mind. He wouldn't sell any land but he might rent it."

"Oh," said Joyce clasping her hands eagerly, "where can I find him? I'll go right away. Perhaps I'll be in time if I hurry."

"Why, no you can't find him anywhere. He's gone to the city. He won't be home till the folks come. He went to meet them. But if you're in such a hurry as all that I suppose you could bring your house here for the night anyway, and then we could see about it tomorrow. About how much were you figuring to pay? Could you pay as much as a dollar a week?"

"Oh, I think so," said Joyce relieved. "I'm expecting to get a position right away."

"Well, you can bring it here tonight, and if it doesn't look too much in the way we'll try it. Our missionary society is getting up a fund to get some chime bells for our church, and each one of us has to earn some extra money some way. If I choose to earn mine by giving up a piece of backyard my husband won't object. The house is really mine anyway. You can come and try it and we won't promise anything on either side till we see how it goes. Now. Can't you hurry right back and help me? I'm almost distracted with all there is to do, and I'm all shaken up with that fire and all."

"I certainly will," said Joyce with almost a shout of glee in her voice, as she turned and fairly flew back the four blocks to her little house, straining her eyes as she came nearer to make sure it still stood whole and fair before her. Yes, there it was, all vine clad. How dear and sweet. But the vine would have to go of course. It could not survive. What a pity. Of course those men would think that was all nonsense. If she only had a little time perhaps she might have managed to get the root loose and maybe it would live, but there wasn't time and she mustn't think of it. She must hurry, hurry back to that woman who had been so good, and help her with all her might.

"She's a comin'," growled Tom as the sound of her swift footsteps drew near, "an' she don't sound discouraged neither."

"What'd I tell ye?" growled the other. "The hour ain't up fer ten minutes yet neither."

"Mebbe she's coming to ask fer more time," urged Tom squinting down the street speculatively.

"No," said the other, "she wouldn't come till the time was up to the minute ef that was it. Anyhow, look at her! She's ashinin' like a robin just back fer spring. That ain't no discouragin' countenance, ur my name ain't McClatchey."

The big auto truck was just lumbering around the corner as Joyce arrived panting and triumphant:

"I've found a nice place," she said joyously, "just down this street three blocks, and one around the corner. It's opposite the side of a row of stores, just beyond the store on the side street. There's a fence, but I thought perhaps you could back right up to it and slide the house over it."

"Most likely we kin," said the boss filling his pipe speculatively, and straightening up to await the truck.

"What! Ain't ya got the kindlin' ready to pile on yet, boys? It's most quittin' time now. You said—"

"Hold your clack!" commanded the chief. "This here is a

house, it ain't no load o' kindlin' wood. You made a mistake. I've sold this here buildin' an' it's gotta be delivered t' oncet. You clamber down, Sam, an' git them jacks an' rollers from behind that hedge, an' get busy."

"Can you tell me how much it will be?" asked Joyce, anxiously remembering that this was a momentous question and might yet present an impossible barrier to her plans. She looked from the driver to the chief in a troubled way, and the chief spoke up gruffly:

"Oh, you kin give him five bucks too ef you want fer keepin' his tongue still, but he has to do what I say, and I say this here house is goin' to be moved t'night. Look out there, Sam, don't you knock that there hangin' garding off'n the end. That's part of the proposishun, an' don't wantta be destroyed. Get me?"

"Oh," said Joyce, quite childishly clapping her hands. "You've saved the vine! Oh, thank you so much!"

"Sure," said the chief, "sold it to you, didn't I? Part o' the house, ain't it? I 'low to keep my contrac's. Now, you kin run 'long, an' be on the spot when we git thar to say where you want her put. This ain't no place fer a girl, while we're movin' her, you might git hurt."

"Shall I pay you first?" she asked opening her little handbag.

"No," said the chief quite crossly, "don't take no pay till we deliver the goods. Down across from the stores you say? Stone house? Picket fence? Yep. I know the place. Ain't but one picket fence in the place. Folks wouldn't sell an inch of ground. You're lucky! But then ennybody kin see you're that kind. Run along. We'll be along in a leetle while. You needn't to worry."

Chapter 10

On winged feet Joyce retraced her steps and entered the dining room she had left a few minutes before as eagerly as if it were her own home.

"I'm so glad I could come back right away," she said. "The men have the truck all ready and said they would be along in a little while, and, oh, I'm so thankful to you. Now, what can I do first?

"I could see you were a little troubled about that ham, never having tasted it cooked that way. Is there anything else we could make to help make up for the chops? Or couldn't I go somewhere and find the butcher and ask him to let me have some more for you. I'd pay for them myself, because I really burned them up you know."

"Well, you're a dear child," said the woman pleasantly. "No, you can't find the butcher. He's taken his wife up in the country for the afternoon, and he's cross as two sticks anyway. Besides, I wouldn't want him to know I had been so careless, and it's none of his business anyway. But I was thinking if there was something else I could make."

"Well, what have you on hand? Let's look in the refrigerator," suggested the girl.

"Not much. There's some cold chicken. I was saving it for Jim and he didn't come home at noon."

She hurried to the refrigerator and took out a bowl which Joyce examined.

"There's half a breast and a drumstick, and both wings. There's the gizzard too. Why don't we make some chicken salad. Have you any celery?"

"Yes, I bought a stalk the other day. I like the top leaves to flavor bean soup, but there isn't much."

"A little will do. I see you have some tomatoes."

"Yes, Jim likes them. I say they aren't very tasty this time of year, not worth the money, but Jim always asks for them."

"Well, why don't we stuff them with chicken salad? That would make a beautiful salad dish and make the chicken go farther. Didn't I see lettuce in the garden? A few leaves will do even if it isn't very big. And how about mayonnaise?"

"Why, I make a boiled mayonnaise, but it's late to get it cool, isn't it?"

"Haven't you any oil? That makes it so much nicer."

"Yes. Mrs. Parsons brought over a can she had left when they moved away last week. There's pretty near a pint in it, just had a few spoonsful taken out, but I can't make real mayonnaise. It won't get stiff for me. It separates. And it takes so long, doesn't it?"

"Well, I can. No, it only takes a few minutes. I know a lovely recipe. Where's the oil? Get me some salt and pepper and mustard and eggs. I'll have it ready in a jiffy while you cut up the celery and chicken. Then we'll fix it and put it on the ice all ready."

The two were soon busily at work, and the mayonnaise whipped itself into a thick, velvety, yellow mass in no time under Joyce's skillful hand. The worried hostess was delighted, and presently a tempting platter of scarlet tomatoes was set on the ice, filled to overflowing with the most toothsome chicken salad that ever went to a feast.

"You're going to have creamed potatoes and new peas out of your own garden. Isn't that wonderful? What's for dessert? Anything I can do about that?" asked Joyce as she turned away from the refrigerator.

"Why, I've ordered ice cream, and I made a cake. That's all right, I just looked at it and the icing is hardening nicely. You see I just got the telegram at three o'clock that they were coming. It went first to the other Bryants up on the hill and they were away. I ought to have got it yesterday. I wonder why that ice cream doesn't come. They promised to have it here at four. I always order it earlier than I need it for safety. It's twenty after four now. I believe I'll call up to make sure."

She went to the phone and in two or three minutes appeared in the kitchen door where Joyce was just putting on the peas, with her face the picture of dismay:

"What shall I do? They can't send it. They say the orders have all gone out this afternoon, and mine wasn't among them. There was some mistake."

"Isn't there some other place? I'll run out and get some for you."

"No," said Mrs. Bryant in despair, "the other two places don't have any fit to eat. I wouldn't offer it to a cat! I haven't even a pie on hand. Isn't this simply awful!"

The poor woman sat down and dropped her tired face in her hands looking as if she were going to weep.

"Oh, don't worry, Mrs. Bryant. There's always something one can do. Let me think. Have you any junket tablets?"

"Why, yes," said the despairing housekeeper, "but what is junket? An invalid's food!"

"Wait till you see mine. It's caramel junket, and we'll serve it with whipped cream. You haven't some preserved cherries or a few strawberries or something to put on the top of each dish, have you? It's the prettiest thing you ever saw. Where is the sugar, quick? We must hurry. Have you some individual dishes that will be pretty to hold it?"

Mrs. Bryant produced some long-stemmed sherbet glasses and a bottle of preserved cherries, saying dubiously:

"It'll never cool. It's way after four now." But she watched the deft fingers as they manipulated the sugar over the flame, until it had reached the right perfection of caramel color and was stirred fizzing into the lukewarm milk.

"It won't set," said Mrs. Bryant. "Mine never does except in real cold weather."

"Oh, yes it will. I put in an extra tablet to hurry it," said Joyce. "Now, I want some cream. Can I take it off those two bottles? It looks rich enough to whip."

"Yes, it whips I guess," sighed the woman, "but I never can get time for such frills. That's why we've decided to sell the cow, it took so much time to tend to the milk. It's really sold, but the man isn't coming for it till next week."

Joyce worked breathlessly, one eye on the clock, and all the while her heart watching for a little house to come riding down the street, yet the time went by and no house appeared. Could it be that the men had gone back on their word, or that they had made a mistake and taken it to the wrong street, or that something had happened to the precious little structure on the way?

The junket set and the cream whipped in spite of the anxiety of Mrs. Bryant, and at ten minutes to five both were on the ice, and the cherries were on a plate with a fork nearby to place them on their setting of whipped cream at the proper moment.

"You had better go and get ready yourself now," said Joyce smiling, as she lifted the potatoes and poured them through the colander, setting them to steam dry for a moment before creaming them. "I'll see to the peas, and the ham is just perfect. I'll have it all on the platter ready to take in and keep it hot. You don't happen to have a white apron you could lend me, do you? That is, if you want me to wait on the table."

"Oh, will you? I'd be so glad. I'm always nervous with city folks. Yes, I've got an apron. I'll throw it down the back stairs. And I'll just run up and change now, and smooth my hair. It won't take a minute. They ought to be here any time now. I'm real relieved. I think things are going to be all right. If you have time you might cut the cake."

Joyce, wearied almost to the limit, yet interested in what she was doing and eager to serve one who had so served her, turned back and put all the last little touches on the table that she well knew how to put, smoothed her own pretty hair as well as she could with only the tiny comb with which her handbag was fitted, washed her face and hands at the sink, and took off the big gingham apron Mrs. Bryant had loaned, to replace it with the white one that presently fluttered down the back stairs. She giggled to herself to think what a change had come over her life in twenty-four hours. Here she was at almost the same hour getting supper in another kitchen for an entirely different set of people, utter strangers. How strange and interesting! How wonderful to have the opportunity to thus work her way into a bit of land for her house! How kind of the heavenly Father to fix it all for her! How good it was that she could cook, and had the ability to help in this time of need!

But there was no time to meditate. The kitchen clock was striking with a businesslike clang, and the honk of an automobile horn could be heard coming down the street. Mrs. Bryant rustled down in a gray crepe dress and her hair fluffed up becomingly. Her eyes were bright and her cheeks wore a pretty little touch of nervous color as she looked out the door.

"I think they are coming!" she said eagerly, and then Joyce glancing out behind her saw looming clumsily in the distance, blocking up the street and grown to most enormous proportions, her little vine-clad office riding down behind the bright little car that was speeding rapidly toward the Bryant gate.

"Oh, Mrs. Bryant!" breathed Joyce in alarm. "My house is coming too, and you haven't told me where to put it yet!"

"Your house?" said the preoccupied lady half impatiently. "Oh, yes. Why, put it anywhere you like for tonight. Just don't get into the garden. You won't have to go out and see to it, will you? Because I can't spare you now."

"Only for a second," said Joyce happily. "I've got to pay the men."

"Well, wait till the meat is on the table and everything passed. Don't forget the coffee. There they are. Now I must go."

Joyce, starry-eyed, tired to death but smiling, began to take up the dinner and carry it into the dining room. She could hear the hum of voices in greeting, the people going upstairs, the splashing of water as the guests made rapid toilets, and all the time her senses were listening for the coming of the truck and trying to time her actions so that she might go out and tell the men where to put the house, and yet not interfere with any of her duties as waitress.

She flew out at last while the guests were being seated and told the chief about where she thought the house should stand.

"I've got to go right in," she said confidingly. "I'm helping

Mrs. Bryant with a dinner. She has company, and they're going to catch a train, but you can put it right in there between those two trees, wherever it is convenient to you. Just so it keeps out of the garden. I suppose I'll have to get someone to fix it steady, won't I? I'll be out again in a few minutes if you need me for anything," and she flew in again, and straightening her white apron entered the dining room with a plate of hot biscuits.

Mr. Bryant was a meek, apologetic little man with a retreating chin and kind eyes. He half arose when he saw Joyce as if he thought this was another guest that had somehow got misplaced, but Mrs. Bryant incorporated her at once into the picture with a glance that placed her as a server, and Mr. Bryant slid back into his chair, his mouth the shape of an inaudible O, and addressed himself to this new and mysterious kind of ham that looked like roast veal and cut like chicken.

The guests exclaimed with delight over their food. They said they had lived in hotels all winter and it was just wonderful to get back to home cooking again, and what wonderful ham! Was it really ham, just *ham*? And how did she do it? Could she give them the recipe? And then Joyce as she came and went with relays of hot biscuits and peas and potatoes heard Mrs. Bryant tell carefully how she rubbed the mustard into the meat, and poured the milk on, through all the performance just as she had done it, and finish up:

"Yes, we think it is the best way in the world to cook ham," just as if she had been doing it that way all her life. She smiled to herself over the salad as she arranged the ice cold tomatoes on the crisp lettuce leaves. Well, it was a pretty dinner and she was proud to think she had helped make it so. The poor burnt chops were utterly forgotten now, lying in the grass at the kitchen door, and sometime within the next few hours she would get a chance to sit down, perhaps to lie down, somewhere, on the grass if nowhere else, and rest. Oh, that would be wonderful!

She took the plates out and brought in the salad, adding some crackers she had found in the pantry, and then slipped out to see what the men were doing.

"What a very superior waitress you seem to have, Aunt Mattie," remarked a niece, eyeing the door through which Joyce had passed. "You don't want to let me steal her and take her up to New York do you? I'd certainly give a good deal to get one that looked like that. She seems a real lady."

"She is," said Mrs. Bryant shortly. "She's not a waitress at all. She's just a neighbor who came in to help me so that I could have all my time with you instead of running out to the kitchen all the time."

There was something innately grimly honest about Mattie Bryant. She might claim the credit of a well-cooked ham, but she would never let a young girl who had been kind to her be treated like a servant. It wasn't in her. She would have liked to have posed as having well-trained servants, but she couldn't.

"A-a neighbor, did you say, Mother?" asked Mr. Bryant. "Why, I don't seem to remember her. Where does she live?"

"No, I guess you don't, Father, she's mostly been here when you were away. She lives on this street. Cornelia, won't you have another cup of coffee?"

And then there came a shuddering, sliding sound, and a dull, reverberating thud, that vibrated along the floor, and seemed to make the dinner table shiver a tiny bit and everybody looked up and said, "Why, what is that? An earthquake?" and only Mrs. Bryant kept her cool indifference, and went on pouring coffee. But outside the little vine-covered house had slid into place between the two maples, and settled to rest exactly where it had been aimed by the three men who had put it there, and Joyce was out in the sunset fluttering three five-dollar bills from her precious hoard and smiling her wistful, wild rose smile:

"I wish I could give you ten times as much," she said. "If I only had it! You've been so kind."

The old chief stood a minute and watched her as she went in, looked at the bill, half folded it to put in his pocket, thought better of it and stepped inside the building. He glanced about, fumbled a pin from the lapel of his old coat and pinned it up on the wall opposite the door. Tom watched him from a distance, squinting his eyes thoughtfully, busied himself with his dinner pail and pickax till the chief was around the corner, when he slipped into the cottage, took a look around, stood thoughtful a minute and deliberately took out his own five-dollar bill and pinned it beside the other. Then he went out quickly and followed his chief down the street.

Over in the kitchen Joyce, too weary to eat much supper, had taken a bite and gone at the dishes pell-mell. She was a swift worker and used to turning things off rapidly, but the last two days had been more strenuous than any in her short life, and now that the immediate excitement of the dinner and the house were over, she was beginning to feel that she had reached her limit.

Mrs. Bryant slipped away from her guests long enough to smile upon her, and tell her to eat a good supper, that everything was wonderful, and she couldn't thank her enough; then went back to the parlor where the chatter of relatives long separated with many years to check up in a short time made a din almost amounting to a church social. There was the uncle who had certain jokes that he had to tell over, and the cousin who boasted, and the cousin who wanted to recount all the past, and the aunt who wanted to forget the past and go on at great length about her house in New York, and her place in Maine, and her winter in Florida and the trip she was going to take abroad this summer, and with it all the poor, eager little Bryants hardly got in a word. The strange young woman in the kitchen might naturally be forgotten under such circumstances, especially as they were planning to take all their guests into the city in time for the late train.

So Joyce washed out the dish towels and slipped out the back door with only the moon to light her to her little new house.

Chapter 11

Joyce wondered, as she went cautiously through the grass lest she stumble in the darkness, whether her house was going to be at all habitable, and what she should do if it were not. She had no mind to trouble Mrs. Bryant any further, neither did she care to have that good woman know how thoroughly she was adrift in the world without a spot to lay her head. Very likely Mrs. Bryant might offer her a bed for the night, it would be like her good nature, and yet, she was an utter stranger, and she shrank from accepting such a favor. Taking an entire stranger into one's home was a big thing to do, when one had no introduction whatever except that one could cook.

She had no time to look out at her new purchase while it was being placed, and now was not even sure they had set it evenly on its floor. It might be on end or toppled onto its roof for aught she knew, and when this thought presented itself she walked on in a growing dismay. But the streetlight just opposite proved a boon and shone right between the two trees to the little white building which was nestled all properly on a level spot, floor down, and even as a die, with its little front porch facing the street and set back about fifteen feet from the fence. When she put her hand on the porch rail it seemed to be standing solidly. She could see, on stooping down, that it was set on some stones with fresh cement. The men had taken trouble to make it right and firm for her. How kind they were! She must try and hunt them up tomorrow and thank them. Then she remembered the vine and tired as she was stepped around to see how it had fared on its journey. Behold it had been taken out of its lard can and set in the ground! They had even found some water and watered it, for drops were glistening on the leaves and an empty tin can lay on the ground. Somehow it brought sudden tears to think that these two rough men had taken so much pains to set out the vine for her, a stranger.

"It is just God," she said to herself as she went back to the front porch. "God is taking care of me!" Then she lifted her eyes to the stars and said in a soft voice as she stood on her own little step, "Dear Father in heaven, bless this little house, and me, and take care of me here for Christ's sake."

It occurred to her as she turned toward the door that it might be locked and then where would she find a key to fit it? But the knob turned and the door opened without any trouble and she stepped inside and closed it softly after her. For a moment she could see nothing. Then her eyes became accustomed to the semidarkness, and the patches of light on the floor that came through the little diamond panes of the windows and door showed the room to be empty save for a wooden box in the middle of the floor, and a great stack of newspapers in one corner.

Joyce had brought a few matches with her from Mrs. Bryant's and now she struck one and looked around carefully. The place was tolerably clean. The floor was dusty of course and a few peanut shells were scattered here and there, but nothing very bad. The walls were lined with compo board and painted white, and in the flare of a few matches presented no unpleasant features. The box was empty and the pile of newspapers seemed to be different lots left over from some newsstand. They were of old dates, folded but once, and quite clean. There did not even seem to be any spiderwebs in that corner, and only the top papers were dusty.

Having satisfied herself so far she deposited the remaining matches on the windowsill for a possible time of need in the night and set to work. Those newspapers were her only chance, and she was thankful for them. She must make a bed out of them.

Her first act was to drag the box across the floor to block the door. There was no key and she had no mind to sleep in a strange place with a door that could be opened by anyone in the night. The box was just high enough to reach under the knob, and heavy enough so that the door could not be opened without making a good deal of noise; and after she had placed it she felt quite secure in her new shelter.

She covered the top of the box with a clean newspaper and put her hat and handbag upon them. Then she attacked the pile of newspapers. She unfolded them sheet by sheet and crumpled them thoroughly, throwing them into the corner and when she had covered a space on the floor about six feet long by three feet wide with these crumpled papers crowded close together, she laid several open sheets smoothly over them tucking the edges well underneath, and began again crumpling papers and putting on the top another layer. These in turn had several whole newspapers laid smoothly on the top and then another layer until she had quite a comfortable couch of springy paper. She even opened out a couple of papers and filled them with crumpled pieces for a pillow.

There were still plenty of newspapers left and she spread them out overlapping one another in layers, until she had a coverlet of good proportions. Then she folded their edges back to hold them together.

"Now, I shan't freeze if it turns cold in the night," she thought gleefully.

Next she went to her little new windows and wrestled with them. They were casements, swinging in, but it required much pounding and pulling to make them swing at all at first. At last she had them all open wide letting in the sweet night air. She looked out into the dark garden a trifle dubiously, it is true. It did seem a little uncanny to sleep there alone with windows wide and the street so close, with not even a curtain to shelter her, but she must have air and there was nothing else to be done. She must just wake up early in the morning before folks were astir. Curtains were among the first things she must purchase. Of course there were the newspapers, but they would shut out the air.

She knelt for a moment beside the wooden box in the path of moonlight that came through her window and prayed for strength and guidance. It seemed a strange thing she was doing, now that she had done it, this buying a little house and daring to set up a home of her own on practically no money at all. A sense of awe was upon her as she brought her deed before God and tried to see it in the light of His wisdom. Had she done wrong to fly off at the unpleasant words of her cousin and seek a new environment? Somehow her soul rang true, however, as she cast once more a retrospective glance back and asked approval and guarding. She seemed so alone as she knelt there in the little empty room in the moonlight. Aunt Mary gone. The death angel standing ever between them and the dear old life they had lived together; the hometown with its dear friends who loved her and whom she loved, forever lost to her because of the presence there of the cousins who had nothing in common with her and who were possessed to spoil everything she tried to do; who were jealous of all her communication with the old friends. There was simply no one or nothing left but God, and she must cling close to Him.

She glanced out her little open window as she rose from her knees, and dismay seized upon her as she heard footsteps coming along the pavement. The street was so near. It was almost as if she were standing in the way of the oncomer. She held her breath and the steps paused for a full minute in front of the new little house in its strange setting, and she shivered nervously as they finally passed on.

Then there came to her mind, as if a sweet voice had spoken, the old words she had learned with Aunt Mary one Sunday afternoon long years ago:

"The angel of the Lord encampeth round about them that fear him and delivereth them. . . . I will both lay me down in peace, and sleep: for thou, Lord, only makest me dwell in safety."

She crept into her strange, rattling couch and drew the crackling coverlet up about her, laid her head upon her rattley pillow and closed her weary eyes, resting her heart upon the words of the book as upon a pillow of peace. Then suddenly, without warning, the tears came stinging into her eyes, as she remembered how alone in the world and desolate she was, and how she longed for her dear aunt and her old home. There in her strange little bed she cried as if her heart would break for a few minutes. Then into the confusion of her sad thoughts came the words, "Even Christ had not where to lay His head."

"And I have!" she said to herself severely. "I ought to be glad and thankful. He gave me this house. It was just as plain as if I had heard Him offer it to me."

So she turned over the little damp spot on her pillow where the tears had fallen, and deliberately settled herself to sleep, forcibly putting away all thoughts of her strange experiences for another time and addressing herself to rest. There might be dangers passing on the street, but God had promised to care for her, and she knew she could trust Him. She needed the rest and must take it. So she slept and night settled down about the little cottage under the maples.

A hundred miles away in the darkness a man stole like a shadow through the night, walking noiselessly down a deserted road to the graveyard, vanished among the graves into the velvety blackness under the trees. Appeared a point of light like a darting firefly fitfully now and then lighting up the spectral marbles for a gleam and going out again as if it had not been there. A soft sound of stirring among the growing things on a grave as one knelt beside it and worked, breathing hard, the light shining once more steadily for an instant on trailing vines and glowing berries, then ceasing entirely. Steps to the back of the graveyard, and strange, muffled sounds dying away into silence and midnight.

Later, in a city cellar lair a meeting of angry, puzzled, incredulous men, and one, resolute, calm, fearless, indifferent, determined, dominating them all. Money going around, more than they had expected, yet only arousing suspicion; and then, before they could protest, the leader going out into the night alone, leaving them to voice their suspicions, and plot against him.

Chapter 12

When Judge Peterson woke up in the morning after a night of restless tossing, and an early morning doze, he called to his wife with a voice much like his old time vigor.

"Miranda, bring me my pants. I want to try how it seems to sit up. I've got to get out of here and find that little girl. There's something queer about this business and I reckon it's up to me to study it out."

The anxious face of Miranda Peterson that had been creased all night with tormenting fears suddenly relaxed and a gleam of joy came into her eyes. This was her old-time husband back again. The visitors hadn't done him so much damage after all, perhaps had only given him an added incentive to get well. With a spring in her step and a light in her eye she swung the old-fashioned wardrobe door open and revealed his baggy trousers hung up by their suspenders just where she had put them the night he was taken sick.

"All right, Father," she said briskly, "there they are. You have your breakfast and as soon as the doctor comes we'll ask him if you can put 'em on. There's ham and eggs this morning, do you feel for ham or only eggs?"

"Both!" declared the indomitable old man. "I've got a lot to do today and I want strength. Mother, did you ever think that Mary Massey suspected her son's wife of not being—well—exactly loyal to the family?"

Miranda Peterson paused in the open doorway:

"Yes, I did, Father. The last time I was up there before she died she kind of tried to apologize to me for asking me to close the door while we talked. She said she knew Nan wasn't very fond of Joyce, and she didn't want her to know we were talking about her future, it might cause jealousy. She said Nan had accused her of thinking more of Joyce than she did of her own son's wife, as of course she did. How could she help it? But I could see she was real uneasy about how they would get on when she was gone, especially when they found out about the house. She said then she was going to explain it all to Eugene right away. But you know she took worse that night and I suppose she never did get the chance. I think myself it was a great mistake, letting the children grow up without knowing all about it, but of course Mary Massey felt she must keep her sister's dying request, and her sister hadn't wanted Joyce to know she had money coming to her till she was twenty-one. She said she was afraid it would spoil her. Well, she isn't spoiled, that's one thing certain, but it always seems to me when you work real hard to escape one trouble, you're like as not to run head on to another that's about as bad. Look what's happened now. I don't blame Joyce Radway one little mite for not standing that Nannette. She's got a tongue like a hissing serpent, and she can wind that light-minded, weak-chinned, bull-headed husband of hers around her little finger. How that poor bag of meal ever came to be Mary Massey's son I can't figure, even with a husband like Hiram Massey, for Mary Massey was the salt of the earth. Talking about salt, do you want your eggs on toast? And hot milk? Yes, I know. I'll have 'em here in the jerk of a lamb's tail, and then you'll be ready to talk to the doctor when he comes."

"All right, Mother. And say, send Dan down. He's about isn't he? Well, I want him to go on an errand. Send him in."

Dan appeared, clean-shaven, kindly eyed, with a square jaw like his father's and a determined set to his shoulders.

"Dan, we've got to find that little girl right away. Understand?"

"Yes, Father. So I told Darcy Sherwood last night. I've a notion we'll be on her track soon. Darcy gets around quite a good bit, and he seem interested. Always thought a good bit of Aunt Mary, you know. Any danger of that poor fish of a Gene lighting out?"

"No, I don't think so," said the judge. "He's too mad. Thinks his dignity has been offended. It's about all he's got left of the family pride, his dignity and he's working that for all it's worth. He likes to be bowed down to, has ever since he was born, and he thinks his mother's Christianity was wide enough to cover him and his fat, lazy family. I don't want to do injustice to anybody, Dan, but I've a notion that chump needs a lesson or two and I'm figuring on being able to give it to him in a few days. I don't know why good women like Mary Massey have to be afflicted with conceited puppies for sons. I suppose she loved him, so she spoiled him. Women mostly do. Take your mother. Dan, you'd have been a ruined man if it hadn't been for the lickings I gave you with the old birch rod down behind the barn when your mother'd gone to missionary meeting. You've never thanked me for that, Dan, but you're a better man for it, you know. Now, Dan, just slip me those pants on the nail behind you, lad. I'm going to surprise your mother. Hurry up. I hear those ham and eggs coming!"

With the help of Dan, Judge Peterson got into his nether garments and was sitting on the side of the bed when his wife arrived with the ham and eggs, and though a bit weak and trembly he insisted on sitting up in the rocking chair without pillows while he ate his breakfast. The old zest for work and fight had lifted him at last from his weakness back into the world again and he was determined to get right into line. Of course the doctor hustled him back to bed again when he arrived, and glad enough he was to get there, though he wouldn't own it, but in the half hour after he had finished the ham and eggs and before the doctor arrived he managed to get quite a number of little things started that meant business for all those who were trying to oppress any of his beloved clients.

When Dan Peterson came home for the noonday meal he was able to report that several lines of secret organizations that thread this land of ours like hidden tracery had been set vibrating with efforts to find Joyce Radway and restore her if possible at once to her home. Meantime, Eugene Massey had been notified that while he would be at liberty of course to remain in the home where his mother had lived for so many years until its rightful owner could be found and should return, it must be thoroughly understood that nothing about the place must be hurt or sold or destroyed in any way.

It was all done very quietly, and nobody in town was told. Judge Peterson was friends with everybody, but he had been able to go about the town for a good many years without letting his neighbors so much as dream that he knew aught about them and their affairs, or anybody else's, and he was not going to begin now by disgracing the family of his old friend Mary Massey. Eugene and Nannette simply were made to understand that they must walk carefully, and that they were under surveillance. Nannette grew to have a hunted, ingratiating look, and stayed at home more than had been her custom. She spent much time writing letters to Joyce and addressing them to "General Delivery" in every part of the country. She even put advertisements in the personal columns of one or two big city papers in parts of the country where her fancy thought Joyce might have wandered. She questioned Dorothea and

Junior nightly on what they knew about Joyce's friends, and habits in the village; and concerning anything that had been said to them during the day about her. They acquired the habit of being sharply alert to any scrap of news that might bear in the remotest degree upon the tragedy in their home. For even to their childish minds this that had happened in their family had assumed the proportions of a tragedy. Their mother cried a good deal and scarcely ever made desserts for dinner. Their father had locked up Cousin Joyce's room and taken the key. They were forbidden to go into the parlor and play on the piano, and anything that had been very especially nice in the way of furniture was guarded carefully. Their father explained to them that it might mean someone had to go to jail if it turned out that they had no right to things and anything had been injured. Scarcely a night passed that their father and their mother did not have a wild orgy of argument ending in a fit of weeping on their mother's part. Dorothea and Junior decided that it would have been better to have Joyce back. Besides, they were hungry for jelly roll. They even set out on one or two expeditions of their own to find their cousin, but only got into some trouble each time, and once Junior barely escaped with his life from under the wheels of an automobile.

But the worst of all to their thinking was when their father decided that they must all go to church every Sunday. Dorothea didn't mind so much because she should wear her prettiest clothes, but Junior hated the white stiff collar his mother made him wear, and the sitting so long without wriggling, for Eugene was very strict, and the time seemed endless.

Quite respectably they filed into the church the first Sunday after Joyce disappeared, just as if they had been doing so regularly during the three years they had lived in Meadow Brook. Of course everyone thought they were doing the proper thing after a death in the family, and would probably never come again. But the minister welcomed them gravely, and Nannette in her new black veil which was almost becoming, dabbed her eyes with a black-bordered handkerchief when he spoke of the departed mother who had been so faithful in her church attendance during the many years. People spoke to them sympathetically, it was not in their scheme of Christian living to do otherwise; but one or two sharp-voiced sisters who believed in "speaking their minds," asked pointedly after Joyce and wanted to know when she would be back. Nannette had by this time concocted a flexible story about her having gone to see several distant relatives of her father's in response to a telegram. Whereupon one keen-minded sister who had a daughter in the telegraph office hastened home to acquire further details. Before night Nannette's version of Joyce's western visit had grown and acquired definite shape, with a definite destination and even the length of time she was to stay. It reached the minister's wife who told it to the minister on the way home from church, and they decided to write to the minister in the town where Joyce was visiting and ask him to call on her and make her feel at home, and incidentally discover if she looked happy and all was well with her. So the ball rolled on, and Eugene, despite his ravings and rantings, was powerless to stop it.

Lib Knox suddenly began to cultivate Dorothea's companionship industriously, using her own peculiar methods for so doing. She brought Dorothea a handful of tulips which she had stealthily extracted from one of the finest gardens in town, and she offered her five minutes' lick from her all-day sucker. Now, although Lib was somewhat of a social outcast, much sneered at by the children who were not in her clique, Dorothea was nevertheless flattered by the unusual attention given her by this notorious outlaw, and was presently deep in the ecstasy of an illicit friendship with a child whom respectable mothers tabooed. Not that Lib at the age of eight had reached any depths of wickedness beyond most, but she had no respect for age and class, she did as she pleased without regard to clothes and manners, and she could sling a fine line of truth uttered in purest Saxon language at anyone who dared attempt to interfere in any of her plans. "Not a nice little girl" was what the mothers met in social conclave said about her, and she early knew it and delighted to distress them by cultivating their young hopefuls and leading them into bypaths of mischief where only her guiding hand could lead them safely out again. Lib cultivated Dorothea until Dorothea was as wax in her hands, and no foreign spy or diplomat could have used advantage with keener skill than did little Lib Knox of the dancing bronze curls and the wicked green eyes. What she did not extract of facts from unsuspecting Dorothea's soul was not worth extracting.

The high school professor felt keenly annoyed. He trusted his intuitions violently, and to have the opportunity to prove them taken away from him by so simple a thing as a girl going on a visit was not to be thought of. In the first place, it was not like a girl with a face like that one to suddenly fly up without any reason and go off on a series of visits to distant relatives, right in the midst of important examinations which he had all reason to suppose she had worked hard for and was anxious to take. In fact, the members of the school board whom he consulted all agreed in his judgment of Joyce's character and the things they said about her showed that she had every reason to wish to pass her examinations well and get a position to teach. There must be something behind all this and he meant to ferret it out.

So he put aside his stacks of examination papers and took his hat and went for the third time to interview poor Nannette. But Nannette saw him coming and fled to the attic, locking herself in, and keeping quiet as a mouse till he grew discouraged knocking and went back to his papers once more. But he did not give up. He searched out Eugene's city address and got him on the telephone, grilling him for fifteen expensive minutes as to the cause of Joyce's leaving, and why he couldn't reach her by telephone or wire if he tried every place that she had expected to visit. Eugene was reduced almost to a state of distraction and came home that night in a worse temper than ever.

That night four men sought out an old haunt where they had been accustomed to meet and sat in dark conclave. They were big, husky fellows and three were dark-browed with heavy jaws, and hands that could break an iron bar or crush a lily, but one had bright red hair and unclean eyes, with a voice that had continually to be hushed by his companions.

"Well, *I* say there's a *skirt* somewhere in all this," he bellowed forth as he raised a glass of ill-smelling liquor to his lips.

"You spilled a mouthful!" hissed out one they called Bill. "He never cleared out alone. D'you know who the dame is, Tyke?"

"I got my ideas," boasted the red-haired one mysteriously.

"Whaddaya know, Tyke? Spit it out. This ain't no time to keep things locked up. You'll get in the same class with him if you go around keepin' things ter yerself, an' you know what that means, Tyke! We ain't to be trifled with. Can't swing that game with us the second time. It's mates or hang, and you understand. Now, let her fly. Whaddaya know?" A heavy hand came down on his shoulder and Tyke shivered in his long length like a serpent taken unawares.

"Take yer hand off'n my shoulder you, Taney, ur ya don't get a word outen me." He shook the rough grip off and shuffled into another position. "You fellers go off like powder. Ef you don't quit yer suspicions I'm outta this fer good, and then where'll ya be? I got brains, an' I know a thing er two, an' when I say I got ideas I ain't sayin' I know it all, but I got a line on it. I think I can foller it up."

"Meanin'?" The heavy had came down once more upon his shoulder.

"Meanin'—well—boys, I seen a girl in the graveyard that night. Splashed my flashlight full in her face oncet. I think he seen her too—"

A low mutter from Bill as he took another drink in big gulps.

"Know who she was?" asked Cottar, the man who had not spoken yet.

"Nope, I don't live around these diggin's, you know, but I'd know her again ef I seen her, I swear I would. She had eyes you don't forget."

The man drank in silence and watched him.

"Get it all off'n yer chest, Tyke—" said Bill at last. "There's more comin'."

Tyke edged in his chair uneasily. He dropped his voice to a whisper:

"She slep' in a hammock that night. I seen her. I follered after he went back to the village. I made an excuse an' cut across to the station. Remember? But I come back after you all left an' went down the road a piece. I think I could find the house again. I seen her in a hammock underneath the trees."

The men bit hard on their pipes and watched him in silence piercing him through with little narrowed eyes in the smoke haze of the room, grilling his soul to see if it were true.

"Well, whaddaya figger?" Taney asked at last.

"Ain't figgerin' yet. Gotta find out more. Gotta find that girl. Gotta find him. Ef they're both gone, they're gone together. You all didn't think for a little minute that guy told a straight story, did you? You all didn't believe he'd give up a business that was rollin' in the money hand over fist jest fer what he called conscience, did ya? Just because he thought it wasn't a nice, pretty little business? Not on your bottom dollar he didn't."

"Mebbe he got cold feet," suggested Cottar.

"Cold feet? That guy get cold feet? Nope, you don't know him. Nothin' couldn't ever make him get cold feet. I know that guy. I seen him in France. He'd walked right outta the dugout just after his bunk had been shot away an' smoke a cigarette as cool as if he was takin' a ride in a pleasure park. Nothin' didn't never faze him. He'd just eat up danger. He thrived on it. No, sir, the only thing he'd ever fall fer was a skirt, an' it's a skirt that's done it this time fer sure, ur I don't know nothin'. No, siree, he's got that last cache all salted down somewheres, good and rich you bet, an' he's throwed us off'n the track an' thinks we can't find out where he got it from ner where he's sold it to, but we'll show him we're too smart fer him. I ain't got red hair fer nothin'. I wouldn't ha thought he'd a lied to me, we was like brothers, we was; in France, I took him back to the base when he got his, an' he brang me a drink when I had the fever an' was left on the field with the little love messages comin' over constant from the enemy all around me, he just walked out calm as you please, just like he always is, an' said, 'Tough luck, kid, but we'll pull you outta here—'"

"Cut that!" said Bill sharply. "We ain't hearin' any soft soap. We come here to get fair play an' justice. He's a sharper he is! He's a slick robber! He promised us a big deal when we went into this here dangerous business, an' he's went back on his word. He let us take all the risks, an' he hung round in the bushes. An' then here he comes along after he gets the business goin' fine to suit him an' pays us a couppla hundreds apiece an' says he's *done*. That he's decided to *leave off*. Now—Tyke, you there, you just might ez well understand what I'm sayin', we ain't takin' no soldier boy blarney about this guy at all. He's turned *yaller*, an' *took all the dough*! Bought us off with a trifle, an' skipped the country! Left us here to face the music while he skips out with a dame an' spends his thousands. No, sir, I ain't no fool. Drink o' water ain't in it. Get him a knockout. That's what he needs, an' we're here to do it, d'ya hear, Tyke?"

"Oh, shure, I'm with ya boys, I was only tellin' ya, he ain't no bloomin' coward, an' don't ya reckon on that. He'll take his medicine with a smile if we ever catch him to feed it to him, an' don't you ferget it."

"Well, I'm a goin' to knock that there bloomin' smile off his pretty face," declared Bill. "Get me?"

"Here too!" declared Tyke lustily. "But we gotta find the skirt."

"We gotta make one more try fer the boodle," declared Bill, "an' that we're goin' to do t'night. I been figgerin' we ain't looked carefully down at that first place we went, out near the point, ya know. There's a spot down behind some hazels—" he lowered his voice and looked around the room at the hazy groups around the tables and finished his sentence in a whisper.

A door opened across the room, a face shone with a white pallor through the blue haze of smoke, and a low, sibilant voice uttered a single sentence:

"Cop's comin'."

A soft shuttle of feet on the sawdust floor, and the gray figures in the room melted like mist from a breath, as if the rushing in of the outside air had blown them all into rings of smoke and carried them away. Mysterious doors opened and closed as if they had not been, and the room was quiet and deserted, the proprietor and his assistant reading the sporting pages with their feet on a table when the cop swung along and looked in:

"Business pretty poor t'night, Jake," he said with a significant look around.

"Yas, Cap'n, pretty poor. Beats all how a man's goin' to live ef this here prohibition keeps up. Have a glass o' sody, Cap'n? Sorry I ain't got nothin' better to offer ya."

Out in the night gray figures melted into black shadows, and a low voice murmured: "Behind the hazel—"

And out at sea a revenue cutter paced the coast, and a little black boat with a silent crew and no lights dropped down after a long wait behind the horizon and stole away, hovered back to watch, and stole away again just before the dawning.

Chapter 13

Joyce did not get up as early as she had planned. She had been utterly worn out with the experience of the last two days and human flesh will have its revenge. The sun stole into her little casement windows, and laid warm fingers on her brown hair, but she did not feel them. She was sleeping deeply. It was the grocery boy with the little yellow Ford from the store across the way that finally reached her consciousness. He was possessed of a clear, sharp whistle, and a jazzy tenor voice and when he was not using one he was using the other while he unloaded boxes from the freight station.

Joyce roused at last, rubbed her eyes and looked around, for a moment forgetting where she was. The little house was full of sweet air and brilliant sunshine, and in the maples overhead two robins were singing with all their might. The world sounded cheerful and busy and she felt rested and more ready for life than when she had crept between her newspapers the night before.

As her eyes wandered over her own painted walls suddenly she saw the two five-dollar bills pinned there, waving a little in the morning breeze. Where could they have come from? Had someone, a former occupant, pinned them there for safekeeping while at work? And must she waste her valuable time going out to hunt for the owner? Then she spied the ragged edge of one bill, and a crooked tear halfway across, and noticed that the other was crisp and new. These must be the bills she had paid the men for their work! That tear was unmistakable. She had been afraid it would tear all the way across before she got rid of it. The other two bills she had used had been crisp and new. She remembered that the man who drove the truck got a crisp, new one. It was the two older men who had left this money for her. The kindly spirit of the rough workmen drew sudden tears to her eyes. To think that such a beautiful act should be done by rough workingmen who were utter strangers to her. Gentlemen at heart they were. Ah, more than that, God's men. Surely her heavenly Father, knowing her need, had let them be His ministers. She knelt suddenly beside the wooden box and prayed a blessing on the men, and a thanksgiving to the Father who had thus given His help, and arose feeling strengthened. Somehow the nearness of God her Father, Christ her Companion had become real to her in a new sense. Some might have said this little bit of money came from the kindness of humanity, and proved nothing about an overruling God. Joyce knew better. She had the inner witness in her soul that God was with her, the spiritual sense that comes to those, and those only, who believe, and who yield their lives to leading because of that belief, which becomes faith, the faith of our fathers. Because faith is the gift of God in answer to our deliberate act of faith. Joyce had no question but that her Father's hand was in every happening of her life and had one suggested that all these things would have happened anyway, whether she believed, or prayed or not, she would have merely smiled as at one who is talking about something he does not understand. So simply had she been taught in the faith while she was yet a little child, and so deeply and truly had the faith grown within her year by year.

Joyce smoothed her hair with the tiny comb and mirror in her handbag, and decided to hunt up the railroad station and wash her face. She did not care to appear at Mrs. Bryant's until her arrangements were more complete, neither did she wish her to know that she was so hard put to it for shelter that she had slept in a newspaper bed all night. It would not look well for her reputation to be poor as a tramp. She wanted to be respected if she was poor, and she wanted to hold up her head and feel independent, not to have people feel they must offer her charity. She must hunt up those two men right away and try to make them take that money back, or thank them at least if she found it would hurt their feelings to restore the money. She felt deeply touched at the thought of their act of kindliness. Perhaps they had daughters of their own, and had noticed her thin little purse. Men who would take the trouble to dig up a vine and make a shelf to keep it safely must have fine souls within them.

Joyce folded her bed into an innocent looking pile of papers, so that it would tell no tales of the night, in case anyone looked in the window, pulled the casements shut, and moving the box against the wall softly opened her door. As she did so she noticed for the first time a key hanging on a nail high up on the door frame. She fitted it into the lock and found to her joy that it worked perfectly. The coast seemed to be clear for the moment. The yellow Ford, without a muffler, had whizzed away after another load of freight, and the only person on the side street was walking away with his back toward her. She cast a furtive glance toward Mrs. Bryant's kitchen door but it seemed to be closed and no one about, so she locked her door, slipped quickly out the gate and around the corner without being seen.

She found on inquiry that the pretty little stone railroad station was only four blocks away. It contained a tiny washroom that was in tolerably clean condition, so that she was able to make herself quite respectable, although her serge dress did look a bit rumpled from sleeping in it, and she realized that a hot iron for pressing must be among the first necessities, if she was to keep neat and presentable for finding a job. An iron would mean some kind of a stove. What kind? There was no gas in her little house, and she hated oil. Aunt Mary had felt it was dangerous. Still, that was probably the only thing possible. Mrs. Bryant would perhaps let her press her dress once, but she did not want to be constantly beholden to her landlady for everyday necessities. Well, a way would come. She must trust and work each problem out as it appeared. She could not face them all at once.

She stepped into a drugstore and got a glass of good milk and three butter thin crackers at the soda counter, and then went out to hunt up the two men who had left the money.

But they were not where they had been the day before, and a careful search for several blocks finally discovered only the truckman who said the other two were on another job that day and would probably not return to that suburb at all as the work was about done there. When she told him that she wanted to thank them for their kindness, she could see by the way he said he would tell them that he knew nothing about their kindly act, and she had to turn away and be satisfied with only this. Looking up to the waving leaves of the trees in the sunshine, and to the blue, blue sky overhead a great thankfulness came into her heart for all that had come to her, and she lifted a little prayer, "You tell them, Father. Make them know I thank them." She wondered whimsically as she walked down the pleasant street, whether she would meet them someday in heaven, and make them understand then how truly she had appreciated what two strangers had done for a lonely girl.

She went back to the little line of stores that was already beginning to make this new suburb look like a commercial center, and found a small utility shop where she bought thread, needles, a thimble, a paper of pins, enough cheesecloth for window curtains, some blue and white chintz that the woman let her have for fifteen cents a yard because it was all that was left, half a yard of white organdy, and a big blue and white checked apron of coarse gingham that would cover her dress from neck to hem and was only fifty cents.

There was a hardware store next door, and here she found a partial solution to her fire problem in canned alcohol and a little outfit for cooking with it. She also invested in some paper plates and cups, a sharp knife, a pair of good scissors, a hammer, a can opener, some tacks, and a few long nails.

She stopped at the grocery store on her way back and bought a can of vegetable soup, a box of crackers, and some bananas, and hurried back to her domicile, excited as a child with a new toy. She had spent just six dollars and twenty-three cents.

But first she must pay her ground rent, so after depositing her bundles she ran to Mrs. Bryant's door and knocked.

Mrs. Bryant welcomed her with a smile:

"I'm real glad to see you," she said. "I didn't pay you yet for yesterday. Mr. Bryant said I ought to have asked you if you had a place to stay all night. He said we owed you a great deal and he left this ten-dollar bill for you. He said it was worth a good many times that what you did, carrying that broiler out of the house. You see it's all wood ceiling up behind that range, and if it had caught fire the house would like as not have gone. You know I had some dish towels hanging up on that little line to dry, and two of them were scorched. I found that out this morning. It wouldn't have been but a minute more till the whole would have been in a flame, and then the wall would have caught. And Mr. Bryant hadn't renewed the insurance. The time was up day before yesterday, and he had been busy and had just let it slip by without realizing till this stirred him up. So he appreciates what you did."

"Oh, that was quite all right, Mrs. Bryant. I didn't want to be paid for what I did yesterday. It was I who distracted your attention and made you forget your meat, and I wanted to make up for it. I couldn't think of taking so much anyway. I just helped you out when you were in a hurry. Anybody would have done that. And I'm sure you helped me out. I came in to pay my first month's rent," and she laid a five-dollar bill down on the table.

"Well, I'll take that," said Mrs. Bryant, "but you've got to keep the ten. My husband put his foot down. Five is for getting the supper, and five is for saving the house. It really isn't much, you know, when you stop to consider it. Why we'd have lost everything. Now, is there anything I can do to help you? When do you move in? Want to borrow anything?"

"Why, perhaps I may need something by-and-by, but I'm all right so far," said Joyce ignoring the question about moving in. "I'm wondering if I can get some water now and then at that outside faucet?"

"Why, sure, get all the water you want. It's right handy for you, and there's a drain out by the back door you can use too, or you can throw your dishwater into the garden. Here, I'll show you—" and she whisked outside and made Joyce acquainted with all the ins and outs of the kitchen shed.

"I don't mind a bit if you come and wash out your clothes in these tubs," she added thoughtfully. "You can't do much washing out there in that little tucked-up place. Besides, you'd have to carry so much water. Better just bring anything you want to wash in here and rub it out. There's the wire clothesline outside, and you can fix it to wash on the days when I don't so we won't interfere. How'd you ever come to buy that little shack, anyway? Some agent sell it to you?"

"Why, no," said Joyce smiling frankly, "I just saw it as I passed by and it appealed to me. A man was knocking it to pieces. I got there just as he struck the first blow and it shivered like a person, such a pretty little house! I needed a house myself, and I asked if I could buy it. They said it had to be taken away at once and finally they agreed to sell it if I took it away in an hour."

"H'm!" said Mrs. Bryant eyeing her thoughtfully. "You were hunting a house were you. Where'd you come from? How'd you happen to come to our town?"

Joyce smiled:

"I just walked till I came to it I guess. You see my aunt died with whom I have lived since my parents' death, and I felt as if I could go on living better if I tried a new place, it wouldn't seem so sad, so when I reached this region I just took a trolley and rode till things looked interesting and then I got off and walked till I came on the little house."

Mrs. Bryant looked interested. Joyce's story was vague but it intrigued her. Her life had never contained such romance as walking off into the world till you found a place you liked and then camping down there. Joyce was a new kind of girl and she liked her. But she also wanted to satisfy her own curiosity and her sense of the conventions, so she proceeded with her inquisition. Also, it was necessary to have an explanation ready to give at the Ladies' Aid that afternoon of the new little house that had come to park on her premises. She knew everyone would ask about it. She could hear them now, "Whoooo—is she? Wheeere did—she—come—from? Whoooo—knows—her? Whiiiiiy—is—she—here? Whoo? Tu-Whit, Tu—Whoooo?" for all the world like so many owls. Mrs. Bryant meant to be ready to silence all voices. Her husband was sponsoring this girl by allowing her on his premises, and she was not going to have anything questionable said about her.

"What you going to do now you're here?" she asked

abruptly. "Have you got means of your own, or do you have to work?"

Joyce flushed but answered without hesitation:

"Why, I've got enough to get along on I think until I get a job. Of course I could have found something easier at home, I suppose, but I thought it would be better to make a change. I guess I'll find something pretty soon. I've got to get settled first."

"H'm!" said Mrs. Bryant. "What's your line? You a stenographer or what?"

"What! I guess," laughed Joyce. "I've been aiming to get ready to be a teacher, but I suddenly decided to come away just before the examinations so I guess I'll have to wait for that. And anyhow it's almost vacation time. I'd have to do something else until fall, of course. I wonder if perhaps I could arrange to take examinations here? I don't suppose you know when the state examinations come off in your public schools here, do you?"

"No, but I could find out this afternoon. I'm going to Ladies' Aid an' Mrs. Powers is always there. Her husband's on the board of trustees, and she mostly knows everything about education. I'll ask her."

"Thank you," said Joyce gladly, "I should be so glad if there was some chance for me to get my tryout before next year, for I really want to teach. I'm hoping for a position. I can get along with almost anything else in the way of a job until then. I'd like to take my examinations while everything is fresh in my mind. I've been studying hard all the spring for them."

"Well, I'll see if that can't be arranged somehow. There ought to be somebody round that has got some pull with the school board. Meantime, if you find a job and want references, just send 'em to me. I'll be glad to tell anybody you're all right."

"But you don't know me, Mrs. Bryant. How could you give me a recommendation?" laughed Joyce in amazement.

"I know you all I need to know," said the good woman decidedly. "You're a good girl and a capable girl. Nine out of every ten girls I know would have screamed and run for the fire company instead of stalking in here and doing something. And I can't be sure of one that would have come in here and helped me the way you did with that dinner when I was hard put to it, not even for pay. They'd have had too much to do in their own affairs. And if they had come after urging they wouldn't have known what to do without being told at every turn. You told me, and you made things go, and I say you're a smart girl and a good girl."

Such praise from a stranger was sweet to Joyce's lonely soul and she found the tears welling to her eyes, but she choked them back with a smile:

"Thank you, Mrs. Bryant, I'll try to live up to the recommendation you're giving me. I only hope you won't ever have reason to take it back."

"Well, I don't believe I shall. Now don't hesitate to ask for anything you want to borrow, and let me know if there's anything I can do for you. By the way, if you want to clean any before you get a stove just come over and get hot water. I'm going out this afternoon, but I'll leave the kitchen key under the doormat and if you want to, just come in and put on the teakettle and get all the hot water you need."

So Joyce went down the short path to her own door with gratitude in her heart and a ten-dollar bill in her hand, saying over to herself the words that had leaped to her lips of a sudden out of the stores of the past when she and Aunt Mary learned whole chapters out of the Bible and repeated them to one another:

"The barrel of meal shall not waste, neither shall the cruse of oil fail, until the day that the Lord sendeth rain upon the earth."

"Isn't it almost funny," she said to herself thoughtfully, "the money comes back just as fast as I spend it for the things I need, faster in fact. It's wonderful to be cared for this way!"

Chapter 14

Back in her house she set to work on her curtains, cutting the cheesecloth in lengths, and hemming it with long, even stitches. It did not take long and her fingers flew rapidly. She was always a fast worker on whatever she took up, and her thoughts kept pace with her work. Suppose Mrs. Bryant should find out that it was still possible for her to take her examinations! Suppose she got a school here! Could she live in the little house all winter? How would she get heat? And light? She would have to work and study in the evenings! How many problems there were to meet when one dropped away from a home and provided it for oneself!

There were strings enough around the packages to run in the hems and hang the curtains, but the windows had to be washed before the curtains could be put up, so Joyce ran over to the store for a few more purchases. A broom, a scrubbing brush, soap, a galvanized pail, and a sponge. She had no rags but a sponge was wonderful for paint and windows. Then a bright thought came to her and she asked if they had any boxes for sale. They took her down to the cellar where there were boxes and barrels of all sizes and shapes. She selected several boxes and two nice clean sugar barrels, besides two delightful boxes with lids swinging on tiny hinges. These would make wonderful closets for her china when she got some. She had to pay ten cents apiece for them.

It was noon when she got back, and all the whistles were blowing. She lighted her little alcohol can and heated the can of vegetable soup. This with crackers and a banana for dessert made a fine meal and while she was clearing it away the boy from the grocery brought over her boxes and barrels, and the place began to assume a look of furniture. Mrs. Bryant came to the door with a roll of old rags as the boy went away.

"I thought you might like some cloths for cleaning," she said, stepping in at the door. "I have such quantities, so I brought some."

"Oh, thank you," said Joyce, "I was wondering if I could make my windows shine with newspapers. Now I won't have to try. Won't you come in and sit down. Here's a nice clean box."

"No, thank you," declined the lady stepping back with a glance of approval around the little room and at the window where Joyce had tacked up a finished curtain to try it. "I'm on the committee for serving luncheon at the Ladies' Aid today and I have to hurry. We serve at one and it's almost that now, but I saw your goods coming in and I thought you might need these so I just ran in. I left the teakettle on and you can just turn it out when you are done. How cozy you are going to be! This is a real cute little house. Well, I must run along."

Joyce drew a long breath as she watched her go. "Goods." She glanced at the barrels and boxes amusedly. So she had thought these were her goods. What would she say if she knew she had no goods in the world? And she had so hoped to get the little room looking habitable before there were any visitors. Well, the woman hadn't noticed the lack of furniture, and perhaps she would be able to do something about it before she came again.

She changed her serge dress for the new gingham apron, got the hot water and went happily to work scrubbing with all her might. In a short time the place was smelling sweetly of soapsuds and gleaming with the whiteness of the paint. Evidently there had not been much wear and tear on the inside of the place since it was painted, for when the dirt was washed off it came out nice and clean. There was an advantage too in having a small place. It did not take long to clean it. The five windows and the door were soon finished, and then she swept and scrubbed the floor, and put up her curtains.

She stood back when the last tack was driven with a sigh of satisfaction and looked around. It certainly did look cheerful and pretty. She could imagine being quite happy in this pretty place. Now there must be some inner curtains to draw when night came on and screen her from the passersby. They could be of cretonne and there would have to be five-cent rods for them, so that she could draw them back and forth. How many things there were to buy! Perhaps she could find some cheap cretonne and get enough for a curtain across one end to screen her bed from view until she could manage to get one that was respectable. Beds cost a great deal, even just cot beds, she knew for she had bought one once for a poor family at Aunt Mary's request. Then there was a mattress and pillows. So many, many things to buy. But there would be a way. See, how her money had increased as fast as she had spent it. Could she trust that such care would continue until she had an income? And the old chant from the beloved Bible story of childhood went over again in her head: "The barrel of meal shall not waste neither shall the cruse of oil fail."

Joyce was not a modernist. She had been taught to believe the Bible literally, and found no difficulty with miracles. She was not dumb nor ignorant. She knew that the academic world was largely inclined to put aside all that was miraculous, and to doubt everything that they had not seen happen in everyday life; but she looked upon such as souls who had not chosen to accept God's way of proof, the proof that comes to the soul of every true believer who takes God at His Word, and cannot doubt because He knows. Miracles never had bothered her, because if God could make *anything* why couldn't He make or do anything else? She had once heard a wonderful man who came to Meadow Brook to preach say that mystery was soomething that God knew but didn't tell right away, and ever after that the mysteries that she found in the Scriptures had been but more beautiful to her. They never troubled her nor made her doubt. She was a bright girl with a more than ordinary mind and a fair education, but she accepted the things of the kingdom as a little child and when someone pointed out to her a spot that seemed a contradiction to facts as she knew them she would smile and say, then *she* had made some mistake, not God, and not His Word. That was how Aunt Mary brought her up. More and more as Aunt Mary drew nearer to the end of this life and saw how miserably she had failed to teach her own son heavenly things did she yearn to give this dear girl something substantial to stand upon when all else failed. And if she had not left Joyce anything else she had left her a great faith in the living God and in His Word.

But it was growing late in the afternoon and Joyce was weary. The night was coming on again and the question of light had not been settled. Perhaps she had better run over and get some candles and a few more things for supper. She was hungry as a bear, and the can of soup seemed a forgotten dream.

So she went to the store again, and when she came back and had eaten some sandwiches of dried beef and bread and butter and drunk some milk she felt better, and set to work to arrange her box furniture to advantage.

There were the two barrels. They were to make easy chairs, one for herself and one for any possible company that might come in. They would have to wait to materialize until she could buy material to upholster and cover them, and until she had time to work over them. They would need sawing. Oh, they must wait, but when they were finished they would stand here, and here—she wheeled them into place. And right here between them should stand a table—she placed the biggest square box there, and imagined a lamp with a pretty shade, and some magazines lying on it.

The two boxes with hinged lids she nailed to the wall in the corner she called her dining room and kitchen. These were her china closets. She carefully placed her paper cups and plates in one and arranged the cracker box, the milk bottle, and other supplies in the other. Somehow she must manage shelves for them. There were some loose bits of boards in one box. These would make shelves if she could manage to borrow an old saw.

In the corner beyond the window next to her bed she placed another box for a dressing table. Someday she would drape it in chintz and get a looking glass to hang over it. Chintz or cretonne was really one of the next things she needed. There must be a curtain to shut off her bedroom. She did not want everybody to know she was sleeping on a paper bed, and a curtain would give a little privacy. Besides, she must curtain off a small corner for a closet.

She was suddenly interrupted in her meditations by a tap at her door.

"I wondered if you were here yet," said Mrs. Bryant as she opened the door. "No, I can't come in, I've got to run back and start supper. But I just stepped over to tell you Mrs. Powers, the lady that in the big brick colonial with tulips in the yard, perhaps you've noticed it—she was at the Ladies' Aid today and was going on something terrible about how she was going to have company from Baltimore tomorrow, and her maid had gone away sick yesterday and isn't coming back for a week. She had telephoned in town for a maid but they couldn't get her any she would have and she didn't know what to do. She said her friend hadn't seen her in a long time and she wanted to take her around in the car and she just didn't see how she was to cook dinner too. Well, she seemed so distressed and all that I finally up and told her how you helped me out last night. I don't know's you'll like it, but she seemed so interested that I went on and told her all about you, and how you were a teacher, and you'd bought this little house and were going to teach school in the fall, and then she looked awfully disappointed and said: 'Oh, she's a teacher, is she? Then I don't suppose she'd be willing to help me out, would she?' And I said, well, no, I didn't suppose you intended doing things like that, that you were a perfect lady, but you might do it once for accommodation. I finally said I'd tell you anyhow. She said if you would come she'd gladly pay you five dollars for cooking dinner, and if you were willing to wait on the table too why she'd pay ten. I really hated to tell you about it after I'd promised, but you can do as you like."

"Why, I'd be glad to help her," said Joyce pleasantly, "and I'd like to wait on the table too. I really want to earn the money of course, and while I don't think I want to be a cook for life, still I don't see that it's going to hurt me to cook a few dinners for other people. I've had to do it in my own home a good many times."

"Well, I didn't know how you'd feel about it. I think it's fine of you. Some folks are so kind of proud nowadays. But I somehow thought you were sensible."

"Well, what should I be proud about?" laughed Joyce. "I haven't any reputation here to lose anyway, and if people want to think less of me because I know how to cook they can."

"Well, I say you're a real fine girl. So that's settled, and I'm kind of glad, for her husband's on the school board, and if she wants to she can do a lot for you. You run right in the house and call her up. Her number is ninety-five and her name is Powers. I told her you'd call."

Joyce ran in to the telephone and came out smiling in a moment:

"Thank you ever so much, Mrs. Bryant. This will help me out a lot. I've just been thinking of a good many things I want to get and I wasn't sure I ought to spare the money. Now I can get them right away. I'm to go to her at twelve o'clock and stay till after the dishes are washed. Which way did you say she lives?"

After most explicit directions have been given Joyce went back to her house and flew at the bundle of chintz with swift fingers. There was about three hours of daylight left—the evenings were long this time of year—and she must use every minute of them for she must have a thin dress to work in and she did not want to burn a light and show that she was staying nights in the place until she had things looking a little more comfortable, both because she did not want anyone to offer her charity, and because she did not care to have them all know how poverty-stricken she really was.

She folded her material crosswise in the middle and spread it upon the driest place on her cleanly scrubbed floor. Then she laid her blue serge smoothly down upon it with the shoulders to the fold and the kimono sleeves stretched toward the selvages. The material reached below the serge far enough for a good hem, and guided by her serge dress she took her sharp, new scissors and carefully cut out a straight little simple slip of a dress.

She had cut many a dress before, on Aunt Mary's big dining room table with a box of shining pins and a tried and true pattern to guide her. But she knew the lines of a simple dress well enough and she could not see how she could go far astray in her cutting. It had to be long enough and wide enough, for it was as big as her blue serge. So she clipped away, and soon had a dress cut out, making the neckline only a curved slit until she should try it on.

Then she sat down and ran up the two side seams on the right side and slipped it on to try it. Of course she had no mirror but she managed to get a vague glimpse of herself in the closed lattice of her window. It needed a little taking in under the arm, but the rest seemed all right, and she slipped if off again and sat down to make the changes and French the seams. Another trial and the fit was found to be better. She hunted out her pins and turned up the hem. This she found rather a hard proposition, but after several takings off and re-adjustings it seemed to swing evenly.

She was growing tired, and her back began to ache with sitting on the hard box after her day of scrubbing and curtain making. She wondered if she could keep at it much longer?

With a weary impulse she flung her paper bed out in the corner and threw herself down upon it.

For almost ten minutes she forced herself to lie and relax, trying to think of nothing and really rest. Then the clock on some distant building struck eight, and she roused up, suddenly aware that she had but a few more minutes of daylight and that if she lay here she would soon be asleep. She simply did not dare leave all that sewing till morning. She must have a neat, washable dress ready by twelve o'clock in which to work. So she stood up and tried to cut out the neck of her frock as best she could, wishing all the time for a big mirror. She finally got out the two-inch bit of glass belonging to her handbag and inspected her work, deciding it would have to do. Then she caught up a newspaper and cut and experimented until she had a pattern for a simple collar to fit the neck of her dress. This she cut from the half-yard of organdy, also cutting organdy cuffs to fit the short sleeves.

It was quite dusky now in her little room and she had to take the pieces of chintz that came off the sides of the dress out on her front step to see what she was doing. Here she cut from the longest piece a string belt, and several long strips of bias binding about an inch wide. Then rolling up these with the organdy collar and cuffs, her scissors, thimble, needle, and thread, she put on her serge dress and hat and hurried down the street. She had thought of a way to work a little longer that night without burning a light. She would just sit in the station waiting room a little while and sew.

The soft evening breeze of the out-of-doors revived her weary body and she felt quite cheered and happy. To think, she was going to earn a whole ten dollars in one afternoon and evening! Here was her Father providing her with more money again just when she had discovered so many things she had to buy, that it overwhelmed her. The "barrel of meal and cruse of oil" again! How wonderful it was!

When she reached the station, however, her plans seemed balked for the station itself was closed and dark. There was a bench, however, down along the platform under a shedlike roof, and a great arc light glowed above it. People were walking back and forth too as if waiting for a train, so Joyce sat down at one end of the bench and took out her bit of sewing. No one noticed her and her swift fingers had soon run on the bias bands around collar and cuffs, and turned down the binding smoothly. She just loved the hemming of them down. It was like a bit of fancy work, and they looked so pretty—the blue edging the sheer white. Of course the dress could have been bound around the neck and sleeves without the white collar and cuffs but this touch of prettiness made it look more comely, and she must remember her appearance if she was to hope to get a school around here sometime. Mrs. Bryant had given her the reputation of a lady and she must keep it up, even if it meant a little more work for her.

By the time the half past nine train had gone she had the organdy bound, and was sewing up the string girdle. She lingered only until the seams were run up before she gathered up her things and hurried back to her little dark house. It was growing lonely on the station platform, and she did not like to stay any longer, but she could turn the girdle inside out in the dark by the help of a safety pin, and then everything would be ready for morning. She would only have to hem the skirt and put on the collar and cuffs.

Sitting in the dark on her box she found a safety pin in her handbag and, fastening it in the end of the girdle, began pushing it through, and when it was turned all the way, creased it carefully and smoothed it between her fingers till it almost looked as if it were ironed flat. Then she took off her serge dress, put on her gingham apron and lay down under her paper blankets for another night's sleep, too weary to do more than thank her heavenly Father for keeping her so far. As she drifted away into sleep she heard a soft, sweet voice, like a pleasant melody in her soul, Aunt Mary's voice long ago, saying over the golden text from Sunday school, over and over again till she learned it, "The barrel of meal shall not waste, neither shall the cruse of oil fail."

"I must have a Bible," she said to herself dreamily. "I wish I had brought mine along."

Chapter 15

Notwithstanding her weariness Joyce did not sleep well that night. She heard the late travelers passing by and the milkman and grocery trucks on their way to a new day, and she tossed on her rattling, lumpy bed till almost dawn. Somehow all the happenings of the last few days seemed to have arrived in concrete form and to be standing about her couch for her to reckon with.

First, there was the matter of her leaving home. Ought she to have left at all? And if she should have left, was that the right way to have done it? The whole problem of her life took on a distorted form in the midnight and darkness that it had never presented before. She thought of her friends back in Meadow Brook who had loved her and Aunt Mary. What would they think of her going? Perhaps she should have waited to tell them all, and yet how could she make explanations? It would only bring discredit upon Eugene and Nannette and that she did not want to do. No, she could not have asked her friends, or even have told them good-bye without more explanation than she was ready to give. There was the minister, and Judge Peterson, the Browns and Ridgeways, and a host of others. They never would have let her go alone out into the world without even a destination, and no chance of a job. They would have worked it somehow for her to stay with one of them. She would never have been free, and Eugene and Nannette would have been furious at her making a display of their family quarrels in the town. No, she could have come away in no other manner. And she had to come. She could not have stayed much longer even if she had not started that night.

These questions somewhat conquered, her thoughts turned to the first night away from home, the awful experience in the cemetery, and the look on the face of her old friend when she had asked him what he was doing.

And now she knew what had been the underlying thorn in her soul that had made the pain ever since.

Long ago, perhaps ten years before, when she had been a little girl, there had been a holiday when she and Aunt Mary had started off with a neatly packed luncheon and a handful of books to spend the day in the woods, a long promised, eagerly anticipated excursion. There were chicken sandwiches neatly wrapped in wax paper. How well she remembered helping to make them! And little blackberry turnovers rich with gummy sweetness. Hard-boiled eggs, tiny sweet pickles from the summer's vintage, sponge cakes, big purple grapes, and a bottle of milk to drink. Plenty of everything. Aunt Mary never stinted a lunch and she always put in enough for a guest if one should turn up.

And that day the guest really came.

It was a warm, sunny day in October and the leaves were just beginning to turn. As they climbed the hill above Meadow Brook and came within sight of the valley, great splashes of crimson flung out like banners across the valley and yellow glinted across the purples and browns like patches of gold in the sunshine. There was a smell of burning leaves and sunshine in the air and the earth was sweet with autumn. Blue and yellow and white asters bordered the road that wound along the hill and dipped again into the valley among the trees. Purple grackles were stalking the fields in battalions, their stiff, black silk armor glinting in the sun, cawing of the weather and their coming need of flight. She could hear their hoarse, throaty voices as she lay and stared at the ceiling in her little lonely house under the maples.

And the air! How sweet and winey it had been!

She and Aunt Mary had climbed a fence and crossed a field till they reached the deep, sweet woods with its solemn cathedral silences and its lofty vaulted ceiling. How far away the world had seemed as they entered and trod the pine-strewn aisles and penetrated deep into the cloistered vistas. She remembered thinking that this must be where God stayed a good deal, it was so sweet and perfect. Above in the branches strange birds sent out wild, sweet notes, like snatches of celestial anthems. Favored birds to live in such safe and holy fastnesses. She remembered wondering if they ever flew down to Meadow Brook and fellowed with the common birds, picking up worms in garden paths, and draggling their feathers in the dust of the world like sparrows, or did they always stay here alone with God and praise?

They had found a mossy log to sit upon and a carpet of pine needles fragrant and deep, and there they had established themselves, the little girl lying full length upon the sweet bed of needles, the older woman sitting upon the log and reading. It was a storybook they were reading, one of Louisa Alcott's, was it *Under the Lilacs* or *Little Women*? *Under the Lilacs* of course, because it was where the little white circus dog Sancho appeared that she remembered first noticing the boy's back.

There had been crickets droning somewhere, and a tinkling brook that murmured not far off, and no other sound save now and then a falling stick or bit of branch from some high treetop hurtling down, until, with the advent of that dog there had been a tiny human stir, an almost imperceptible sound of giving attention, and her eyes had been fastened on the gray-brown back, the tousled bright head topped by the torn old baseball cap just a few steps away in the dim shadowed aisle down which she was looking. At first she scarcely recognized it as not a part of the woods, so still it sat, that square, young back in its faded flannel shirt, held in a listening attitude. Then gradually she had become aware of the boy's presence, of the fishing rod in his hand, of the bank that he must be sitting on which had seemed but a level stretch to her first vision. She had turned a quick glance to Aunt Mary, but Aunt Mary only looked up an instant, paused to recognize that there was someone there, smiled knowingly, and went on with the story.

It must have been an hour they sat thus listening to the reading, the boy and the fishing rod not moving, the little girl watching with fascinated, dreamy eyes as if she were looking at a picture that might come alive any minute, and then suddenly something happened. The rod bent quickly down with a jerk, the boy's arm went out with a quick, involuntary motion, and a fish swept up from below somewhere in a great circle and landed floundering on the grassy bank.

Joyce sat up quickly with round eyes watching the boy's maneuvers with the fish, and Aunt Mary stopped reading and looked on with interest too. The boy looked up at last shamefaced and flushed:

"Aw, gee!" he said. "I didn't go to interrupt you. That fish just got on my hook an' I pulled it before I thought. That's a crackerjack story you're reading."

"Why, I'm glad to be interrupted by such an interesting happening," Aunt Mary answered him. "What a beautiful fish! What kind is it?"

"That's a trout. You don't find many of 'em anymore. They been all fished out. Want it? I c'n find some more when I want 'em."

"Oh, thank you, I couldn't take your fish," said Aunt Mary with a smile, "but I've enjoyed seeing you catch it. You better take it home to your mother."

The boy's head bowed a little lower and he said in a low, gruff voice:

"Haven't got any mother. She's dead. They don't want to bother with fish at home. D'you like me to cook it for you? They're awful good cooked outdoors like this right on the coals."

He began to gather sticks and twigs together, and placed them in a little pile.

"Well, that certainly would be wonderful," said Aunt Mary smiling. "Then you can take lunch with us. We always bring along enough for a guest—"

The boy looked up wistfully and grinned, and then was off for more sticks.

In a little clearing he built a fire while the little girl watched him, and put his fish to cook, and then they spread out the lunch on a big white cloth on a rock the boy showed them, and they had a great laugh over the bugs and ants that kept coming to dinner with them.

The boy ate lunch with them, carving his fish proudly with a big jackknife and serving the biggest portions to his guests, saying he didn't care for fish anyhow, he could get it whenever he wanted it. But he ate the sandwiches and little pies and cakes hungrily, and watched the little girl with shy, furtive glances.

Afterward he washed the dishes for them in the brook and packed them back in the basket, then curled down at Aunt Mary's feet while she went on reading.

Oh, the memory of that long, beautiful afternoon among the pines, with the sun sifting down through the leaves and the taller trees waving way up almost touching the sky it seemed, and the drone of bees somewhere, the distant whetting of a scythe—how it all came back as she thought it over!

And then the book was finished and they sat back, sorry it was done, dreamy with the loveliness of the story in which they had been absorbed.

"That's a crackerjack tale," declared the boy. "Gee, I'd like to have that dog. My dog died," he ended sadly. "Got run over by a truck."

They talked a little about the dog and the boy got out a dirty little snapshot of himself with the dog in his arms when it was only a little puppy, and the little girl smiled and said it was a darling.

Then somehow Aunt Mary led them around to talk of other things, and how still it was in the woods, and how beautiful, and how God must love it there. The boy's face grew sober and wistful and wonder came in his eyes with a kind of softness. Aunt Mary got out her little Testament and read the story of the healing of the man who was born blind, in the ninth chapter of John. How they thrilled to the story all the way through, as the different actors came and went, the blind man himself, his wondering neighbors, the scornful Jews, the cowardly parents, Jesus, who came to find him after they had all left him, even down to the words that Jesus spoke to the faultfinding Jews: "If ye were blind, ye should have no sin: but now ye say, We see; therefore your sin remaineth." How strange that those words should sound even after these years, with the murmuring of the pines among the words, and the holy stillness afterward, while the shadows grew long and violet within the sanctuary of trees where they sat, and dusk was all about them. The boy's lashes drooped thoughtfully and his whole face took on a faraway look. Then Aunt Mary's voice came again softly praying: "Dear Jesus, we know You are here today just as then. Help us for Christ's sake to have our eyes open to sin, so that we shall always know when we are not pleasing Thee. Amen."

They had gone out together silently through the quiet aisles with only the tall singing of the pines and the distant melody of thrushes in their evening song above them. The boy had gathered up the basket and his fishing rod, and helped them over the fence with a kind of reverence upon him.

They had walked down the road to the village with that beautiful intimacy still upon them, like friends who had seen a vision together and would never forget. All the way to their door the boy had gone, saying very little, but with an uplifted look upon his face. Aunt Mary had asked him to come and see them sometime, and he had suddenly grown shy and silent, dropped his eyes and set his young shoulders as if he had come to a hard spot. "Well, g'bye!" he said gruffly, and turning, darted out the gate and down the street, flashing them a wonderful smile as he went. He had become suddenly all boy again.

He had come again several times with gifts—a splendid plant of squawberry vine with bright red berries hanging to it, a great sheaf of crimson leaves and sumac berries, a handkerchief full of ripe chestnuts.

When winter came again they sometimes found their paths shoveled around the house very early in the morning and caught a glimpse of a red sweater and gray cap going down the street as they arose.

There had been several times at school when Joyce felt his protection against the larger boys who snowballed most unmercifully.

Once he drew her on her sled through a drifted place. And once she found a rose upon her desk and looking up saw his eyes upon her suddenly averted and knew he had put it there. But he never came again into their intimate family circle as he had done that wonderful day in the woods. His family moved to another part of the town, and she seldom saw him, yet they always spoke when they met, and something would flash from eye to eye that was different from an ordinary acquaintance. They could not forget that day and that holy cathedral of the woods where they had companioned so richly together.

She had not seen him often through the years, but he had come to Aunt Mary's funeral, and at the cemetery stood close to the open grave looking down with bared head as if he loved the one who was being laid to rest. A handsome fellow with a distinguished look about him, and that wonderful wistfulness in his eyes that had not lost the child look and could still flash a smile that lit the hearts of those who saw it.

That! And then to see him there in the dark—at a gruesome task of some sort, and to have seen his eyes as she asked him what he had been doing!

She had not spoken to him in years. Their sole communication had been through smiles till she asked him that question wrung from her lips at cost of pain. Somehow her words seemed to strike a blow at the dear past and shatter something that had been most precious.

And now she had gone over it again in the watches of the night and the pain was still there. He had somehow gone wrong. She had to admit that to her loyal heart. Perhaps he had been wrong all the time, a bad, wild boy. She had sometimes heard hints of that floating about the village but had not believed it. She had clung to that day when they had read *Under the Lilacs* together, and then heard the story of the blind man and gone out together again into life with the blessing of Jesus resting upon them. She could not bear to think that the boy who had been so gentle and kind, so interested and happy in that sweet, simple place, could have been bad all the time, and only dropped out of his regular life for the day just out of curiosity. He must be right and true somehow. And if he had been doing wrong he must be sorry perhaps, for he had looked ashamed. She could not get away from that. She covered her face with her hands to pray and found there were tears upon her cheeks, and then she prayed with all her heart, "Oh, Jesus, go and find him and make him understand. Open his eyes that he may see and sin no more."

About that time a man under cover of the darkness came down the road from the Meadow Brook cemetery and stole into Julia Hartshorn's gate, and silently over the grass to the hammock under the trees; pausing a moment to look furtively up at the dark house, he stooped and felt all over that hammock. He had passed the house that day, slowly, in his automobile and he was sure he had seen the form of an object sagging in the middle. He had observed it most minutely. He was come now to find out. It might give him no clue even if he found it, but he was here.

His hand moved carefully and came in contact with a book, yes—and something soft like cloth, a handkerchief with a faint smell of lavender drifting from it. He slipped them in his pocket and went silently away into the night on rubber-shod feet that made no sound, and after he was gone for a season, came another shadow, stealing as silently into the yard and up to the hammock. It is doubtful if Julia Hartshorn and her niece would have ever recovered from the fright if they had known what went on in their yard that night. But they were slumbering deeply and did not even see the tiny spot of light that flashed over the hammock, and down upon the ground, bringing out in clear relief a scrap of paper with writing across it. A hand reached for it, and again the flashlight focused for a scrutiny. "oyce Radw" the paper read and that was all. It was torn on all its edges, and evidently a part of a larger writing. The man searched again, but could find nothing more. So he stole away as he had come, but he kept the paper safely for future reference.

Chapter 16

When Joyce awoke the next morning it was with a feeling of trepidation lest she had overslept and would not be able to accomplish all that she must before twelve o'clock.

She hurried around anxiously, folding her newspaper bed into an innocent-looking pile, putting away her things carefully for any possible scrutiny, and eating a hasty breakfast of crackers, cheese, and what was left of her bottle of milk.

When everything was neat and trim she took out her dress and sat down to sew, wondering if perhaps she ought not to run out and find what time it was before she started to work. But fortunately the town clock settled the matter by chiming out nine o'clock. Three hours before she must be at Mrs. Powers's! Well, there was only the collar and cuffs to sew on, the skirt to hem and the pockets to make. She could get along without pockets if necessary but she really needed them. If only the collar would fit and not have to be made over again or cut down or anything.

She put in the hem swiftly. That was plain sailing, as it was carefully pinned. Then she put on the cuffs and tacked them in place, and donned the gown. Yes, the collar fitted nicely. With a relieved mind she took it off again and faced on the collar. While she was doing so the clock struck ten. If she hurried there would be time to make the pockets. It was half past before she finished the collar and tacked on the girdle. Somehow her fingers seemed terribly slow. She cut two strips from the organdy, bound them with blue and sewed them at the top of two patch pockets. It was striking eleven as she pinned the pockets in place and began to sew them on with strong, firm little stitches, but ten minutes would see it finished. She drew a long breath and began to think of what was before her. Mrs. Powers had sounded pleasant but condescending. Well, one could keep still and obey orders, and after all, condescension didn't hurt anything but one's pride. What was pride? She could stand almost anything for just once.

She must stop at the store on her way and get a clean gingham apron. She ought to have a white one for table waiting also. If there was anything cheap enough she would get it. If there was only another two hours she could easily make one. But there wasn't. She broke off her thread for the finish, and laid aside her thimble and scissors happily. Well, the dress was done anyway.

She wasted little time in putting on the new garment and smoothing her hair, feeling quite neat and trim as she locked her door and hurried down the street. Mrs. Bryant eyed her approvingly from her kitchen window.

"She certainly is a pretty little thing," she said to herself. "I wish I had a daughter like that. It's going to be a real comfort having her right near this winter when Jim is away. I'm glad we let her have the lot."

Joyce bought her other gingham apron, and found a tiny white one, coarse, but neat, for fifty cents, and with her two aprons presented herself at Mrs. Powers's door at exactly twelve o'clock.

Mrs. Powers herself opened the door, her hair in crimpers, herself attired in a somewhat soiled pink silk kimono:

"I forgot to mention that you might come to the side door," she said loftily, "but it doesn't matter this time."

Joyce paused on the threshold and surveyed her silently. She had never met anything quite like this, nor dreamed that people who served others had to endure it. She was minded to flee at once, till she remembered that she had promised to get the dinner and that it was probably too late for the woman to get anyone else now. She must be a lady, even if her employer was not.

Before she could speak, however, Mrs. Powers entered upon her introduction to the work.

"You don't object to washing dishes I hope. The lunch and breakfast dishes will have to be cleared away before you can do much. Here's the menu for tonight, I've written it out so there won't be any mistake. I never like to have to give directions twice. Fruit cup. You'll find the things in the storeroom, oranges, grapefruit, some white grapes skinned and seeded, I like plenty of grapes in it, and there's a can of pineapple. Then we'll have a clear soup. Do you know how to make soup? I'm sure I don't know what you'll make it out of. You can look around and see. Perhaps there's some stock. Then for the meat course we'll have chops and creamed potatoes and peas. There's lettuce in the garden, and tomatoes in the refrigerator. You make mayonnaise, do you? Mrs. Bryant spoke of that I think. Well, that fixes the salad all right. Then ice cream and cake and coffee. I've ordered the ice cream, of course, but I'll need two kinds of cake. I always like to have two kinds. That's all, I believe. Now, I'm going up to lie down. I really must or I'll look like a rag, but I shall expect you to have the dining room and kitchen cleaned, the peas shelled, and the mayonnaise on the ice by the time I come down. Then I shall feel easy. You'll need to scald and skin the tomatoes too, and get at your cake as soon as possible. It'll need to get cold before icing. Now, do you think you understand it all?"

Joyce looked at her with frank amusement as she rolled out the sentences, tolling off the tasks as if they were trifles and expecting, actually expecting all that work to be done. In spite of her a fresh young laugh rang out as if it were all a joke. The lady eyed her curiously, uneasily. What kind of a young working person was this anyway that laughed at her tasks and came to the front door for admission?

"I want dinner promptly at seven," she said haughtily. "Do you feel sure you will remember all I have told you?"

"I'll do my best to accomplish as much as possible, Mrs. Powers," said Joyce, remembering the ten dollars and sobering down. "There isn't any too much time, I guess."

Joyce undid her bundle and enveloped herself in her clean gingham apron as she spoke:

"Now, if you'll show me where to find your materials."

"Yes," sighed the lady comfortably, leading the way to the kitchen. "I hope you'll let me know right away if there's anything else you need, because I hate to be disturbed when I'm taking a nap."

She trailed away from the scene before Joyce realized the whole situation, or it is doubtful if she might not have fled even yet.

The kitchen was stacked with soiled dishes in every available spot, and soiled dish towels, grocery bags huddled together between piles of plates and pans and potato peelings. It was evident that not only the breakfast and lunch dishes were unwashed but also the dinner dishes of the night before, and possibly some from lunch of the day before. It was a wreck of a kitchen and no mistake. Joyce stood still in her pretty new blue dress in the midst of it all, appalled at what was expected of her. It seemed to her that no two girls could accomplish all that had been given her to do before seven o'clock. The cooking alone was enough to keep her on the jump, without all the cleaning. She was minded to get at the preparation for dinner first and leave the clearing up to take care of itself when the lady came down again, only that absolutely nothing could be done until there was a clean place in which to work.

Joyce had been in hard places before, with a meal ahead to get for company in a short time, and had rather enjoyed the sharpening of her wits to win the game and get it done in time. But never had she had such a kitchen as this to deal with. At first glance her soul revolted from having to touch it. The floor was grimy and messy with things spilled on it. Numerous dishes standing under the sink out of the way with fragments of food burned hard to them showed discouraging impossibilities ahead. The sink was filthy with grease and the dishpan filled with greasy water. It was all simply unspeakable. She scarcely knew where to begin.

Investigation showed there was no hot water, and that the source of it was a tank heated by a small laundry stove in the cellar, which was out. Joyce descended the cellar stairs, found an axe, and split up a box, and finally got the laundry fire going. Then she came upstairs, and put three pans and the teakettle full of water to heat on the gas range. While they were heating she went to the refrigerator to see what was on hand for that soup which she was supposed to make.

The refrigerator proved worse than anything she had yet seen in the house, and greatly needed a good cleaning, but there was no time for refrigerators. She was weary in every bone and sinew now thinking of all that must be done before six o'clock. But she gathered out whatever was worth using, some chicken bones, a small piece of boiled beef, a leftover lamp chop, a bowl of chicken gravy, a few lima beans, and a cup of mashed potatoes. Not a very promising array. She cleared a spot on the kitchen table, skimmed the grease from the gravy, cut the fat from the meat, and put the whole array on to simmer with a little water. A little foraging brought some onions and carrots to light, which she diced and put in with the mixture. By this time the water was hot and she scalded the tomatoes and skinned them, putting them on the ice to harden. Then, with her soup and salad well under way, she felt more at her ease to go at the cleaning.

The first job was the sink, and it took fully ten minutes to reduce it and the dishpans to order. Then, as she could not find any clean dish towels, she washed out those that were soiled and hung them out in the backyard. They would be dry by the time she needed them, for there was a good breeze blowing. She glanced at the clock as she came in. Forty minutes of the precious seven hours was gone and scarcely an impression made on the dreadful-looking place. She looked around in despair. The second relay of hot water was ready, and she went to work gathering first all the soiled silver and putting it to soak in a panful of suds while she scraped up the dishes and sorted them in orderly piles. Everything would have to soak before it was washed, for food had been smeared over them all and left to dry. By the time the sorting was done the silver washed easily, and she put them into the rinsing pan, and filled the first pan with a pile of plates to soak while she washed off the drainboard and shelf and made room to drain her dishes. Inch by inch she cleared places and filled them with clean, steaming dishes, filling her pans again and again with hot water. The laundry stove was getting in its work by this time and the water from the faucet facilitated matters, nevertheless, it was half past two before she had every dish subdued and standing in clean, dry rows on a clean dry table ready to be marshaled into pantry shelves that sadly needed cleaning, but could not have it now. She must get that fruit dug out and on the ice at once.

She turned her attention to the cake next, and when it was in the oven went at the mayonnaise dressing. She had made a chocolate layer cake, rich and dark, with a transparent chocolate filling and thick, white icing, and was just taking a sponge cake, light as a feather, out of the oven when the mistress arrived, fine and cool in a light crepe de chine, her hair marcelled and her face powdered to the last degree, leaving a perfume of luxury in her wake as she moved.

"Mercy!" she exclaimed. "Is that all the cake you've made? And look at the time. You'll have to frost that, of course. It's too plain that way. Have you fixed the salad? And, oh, I forgot to say—There'll have to be hot biscuits. I hope you can make good ones. Mr. Powers is very particular about his biscuits. He likes them light. I must say you might have scrubbed this floor a little bit, and by the way, I wish you'd run up by and by while your vegetables are cooking and wipe up the bathroom tiles. My son took a bath this morning just before he went off on a trip and he left water all over the floor."

Joyce turned suddenly from setting the hot cake carefully on a cake cooler and faced the lady. Her cheeks were two pink flames and her eyes were bits of blue ice. For just one second words trembled on her lips, words that were not humble nor gentle. Here was a woman much like Nannette, who appeared to think the world was made all for herself. Joyce longed to lay down the knife with which she had loosened the cake from its pan and walk out of the kitchen as she had walked out of her cousin's kitchen a few days before, never to return, but she reflected that she could not go on walking out of situations all her life that she did not like, and moreover it would be a mean thing to leave the lady with her dinner only half got and company coming. It was obvious the lady was unfitted to get it. And then, she had promised to do it. The lady had depended upon her and she must stick. Why not make a game of it, something that had to be overcome and won? So she let her lips soften into a smile and answered with a twinkle of amusement:

"Why, I'm not sure I'll have time, Mrs. Powers, but I'll do my best. Things were pretty badly messed up here, you know, and it all took time. By the way, Mrs. Powers, Mrs. Bryant told me that your husband was on the school board. I wonder if you could tell me whether there is likely to be any opening for a teacher next fall? You know I am a teacher. That is, that's what I've been getting ready to be."

There was something, just a shade of fineness perhaps, in the way Joyce spoke, a kind of sense of being above littleness and an air of being there to help her purely as a favor, that made the lady the least bit ashamed of having asked her to wipe up the bathroom floor. She stared at Joyce a minute in that superior sort of surprised way, as if suddenly some ribbon or powder puff or bit of lace she had been using had risen up and claimed a personality, and then she answered in a cold little tone:

"Why, I'm sure I don't know. There might be. If you put this dinner over well and get it all done on time I'll try and remember to speak to him about it. Mr. Powers loves good dinners, and he might do something for you. I'm going down in my car now to meet my friend and I wish you'd answer the telephone while I'm gone and keep an eye on the front door.

And don't for mercy's sake let anything burn. I just hate to have the house smell of burned food when guests arrive. Don't forget the bathroom floor, and have plenty of biscuits."

The lady sailed away again after having peered into the refrigerator at the tomatoes and fruit cup getting chilled, and sniffed at the kettle of soup on the back of the range, with never a word of commendation. Something strangely like tears came into the girl's eyes as she turned back to the kitchen and reviewed the work still to be done, looking despairingly at the clock. Quarter to five! Could she do it? One thing she was sure of, she would never work for this woman again if she could help it. There seemed to be no pleasing her. It had been quite another thing to get dinner for Mrs. Bryant, who was delighted with everything she did. This woman treated her as if she were the very dust under her feet. Perhaps she had made a mistake in consenting to do kitchen work. Perhaps she had lowered herself in the woman's eyes and hurt her chance of getting a school. Well, she must forget it now. It was all in the game and she was out to win. It was just another hindrance put in her way, a net to get her ball over, a wicket through which she must pass. She would win out in spite of it. So, trying to coax a laugh into her throat instead of a sob, she went to work with redoubled vigor.

When the cake was frosted and standing white and beautiful in the window to dry she slipped up to the bathroom, wiped up the floor and tidied it a bit. It needed a vigorous cleaning but she had no time to give it. Then she hurried down to shell the peas and scrape the potatoes. When they were on she would feel easier in her mind. There was a stalk of celery in the storeroom and a few English walnuts. The salad would look prettier if she diced the celery and stuffed the tomatoes with celery and nuts. She must try to get time. It wouldn't take a minute. Then the lettuce must be got from the garden. It ought to be in salt water this instant.

The next hour was a wild whirl. It seemed, as she rushed from table to range and from refrigerator back to the kitchen, that she had been rushing, rushing, ever since she left home, and she was tired, oh, so tired.

The biscuits were in the oven and the potatoes and peas bubbling gaily on the stove, the chops were in the broiler and Joyce was trying to set the table, when Mrs. Powers returned with her guest. After taking her to the guest room upstairs she came languidly down to see how the dinner was getting on.

She said no word of commendation, but a look of satisfaction dawned in her eyes as she saw the orderly row of salad plates, daintily and appetizingly arrayed on the kitchen side table, and caught a glimpse of the two cakes in the pantry window smooth and glistening in deep frosting. Joyce caught the look or perhaps she would not have been able to go on through the next trying hour.

"Mrs. Powers, I can't find but one of those rose napkins you said you wanted to use. Could you tell me where else to look?" she asked as the lady returned to the dining room.

"Why, I'm sure they are in the drawer," said the lady sharply as if somehow Joyce must have lost them herself. "They're always right there." She came and looked herself.

"Well, I guess they didn't get sent to the laundry," she admitted at last reluctantly after a hasty slamming of sideboard drawers. "Oh, here they are. How tiresome! Well, you'll just have to take them down to the laundry and rub them out. There's no other way. The others simply aren't fit. Here, take these. You'll find the electric iron right down there and you can iron them dry."

Joyce paused aghast.

"But the dinner," she said. "Things will burn, and I'm afraid it won't be on time if I wait to do that."

"Well, you'll have to manage somehow. I'm sure I don't know what else you can do. We'll have to have dinner late then I suppose, although Mr. Powers hates that. He always says never hire a person twice who can't get meals on time. It's the worst fault—"

But Joyce had seized the napkins and was already on her way down to the laundry, her lips set in a hard, determined little line. The school board should never be able to say she couldn't be on time, even if it was the school board's wife's fault that she couldn't be. She would win out and have dinner on time anyway.

So with a quick turn of the faucets, and a fling of soap, she rubbed out the necessary napkins, and while they were soaking for a minute, hunted out the electric iron and set it heating. Up the stairs again to her dinner to watch the chops and turn the lights under the vegetables a little lower, breathlessly down again, such a wild scramble! Quarter to seven it was when she came up again with the three neatly ironed napkins in her hand and wildly flew into the dining room to finish setting the table. The sweet potatoes were browning in their sugar bath and she had to watch them closely that they did not burn. It meant flying back and forth continually—and, oh, there were the olives, the ice water, and cream for the coffee. Would dinner ever be ready and served? And where was her apron?

The last five minutes were a nightmare. She could hear the front door open and the voice of the two gentlemen as they entered. Which one would be Mr. Powers? The gruff, deep one, or the high falsetto? And then came the awful minute when she donned the new white apron, and came to sign to Mrs. Powers that all was ready. The clock in the living room was chiming seven with silvery tones as she signaled her readiness, and she thought she saw a look of surprise and relief in the languid eye of the hostess, but she stayed not to make further discoveries. She would have her hands full for the next few minutes without knowing whether the lady was pleased or not.

"Surely He shall deliver thee—"

What was it that Bible verse said that ran through her head with every pulsation of her racing blood? Why should a Bible verse come so persistently into her mind just now when she was too busy to think about anything? "Surely he shall deliver thee from the snare of the fowler, and from the noisome pestilence"—that was it. The snare of the fowler was the little things that caught one. Well, He had delivered her. He had helped her to smile instead of to be annoyed. Was she winning out? Dinner was on time anyway.

Chapter 17

The guests were eating away at the fruit cup with a relish. It was delicious, Joyce knew, for she had tasted it when it was finished. She was hot and thirsty and she longed for some of it now, but there was none left. She had filled the glasses as full as possible. She heard one of the guests say how delicious it was, and the hostess reply in her languid drawl that it wasn't what it ought to be, that she had a new maid, and she was sure she didn't know whether they were to have anything fit to eat or not. She was brand-new, and green, and what was worse, she was *literary*. "Fancy, Clement," and the lady turned to the tall man with the deep, growling voice and her laugh rang out, "fancy, she wants me to recommend her to you as a teacher in the high school! Isn't that the limit?"

Joyce was just coming in to take the glasses and replace them with the bouillon cups filled with a delicious concoction that came out of that mixture of bones and meats and vegetables with the addition of a bit of tomato, onion, celery top, and parsley, and she stopped short in the pantry with flaming cheeks and quick tears in her eyes, and then stepped hastily back into the kitchen and paused in dismay. What should she do? How could she face that tableful of hateful people with their laughter still upon their lips?

There before her stood the kitchen door wide open to a garden path that led around the house to the gate. She could walk out and leave this impossible woman to her fate. Let her get up and serve her own guests, and wash her own dishes afterward and keep her own ten-dollar bill, and yes, and her school positions too. There were other people in the world— and the tears rolled down her hot, angry cheeks.

"Surely He shall deliver thee—Surely—Surely—"

It rang in her ears like a voice, a reminder.

"Yes, I know—" said her tired heart. She mustn't get into the habit of walking out back doors when she didn't like things. She really mustn't. "Dear Jesus, please give me strength, courage—" She dashed the tears away and splashed cold water on her hot cheeks, then in answer to the third ringing of the buzzer appeared in the dining room as if nothing had happened and quietly removed the glasses from the table.

In her pretty little blue dress with her white collar and apron she looked a slender vision as she entered with her tray and was conscious at once that every eye was fixed upon her, whereupon her cheeks flamed the rosier, but she kept her eyes down upon her work and managed to get through the door with her heavy tray of glasses without breaking down.

"Jove!" she heard the gruff voice say. "She looks as if she could teach if she wanted to."

"Yes, yes," chimed in the falsetto, "quite pretty for a kitchen maid, I should say."

"Quite too pretty, I should say," said the cool voice of the lady guest, like a sharp, dividing steel, significant, insulting.

Joyce trembled as she heard Mrs. Powers respond in her affected drawl:

"Yas, I thought so myself. But what could I do? I'd have had to get dinner myself—"

"Well, she seems to know how to cook," growled Mr. Powers. By this time his soup was steaming at his place and he was regarding it with interest.

Joyce caught his glance fixed pleasantly upon her as she went about placing the soup, and took heart. Perhaps all hope of a chance through Mr. Powers was not lost after all.

"Surely He shall deliver thee. Surely—" The words kept ringing as she went back and forth from kitchen to dining room, dreading each encounter more than the last.

As the meal progressed it became evident that all were enjoying it and the men at least were loud in their praises of each new dish as it arrived.

"Well, I say. These peas taste as if they had just been picked," said the guest, and his host replied:

"Say, Anne, these sweet potatoes beat anything we ever had. Get her to stay if you can. Pay her fifty dollars a week if you want to, only get her to stay!"

Mrs. Powers turned a languid smile of disgust on her woman guest and answered scornfully:

"Now, isn't that just like a man? Candied sweet potatoes and a pretty face! That's all they think about. I wish you'd see how she left the kitchen floor! And she had *plenty* of time to clean it up before she began to get dinner."

"Well, if you ask me," said her husband heartily, "I'd say cleaning kitchen floors wasn't her job."

All these things she heard in stage whispers that were not intended for her ears, as she went back and forth bringing dishes and serving new courses.

At the salad even the ladies waxed a little kindly, but when the ice cream came on and with it the two great luscious cakes there was loud applause from the gentlemen, and it was evident that if a position in the high school depended upon making good cake Joyce had won it. She hastily placed the last coffee cup and retired precipitately from the dining room, afraid that after all she was going to break down and cry. She was so tired!

But cry she wouldn't. She had one more thing yet to do before anybody had a chance to come out in that kitchen. She would scrub that kitchen floor if it took the last bit of force she had left in her body.

So she closed the pantry and kitchen doors, donned her gingham apron again, and got down upon her knees with hot water, soap, and scrubbing brush, and a great drying cloth she had found in the laundry. Such a scrubbing as that inlaid linoleum had it never had had before and never would likely have again!

She laid a newspaper down by the sink to keep it clean when she was done, and then straightened herself up for a moment, wondering if the ache would ever go out of her back and knees again. It wasn't just the scrubbing the floor, nor the working hard to get dinner; it was the culmination of the days since she had left home.

But she must not take time to think how tired she was. There were dishes yet to wash, and the table to clear. All those dishes! How long the evening looked ahead! They were rising from the table at last and she must hurry with the dishes already there and get them out of the way.

So she went at the dishpan again, her fingers flying as though she had just begun after a good night's rest. And one by one, dozen by dozen, those dishes were marshaled again into shining freshness, and the table cleared.

She had just decided that she would slip out the back door and let Mrs. Powers send her the ten dollars when she got ready, when she heard the pantry door open and Mrs. Powers stood in it, surveying her coldly, a crisp ten-dollar bill in her hand.

"Oh, you're going! I was going to ask you to wipe up this floor before you left—"

She paused and glanced down at the shining floor, from which Joyce had just removed the newspapers. She seemed a trifle flustered.

"Oh, you've done it. Well, that's all right. I never feel that a girl has finished until she has cleaned her kitchen."

She handed out the money and Joyce took it as though it had been a hot coal that she wasn't sure but she wanted to throw out the back door. Of course she had earned it, earned it hard, but it went against every grain in her body to take it. She felt humiliated and dragged in the dust.

"Surely He shall deliver thee!"

She drew a long breath. It was almost over. She was free to go at last.

"I was going to tell you," went on the lady as Joyce rolled up her apron preparatory to leaving, "I'm giving a little dinner tomorrow and I shall want you again. You might come over about ten. We don't get up before that, and then you can clear away the breakfast things. We have dinner about five on Sundays. My husband says the day is so long if we don't have a good many meals. I'm calling up my butcher to get some chickens. Of course he's closed, but he always serves me after time if necessary. He knows he has to or lose my trade. I think we'll have some more of those biscuits, and—"

Joyce suddenly broke into the monologue:

"Mrs. Powers, excuse me, but it isn't necessary for you to finish. I couldn't possible come."

"You couldn't possibly come? I'd like to know why not? I suppose you have some date or other with some young man—I might have known a pretty girl would be troublesome—"

"Stop!" said Joyce, her voice trembling, and just then above the wild beating of her angry young heart she heard the words:

"Surely He shall deliver thee—"

It steadied her so that she was able to control the flashing of her eyes and to speak quietly, albeit with a trifle of hauteur in her steady voice.

"Excuse me, Mrs. Powers. You have no right to speak to me in that way. I have no young men friends nor any others in this vicinity and no dates with anyone, but I do not work on Sunday. I don't think it's right. I was brought up to work only six days in the week."

"For mercy's sake!" sneered the woman, "and so you refuse to help a person out in a tight place? What possible wrong could that be? We have to eat, don't we?"

"We don't have to have dinner parties," said Joyce quietly.

"Well, I think you're impertinent," said the lady angrily. "It is none of your business when I have dinner parties. I suppose it's more pay you want, and I think that's extortion, but of course seeing you've washed the kitchen floor and seeing I can't very well get anyone else I suppose I'll have to pay it. What do you want for your valuable services?"

"Nothing, Mrs. Powers. I am not going to work. If you were sick or in trouble or starving I'd be glad to help you out, but I shouldn't accept pay. I am not working on Sunday."

"Well, I'll pay you fifteen dollars for the day if you'll come. That's outrageous but I'll pay it because I have to. And if you'll come early enough in the morning to get breakfast I'll make it twenty. Come, that's about as high as any girl could ask."

"It is impossible for me to accept any price for Sunday service, Mrs. Powers."

Joyce had retreated toward the door and picked up her bundle.

"I don't see how you can possibly expect me to use my influence to get you a school when you act like that," said the angry woman as a last resort. "I shall tell my husband how unaccommodating and impertinent you have been. You are not a fit person to set over young people. And if you refuse my request I shall take pains to see that you get no position in our schools. As for all this nonsense about working on Sunday, don't you know, my poor girl, that all that belongs to a bygone day? The Sabbath was made for man, and not to be long-faced in. I am in a far better position than you to know what is right and what is wrong, and I tell you that it is perfectly all right for you to help a person out when they have company, and at the same time help yourself out, and I've offered you very liberal wages. I'm perfectly willing also to see that you get a place to teach if you prove to be at all fitted for it, provided you go out of your way to help me."

Joyce looked at the woman steadily.

"Mrs. Powers, I would rather never have a position to teach than purchase it at the price of doing something I think is wrong. Besides, I couldn't help hearing what you said about me at the dinner table, and I've no expectation of your using your influence to help me in any way. In fact, I think I'd rather you wouldn't. Good night, Mrs. Powers."

She was actually gone, out the back door, through the moonlit garden, out the little back gate, and down the street, before Mrs. Powers recovered and realized that she had lost her.

"She won't come," she announced, going back to the living room, where her guests and her husband were awaiting her return to the game of cards in which they had been engaged, "and she actually had the nerve to try to preach a sermon to me about having dinner parties on Sunday. Did you ever? Aren't help the limit these days? I suppose it made her mad for me to ask her to scrub the bathroom floor. She's quite inclined to be above her station. But isn't it ridiculous? Now I'll have to get Martha Allen to cook the dinner and she can't begin to make mayonnaise like this girl!"

"I thought you told me she wasn't help," said her husband. "You said she was a schoolteacher."

"Oh, well—" said the wife indolently, "you know what a schoolteacher is that has to go out to work to make a living. Just as soon as I knew she would come I set her down where she belonged, and made up my mind if she was any good I'd get her permanently."

"Well, that's a laudable ambition. Coax a girl to come and help you as a favor, and then try to keep her down to the station you've put her in! I must say I admire a girl who is willing to cook when she hasn't anything else to do, and especially when she knows how to cook like that. I believe I'll look into her case. If she applies for a job in the school I'll vote for her. I like a girl with ambition and without notions, and I'll bet she earned her money today."

"Now, Hatfield, that's just like you," complained Mrs. Hatfield Powers. "I take the trouble to tell you what a good-for-nothing girl she is and then you go and vote for her just for sheer stubbornness. Just to oppose me. Just to show you how wrong you are about money, I paid her *ten dollars* today for getting that little bit of dinner, and I went so far as to offer her double that if she would come early enough to get breakfast and stay all day tomorrow!" She looked around the room in triumph amid the admiring exclamations of her guests.

"Well, I still say she earned her money," said her husband.

Joyce Radway let herself into her little dark room, locked her door, tossed her hat on the box table, flung herself on the heap of newspapers in the corner and burst into heartbreaking sobs.

By and by her tears were spent and she grew quieter, and above the tumult of her soul a still small voice seemed saying over the words softly to her troubled heart:

"The eternal God is thy refuge, and underneath are the everlasting arms."

How wonderful that that should come to her now!

Once, a long time ago, when she was a little girl and was learning verses with her mother and her aunt, they had told her that these verses they were teaching her were to be stored up for a time of need, and that when any distress came, if they were safely in her heart and memory, they would come out to comfort her or show her the way out of a difficult situation. She had not thought much about it then, but now that all came

back. She was in trouble and comfortless, and the verses were
coming like a troop of angels to comfort and guide her and help
her through temptation—to show her that God was not a God
afar off, but was nigh to each one of us, even in our hearts. So,
comforted, she fell asleep.

And the next day was the Sabbath.

Chapter 18

When Joyce awoke that first Sunday morning in her new home
the sun was streaming broad across her bed. By that she knew
it was very late. It suddenly came to her consciousness for the
first time that she had been so busy getting her dress done in
time to reach Mrs. Powers's at twelve o'clock that it had never
occurred to her to do any marketing for Sunday, and of course
everything had been closed up tight when she came home at
half past ten. Well, there was enough in the house to keep her
from starving, and she would just have to get along. There were
probably restaurants open, but why go to a restaurant on Sunday? She had not been brought up to be much away from home
on the Lord's day, and while she understood that it might be
necessary sometimes for restaurants to be open on Sunday for
some poor homeless ones, still, she didn't see patronizing
them if she could help it.

Examination of her larder proved that there were still a few
crackers, a small piece of cheese, two slices of dried beef, one
banana, and almost half a loaf of bread. There was a little milk
left in the bottle too, and she could have that for breakfast. It
was not an extensive array for a Sunday dinner, and probably
Mrs. Powers's menu would have offered a more tempting list,
but she drew a relieved sigh to think that she did not have to
get Mrs. Powers's dinner that day, no, nor eat it, either.

She ate her breakfast of crackers and milk hungrily, for one
cannot work as hard as she had worked for the past three days
without developing an appetite, and by the time she was
finished, and everything put away, the church bells were ringing.

It was interesting to be going to a new church. All her life she had attended the same church. It came to her while she was brushing her shoes and putting on her serge dress and hat that, perhaps, some of the dear people would miss her and wonder. Perhaps sometime she would write to the minister or her Sunday-school teacher and explain that she had felt an entire change would be good for her, less sad; and that she had gone thus quietly because she dreaded the good-byes. Yes, that would probably be the right thing to do after she had once established herself, and had a good paying job, and could report herself as doing well. It made her almost homesick to think of how all the old friends were on their way to Sunday school just now—how her place would be vacant in the class and her spot in the pew empty.

It wouldn't be the first time though, for Nannette had contrived both Sundays since Aunt Mary's death to keep Joyce at home, the first time because she had a sick headache and wanted Joyce to stay and wait on her, the second time because she and Eugene were going somewhere and demanded that Joyce remain at home with the children, who were supposed to be under the weather. People would not think it strange that she had not come this Sunday either, perhaps, and she knew Nannette well enough to be sure that by this time there was some well-arranged story about explaining, with perfect plausibility, her absence. So she had no uneasiness on the score of her friends.

She chose the pretty church with the stone arches and ivy wreathing for her first entrance into religious worship in her new home. It bore the name of her own denomination on its bronze tablet outside the door, and she entered with a kind of feeling that it partly belonged to her.

The church was filled with well-dressed people, and a vested choir was singing an anthem as she entered. She was annoyed to be late and slipped into a seat near the door.

The vested choir would have been an innovation in the old church in Meadow Brook, but she thought it rather pretty. The church was artistic and beautiful, with deep-toned woods, vaulted ceilings, and gleam of jeweled windows picturing forth sacred themes in memory of certain departed church members. She sat in the softly cushioned pew and listened to the glorious music, the rich tones of the organ, the well-trained voices. Now, indeed, was her soul to find rest and refreshment for the hard times of her life. She relaxed and found peace and a sense of nearness to God in this, His house.

The Powers family entered, to her surprise, a bit noisily, with their guests, and made quite a flutter getting certain seats. They seemed to be important personages, for whom the ushers hurried to find the place in four hymnbooks, and present calendars of the day, with smiles and obsequious bows. The men were fresh from a round on the golf course, and had that air of bored patronage and indifference that so many men wear on Sunday morning, as if virtue fairly exuded from their rosy faces because they had come in from the velvety green to this somber stuffy dullness for a little while to patronize God. The women were attired in spring array and filled the air about them with the faint, sweet perfume of the well-groomed. The eyes of their envious sisters were fixed upon their hats and coats in earnest study from the minute of their entrance, and many a woman forsook her mild attention to the service and tortured her mind with such problems as how she could get together a becoming hat like that without paying the price of an imported one, or whether there was enough in the breadths of grandmother's old silk gown to cut a silk coat like the one Anne Powers was wearing.

Joyce, in her back seat, was surprised that her employer of yesterday should be in church. She had unconsciously labeled her as a non-churchgoer. In Meadow Brook the people who gave dinner parties on Sunday did not pay much attention to churchgoing, and as she watched from her shadowed seat under the gallery and saw Mrs. Powers's delicate airs, and the way she held her book and sang, she marveled that this pretty woman, with the rapt expression, could be the same one who spoke so contemptuously to her the day before.

But when the minister ascended the pulpit for the sermon she tried to put such thoughts away from her mind and to listen to what was being said. It was not for her to judge the people in God's house, and God Himself might be able to see something acceptable in the worship of these people that was not apparent to her.

The minister had read the story of the man born blind, and it had given her a warm feeling about her heart to remember the dear old story, so linked with thoughts of her Aunt Mary, and especially of that wonderful day in the woods, so she settled herself to enjoy the story once more, and to thrill over the miracle of the healing as she had always been able to thrill over this particular story even after she had grown up.

As the sermon opened up with an eloquent passage descriptive of the oriental day and setting of the story her mind was back in the aisles of the grove with the boy and Aunt Mary, and the birds singing far overhead. Her own sweet thoughts leaped ahead in the story, till suddenly, she became aware of words that were being spoken, words that did not seem to fit the thread of the story at all. What was this? No miracle? Common sense? Jesus used clay to give the man something to do himself, possibly it might have had some medicinal qualities as some clays known to the medical profession of the day are known to have healing qualities. But more likely the clay was a mere agent to bestir the man, to awaken him to a sense of himself, and stimulate his nerves to action—a mere psychological effect on the man's spirit, something that Jesus, with His unusually keen insight into men's natures, saw was needed. Such cures were often performed today, by shock of fire or fright, by inducing the subject to in some way believe that he was healed. There was a great deal in willpower and in the state of mind, and Jesus used common sense and set men right with *themselves*. Perhaps the man had not been really blind at all from his birth, but had merely got in the habit of keeping his eyes shut and thinking he was blind, until he and his friends had come to believe that it was true. There was much proof for this theory in the way that his cure was accepted by his friends and neighbors and even by his parents. If there had been a real need of a cure it was not at all likely that the parents of the invalid would have taken the cure so lightly and even professed that they knew nothing at all about it. The matter was evidently held lightly among them. The work of Jesus on this earth was really to bring men to *themselves*, to awaken them to a sense of what they could *do for themselves*, in even rising above weakness and physical infirmity. They called Jesus divine because they could find no better word to call Him, but we were all divine, all the children of God as was Jesus, and all able to do what Jesus did. Perhaps not in the same degree, for he was the greatest Man that ever lived, but still, in a sense, we could do for suffering humanity just what Jesus did. If we were not actual physicians, able to heal disease, we could yet persuade men to common sense, awake them to open their eyes to things about them.

Joyce sat straighter in her seat and her cheeks grew hot with excitement. She felt as if some exquisite, sacred fabric, that was beyond price, and had always been most dear to her had been torn in tatters and scattered to the four winds. She felt as if she must arise and cry out to the man that what he was saying was false—that he was blaspheming!

She looked around startled on the indifferent audience composed in a dreamy silence of peace, eyes intent upon the preacher, lips placid, no look of protest in their faces! How strange! How awful! Was there no one, not one, to stand up for the Bible, for the miracle of healing, for the matchless God-nature of Christ?

But other words suddenly arrested her, standing out from the drab background of the sermon sharply:

"The time has come when the world no longer needs a bloody atonement to appease an angry God. The world has grown beyond that ghastly idea. The death of Christ was to show the world how much He loved it, not to wash away its evil deeds in some mysterious way. People must undo their own evil deeds. No one could do that for them. We must work out our own salvation with fear and trembling, for it was the God in us that works. We all have God in us, only we are not letting Him work, just as that blind man had sight, but he was not using it—"

Joyce almost started to her feet. She seemed to be crying out in her throat so that it hurt: "That is not true, oh, that is not true! Will no one tell him what an awful thing he is saying?" But not a sound came from her lips, of course. She found that her limbs were trembling and she felt as though she scarcely dared look up. To think that she was here in God's house listening to this and no one making any protest! She looked around again, aghast at the smug, satisfied faces of the congregation. It was almost as if they were not listening.

The minister's voice broke again upon her troubled spirit:

"No man's death can do away with my guilt. No amount of shed blood can cleanse me from sin. I've got to do that *myself*. As Jesus made the man go to the river and wash the clay away, so you and I must wash away our own sins in the sweat of our brow, working for Him. We must feed the hungry, clothe the naked, be kind one to another, uplift the fallen, uplift and broaden humanity, put away sin from our lives, and in its place put deeds of kindness such as Jesus did. That life and that alone can atone for a sinful past. Let us pray."

During the prayer that followed tears came into the eyes of the wounded girl, but a choir of the angelic host seemed somewhere far away to be chanting, and the words they spoke were clear and distinct:

"The blood of Jesus Christ his Son cleanseth us from all sin."

"He was wounded for our transgressions, he was bruised for our iniquities: the chastisement of our peace was upon him; and with his stripes we are healed."

"All we like sheep have gone astray; we have turned every one to his own way; and the Lord hath laid on him the iniquity of us all."

They rang in her heart with triumph as she lifted her head for the closing song, whose words she could not see because of the tears in her eyes, and when it was over, and the benediction was spoken, she turned, humiliated and sad, to go out of the house of God. Just behind her came a clear, languid voice, drawling:

"Yes, wasn't it a sweet sermon? Perfectly lovely. I just love to hear Doctor Darling preach; he is so refined, and he makes one feel so good—"

And out in the sunshine the young girl walked back to her little house stricken, almost sick, with the experience of the morning. This was her first experience of Modernism in a Christian church. Summer visitors in Meadow Brook had complained that the minister there was old-fashioned, and they really ought to have a young man who would be broad in his views and educate the young people in up-to-date religion. But the people of Meadow Brook loved Doctor Ballantine and his wife, and did not want to see them leave. He had been there a long time and the elders in the church all thought as he did, so until some of the younger generation who had not been taught by him in the Scriptures grew up he was not likely to be ousted.

Joyce had read a little about the state of things in the religious world, but she had thought of Modernism as one thinks of leprosy, or the starving Russians, as something far, far away and awful, to prevent which one ought to give money and send missionaries, but which one was never likely to meet with in daily life. Now, suddenly brought face-to-face with it, she was shaken to her soul.

Not that the sermon of the morning had given her any doubts. It could not have done that even if it had been strong in arguments and logic, and not weak, garbled statements of half facts she had known all her life, for Joyce was a Christian, rooted and grounded in the Word, and had lived too many years in a sweet communion with her Saviour to have been shaken even a little in her sweet faith. No, it had made her angry, tremblingly, impotently angry. She felt as if she could not stand it that words like those should have been preached in a Christian pulpit under the name of an orthodox faith, and no one put in a protest. She longed to be a man that she might do something about it, a prophet that she might cry out; a wise leader that she might come to the people and tell them how the curse of God would be upon them if they listened to words like those—how their souls would be lost—!

She sat down on her wooden box in her small home, going over it all with sorrowing heart. She did not even take off her hat, so absorbed and excited she was. She went over the Bible verses that she knew that proved the minister had been wrong, verses that she had learned when a child, and her heart began to swell and triumph over the wonder and the joy of the salvation that was hers.

"He that heareth my word, and believeth on him that sent me, *hath* everlasting life, and *shall not* come into condemnation; but is passed from death unto life."

"For by the works of the law shall no flesh be justified."

"For by grace are ye saved through faith; and that not of yourselves: it is the gift of God: Not of works, lest any man should boast."

"Who hath saved us, and called us with an holy calling, not according to our works, but according to his own purpose and grace, which was given us in Christ Jesus before the world began."

How her heart thrilled with the words as she said them over, and how she rejoiced that she had been taught in the Word. Sunday after Sunday during her little girlhood it had been the regular afternoon employment for her and Aunt Mary to learn a chapter in the Bible, or a group of verses that Aunt Mary had selected during the week on some special topic. Sometimes she had done the selecting herself and had taken such joy in finding out a group of verses on a certain topic. Now they came flocking from her fine memory like a troop of strong angels sent to protect her.

"Not by works of righteousness which we have done, but according to his mercy he saved us, by the washing of regeneration, and renewing of the Holy Ghost; Which he shed on us abundantly through Jesus Christ our Saviour."

How she wished she had her Bible that she might spend the afternoon hunting out other verses! What else was there about the blood? Ah!

"Without shedding of blood there is no remission (of sins)!"

"For this is my blood of the new testament, which is shed for many."

"God commendeth his love toward us, in that, while we were yet sinners, Christ died for us. Much more then, being now justified by his blood, we shall be saved from wrath through him."

"For if the blood of bulls and of goats, and the ashes of an heifer sprinkling the unclean, sanctified to the purifying of the flesh: How much more shall the blood of Christ, who through the eternal Spirit offered himself without spot to God, purge your conscience from dead works to serve the living God."

She could remember the very afternoon when she learned that, curled up on the foot of Aunt Mary's bed while she took a little nap, in the days when Aunt Mary was just beginning to be frail and had to rest more than usual. And how proud she had been to think she had found this wonderful verse all by herself. And now she had an inexpressible longing to take that Bible verse to the minister who had preached that strange dead sermon that morning and show him. Perhaps he didn't know. Perhaps he never had heard. But of course he must. And he was one of those men they called Modernists, who were taking the heart and life out of the faith of today, who were helping to fulfill the prophecies about the latter days, when men would prefer teachers with strange doctrines.

She was half frightened at the thought. It seemed to her that she must turn and flee back into the safe harbor of Meadow Brook, where dear old Doctor Ballantine preached about the cross of Christ every Sunday, and everybody knew and believed the old doctrines. It seemed as if perhaps she had run away into danger and horror, and the tempter might be preparing a snare for her feet.

She did not feel safe until she had dropped upon her knees and asked for guidance and strength to keep true to Christ, even though she might have to pass through a portion of the world where there was no faith.

As she rose from her knees it occurred to her that Elijah, the prophet, had once got into some such a panic, and thought he was the only loyal prophet left, and the Lord had told him he had yet seven thousand other prophets who would not bow the knee to Baal. There were very likely many Christians in this town, and by and by she would go out and find them.

So she got up cheerfully and went about getting some dinner. She hadn't a great appetite, for she had worn herself out for several days past, and when she had eaten she lay down on the heap of papers and fell asleep. When she awoke she realized that the paper bed was getting pretty hard, and she really must do something about it tomorrow; one could not sleep on newspapers indefinitely. She shook the papers out, and crumpled them anew, until they had some spring in them again, and smoothed it nicely for when she should come back that night, and then, with a couple of crackers and some cheese folded neatly in a bit of wrapping paper and tucked in her pocket, she started out.

He first object was to find a church. She wasn't quite sure how she was going to tell whether it was the right kind of a church from the outside or not, without listening to another sermon, but she prayed in her heart as she went that somehow she might drop into a place where she would find help and comfort to her soul, and might, if possible, find it without having to listen to more words such as she had heard that morning. It seemed to her that it was disloyal to her Lord even to listen to such things.

The day was wonderful, and the spring air was sweet with the breath of flowers. As she walked down the pleasant streets the blueness of the sky and the greenness of the grass made a kind of ecstasy for her spirit. The little lazy clouds floating, the flight of a bird across the blue, the redness of the maple buds on the trees, all gave her joy. There were tulips in some of the yards she passed, red and yellow, pink and white; and hyacinths made delicate the air, and she thought what a wonderful God to make so many beautiful intricate flowers, each with a different perfume. Little blue crocuses were sticking up their gallant buds from lawns here and there, quaint processions of blue and white and yellow. The town was in its Sunday best, and everything promising a gorgeous summer. One could not help being glad on such a day even though one were all alone.

A church steeple loomed ahead and Joyce quickened her step. It was a plainer church than the one she had attended in the morning and she thought as she approached, perhaps here she would find a company of live Christians who were awake to what was being preached in the other church and would have the good old gospel. Her eyes eagerly sought the bulletin board posted up just outside the door. The hours of service were there, the usual hours, but everything else was completely covered by a large card announcing the Brotherhood

Minstrel Show to be held on Tuesday, Wednesday, and Thursday evenings of that week, tickets fifty cents a night.

Joyce turned away disappointed. The minstrel show might be all right. They had entertainments at home sometimes, of course, for the young people, but people who were really alive to the terrible things that were being preached in another church of their own town would surely be interested in something besides minstrel shows. Of course they might be, and just not have put it on the outside of the church, but she didn't somehow feel that here was her place of worship.

She walked on for at least a mile, passing, as she did so, out of one suburb into another. She was interested in the pretty little bungalows she passed, and in the finer houses when she turned to another street, but she was looking for churches. Presently she came to another, a smart yellow brick affair out on the street with the doors open and a brisk air of business around the place. Groups of young people were wending their way toward it, and going in the door. A large blackboard outside the entrance announced the various activities of the week. Monday evening there was a rehearsal for the Christian Endeavor pageant, and all costumes were to be brought. Tuesday evening Class A was holding a bazaar and supper for the benefit of the new basketball team. Wednesday evening there was to be a lecture by a professor from a famous university entitled, "Why I Know That the World Is Growing Better." Thursday there was a choir rehearsal, and a meeting of the Ladies' Aid to arrange to cooperate with the Red Cross for the annual fair, Friday there was a church social, and Saturday there was a picnic in one of the amusement parks with a moonlight ride home in automobiles. Joyce read it carefully through, searching in vain for a word that would show the faith of these people of great activities, but found nothing, not even a prayer meeting. Probably that lecture was in place of one. Well, it might be all right, but she had been taught that the world wasn't growing better, and never would till Christ came to make things over. Lifting her eyes above the blackboard, she saw that the church bulletin announced the minister's topic for that night, "The Political Situation Today." She turned away with a sigh. Well, it might be all right, but it promised nothing from the outside. She walked on, turning down another street.

Two hours she walked, keeping the general direction of her home in mind so that she would not get lost. She found several little churches, all more or less attractive in a way, but none of them giving any clue to what was preached inside, and at last, with a heavy heart and weary feet, she turned her steps homeward, coming back by a different street.

It was when she was within four or five blocks of where she judged her little house must be that she came upon another church built of rough stone, rugged and substantial, but beautiful in its simple lines. The door was open and a burst of song from young voices greeted her:

> What can wash away my stain?
>   Nothing but the blood of Jesus.
> What can make me whole again?
>   Nothing but the blood of Jesus.

Joyce turned in at the door as a bird flies home to its nest.

Chapter 19

The man called Teneyke had decided to give his confidence to Cottar. He had reached the limit of his detective powers and needed aid. All research in the way of telephone books and directories of the region round about Meadow Brook had failed to bring forth anyone whose name fitted the letters of the paper which he treasured carefully, wrapped in clean tissue paper and further enshrined in a dirty envelope, in his inside pocket.

He sought Cottar early in the evening in his own home, a dull little clapboard house with a side gate and a brick walk. The front door was always locked and one entered by the kitchen door at the side into a room lighted by a kerosene lamp on a little high shelf, and misty with the smoke of Cottar's pipe. Cottar's old wife was deaf as a post, and went pottering round with a little shoulder shawl across her neck and took no notice of anybody. When Teneyke came in Cottar signed to her and she lit a candle and went up a shallow stairway into the hall. One could hear her shuffling tread overhead. The two men waited till the boards overhead stopped creaking. Then Cottar lifted his bushy eyebrows, and let his beady, wise little eyes peer out speculatively.

"Wal, Tyke?"

"All safe?"

"All safe."

Tyke got out the paper and unwrapped it. Cottar put on his spectacles. Together they silently studied the writing. "oyce Radw." It seemed to mean nothing to Cottar at first. But Tyke produced a page filched from a public telephone book. There were three R's that might have been possible, Radwan, Radwanski, and Radwell. The shrewd Cottar decided that the first two were too foreign. The handwriting looked plain and well formed, not as he thought a foreigner would write. Radwell might be the name. He could think of no other. The first name they decided must be Boyce, although that was a boy's name and not a girl's, and would, if correct, throw them off the track altogether. Perhaps it was a middle name. So they speculated.

Cottar made a careful, painstaking copy of the writing and folded it away in his grimy pocket for further use.

"Well, I don't figger it out *yet*, but there's ways. If she's a Meadow Brook dame we'll find her out. Just keep yer mouth shet an' yer eyes open an' most things come out. Gimme time."

Came a tap on the door, and Bill entered:

"Man, I had a hard time findin' ye!" he said, casting a furtive glance about with his restless, bloodshot eyes. "Hey there, Tyke, I thought you got pinched!"

"What, me! Think again, Bill. Takes a slicker guy'n that cop to lay hands on me. I double-crossed him, I did. Seen Taney?"

"Yep. Got him hid in the Hazels down on the Point. Gonta watch all night. Taney's all right fer that. He's on the job. Nothin' won't get by him. We figger this would be the night fer another lot to land there if they had any sorta greement about it. There ain't no other spot this side o' the lights, an' he's bound to connect along this coast somewheres. He ain't goin' fur away, you needn't think. He's got his good buyers all around this part. No, sir, he thinks he's got us buffaloed all right with that there two hundred bucks, an' now he's figgerin' to work it alone, the young devil!"

"Been to the cem'try, Bill?"

"Yep. Went this A.M. fore dawn. Jest light 'nough t'see t'spade. Opened her all up. Nothin' there but a bed of broken glass. Slick job! Cleaned the whole thing out. Must think we're takin' nourishment out of a bottle yet, we can't see through that. Say, boys, whaddaya say we take a little trip through the old buryin' ground up by the state road? He's bound to get another location fer his business, an' that's good an' lonely. I found out he's got a sister an' she's got some kids. Be a good idee to buddy up to 'em, Tyke. You're good at that business. They live down to Meadow Brook on Orchard Street, third house from the corner, opposite to the garage."

Tyke narrowed his eyes and nodded.

The next day Tyke happened along Orchard Street as Lib Knox was starting to school.

"Yer uncle at home?"

She eyed him shrewdly.

"Whaddaya wanta know for?" she demanded, cold-eyed.

"Just wantta see him on a message."

"Well, he ain't in," she said loftily. "You better leave the message."

She started down the street with her armful of books, and Dorothea, approaching from the corner, joined her. Tyke followed them and lounged along beside them.

"Say, kid," he said, bringing out the greasy envelope, "donno but I will. I c'n confide in you. I see you're a pretty good sort o'kid. Looka here!"

But Lib Knox was not the easily flattered sort. She eyed him with suspicion, and looked coldly at the bit of paper he held out to her. When she caught sight of the writing her eyes narrowed and she gave him a quick, veiled glance beneath their fringes. Dorothea, behind her, as ever curious, stretched her neck to see the writing also.

"Know whose name that is?" The man asked the question with alluring mystery in his tone, as if he knew the name himself and had some wonderful information to impart concerning it. But Lib was a smart girl.

"Don't look like any name at all to me," she said contemptuously. "Looks like just a piece of writing. Where'd you get it?"

"That I ain't tellin' till I find out what you know about it. If you can tell me the name I'll tell you something your uncle would like real well to know. Most like he'll give you a box of candy if you tell him."

Lib tossed her head angrily.

"My uncle ain't that kind and I can get candy when I want it.

I tell you that ain't anybody's name at all. It's just scribbling. Come on, Dorrie, we'll be late to school."

But Dorothea had got a good vision of the writing at last.

"Why, that's my cousin's name!" she exclaimed eagerly, wondering if she could possibly get that box of candy. "Joyce Ra—"

But a firm little hand was laid smotheringly over her mouth.

"Shut up!" said Lib Knox fiercely. "Don't you know you mustn't talk to strange men on the street? Come on, I hear the last bell ringing—" and she seized her young slave and dragged her at full tilt down the street.

Tyke stood still on the pavement, his red hair reflecting the morning sun, and his unholy face broad with a leer of triumph. Let them go. He had his clue, Joyce! Strange he hadn't thought of that name before. Even when he used the whole alphabet, somehow he didn't figure out that name. The rest would be easy to get. He sauntered down after the flying children and noted the location of the schoolhouse. School would be out at noon of course—or would afternoon be better? Ah, there was a tall hedge across the way, an excellent point of vantage to watch as the children filed out at the end of the day.

And so it happened, quite late in the afternoon after Lib Knox and Dorothea had written their misspelled words five hundred times and stayed in an extra half hour for talking deaf and dumb language in class, and when they had visited the public garage for an hour and played with the five blind puppies that had recently arrived there, and had said a lingering and fond farewell for the afternoon and parted, that Dorothea started on her reluctant way home to supper.

As she turned the corner out of sight of Lib Knox, Tyke stepped up as if he had just been walking down that way.

"Hello, kid," he said in his insinuating way. "I jest been lookin' fer you. Bought that box of candy awhile ago an' thought I'd like to give it to you. You like chocolates, don't you, kid?"

Dorothea quickly assured him that she did, her eyes round with eagerness.

He produced a pound box tied with a red ribbon.

"Well, you're a nice kid," he went on. "I knowed it the minute I saw you. So that girl was your cousin, was she? Joyce, what did ya say her name was? I ferget without the writin' in front of me."

"Joyce Radway," eagerly supplied Dorothea, her eyes on the candy box.

"Yes, that's it, Joyce Radway. Of course. How did I come to ferget that? Well, now this Joyce Radway, she's a great friend of that other girl's uncle, ain't she?"

"Why, I guess so," said Dorothea. "He came to the house to see her the other night."

"Oh, he did, did he? Yes, of course he would. Then your cousin is home, ain't she?" insinuatingly.

"No, she ain't home, not now," said Dorothea, annoyed, wondering when he was going to give her the box. "She's gone away."

"Oh! She has?" his eyes narrowed as he watched her. "Did she go away with him?"

"Oh, no," said Dorothea garrulously. "She just went away by herself. She was mad. Daddy scolded her, and she just went."

"Yes?" said the young man ingratiatingly, fumbling with the red ribbon as if he were about to untie it. "Suppose you tell me all about it, and then I'll give you the candy. You say your daddy scolded her? What for? Didn't he like the boys coming to see her?"

"Oh, no," said Dorothea quite earnestly, trying to think how to answer so that she would get the candy quickly. "She never had any boys. It was just the 'lectric light. Daddy said she burned it too much, and he didn't like her taking 'zaminations and all. Where'dya get the candy? I saw a box like that down to the drugstore."

"Yes, that where I got it. It's good candy. I suppose you'll give your cousin some when you get home."

"Oh, she hasn't come home. I couldn't—" said the little girl with virtuous satisfaction.

"Hasn't got home? Why, where is she?" plied her questioner.

"Why, we don't know. Daddy's most crazy. Say, if you know where she is you better tell me, fer there's something 'bout her having to be home for Judge Peterson to read the will and give us our house. Do you know where Cousin Joyce is?"

"Why, I might be able to find out, kiddie," said the oily voice. "Where do you live? You tell me where you live and I'll let you know if I find she's in the place I think she is."

"Why, I live right up there in that white house with green blinds," said Dorothea eagerly. "I wish you'd let me know tonight. I'll come out to the gate and wait for you if you will. Daddy would be awful pleased with me if I told him where Joyce was. I think he'd get me a new bicycle if I did."

"Well, we'll see what can be done," said Tyke wickedly. "Here's your candy, kid, and p'raps ye'll hear from me soon."

Tyke handed over the candy and Dorothea flew home, pausing behind the lilac bush to extract one luscious mouthful from the box, then rushing up to her room to secrete the rest where Junior would not find it, under the mattress of her bed.

Tyke went on his evil way rejoicing. Shrewd little Lib Knox saw him as he passed her house and scuttled behind the hedge, sticking out her tongue behind his back as he passed, and thought she had frustrated his intentions, while five blocks away Dorothea was gorging herself on Dutch creams and wondering why Lib didn't like that nice young man.

Chapter 20

Six weeks later found Joyce well established in her comfortable little home, and spending her mornings teaching in a summer Bible school connected with the church which she found that first Sunday evening of her stay in Silverdale.

It came about in this way:

Christian Endeavor was in session when she entered the church and an enthusiastic set of young people were conducting it. The pastor sat in front near the leader in pleasant accord with all that went on. He seemed to be an intimate friend of every boy and girl present. Joyce looked on wistfully. This was like home. Doctor Ballantine had been like that with all the young people of the town.

At the close of the meeting he made several announcements. One which interested Joyce was that there was need of another teacher in the Bible school to take the place of Miss Brown, who had recently lost her health and been obliged to go away for a year. He told them to remember that it meant giving every morning for five days in the week for six weeks to actual teaching and some time to preparing for teaching; that there was a renumeration of ten dollars a week for the work; but that no one need apply who was not a Christian, or did not intend to be present at every session, or who had not had some experience and preparation for teaching.

The pastor, by some magic, was at the door as soon as the meeting was over, and took her hand cordially in welcome. She looked into his grave, pleasant face and impulsively spoke the wish that had been in her heart since she had heard the announcement.

"I'm so interested in your Bible school! I wish I could teach in it, but I don't suppose you'd care to try a stranger, would you?"

The minute she had spoken the color flooded her face, for she felt as if she had been presumptuous, but the minister's eyes lighted and he smiled in a kindly way.

"Are you a Christian?" he asked, his pleasant eyes searching her face.

"Oh, yes," said Joyce, with a proud ring to her voice as if he had asked her if she were the daughter of some great man.

"Have you ever taught in public school?"

"No," said Joyce wistfully, "but I've been preparing to teach for several years. I love it. I'm hoping to get a position near here this fall. But I haven't any credentials yet. I would have to take examinations—"

"Come and see me tomorrow at my house. Any time. It's right next door to the church. If I don't happen to be there Mrs. Lyman will talk with you. It's all the same. Can you come at nine o'clock? Well, I'll be there then. Glad to have you come. Perhaps the Lord has sent you in answer to our prayer."

So Joyce went to see the Lymans and as a result was engaged to teach in the Bible school, which would begin as soon as the public schools closed, and be in session for six weeks. She would have to be at the church at half past eight and stay until half past eleven. The pay wasn't great, but it took only half her day and she loved the work. She might be able to get something else afternoons occasionally to help out. In the meantime she could live on that ten dollars if she had to, and she meant to. As for the interval before the Bible school opened, there would be something to do, she was sure. And, anyhow, the barrel of meal hadn't wasted yet, and she felt sure the Lord would take care of her. Besides, she needed some time to fix up her little home and make it livable. One couldn't just exist if one was working, one had to have things tolerably comfortable for resting and eating or one couldn't do good work.

So she went back to her little house and sat down to think. The conclusion of her meditation was that she decided to buy a saw.

Consulting Mrs. Bryant that Monday morning, she finally decided on a trip to the city, and armed with minute directions about stores and prices, she took the noon train.

Her first purchase was a Bible.

She had asked about a bookstore where things would not be expensive and Mrs. Bryant had named a secondhand place where things were very nice and very cheap, she said. Joyce found a Scofield Bible, new and clean, and scarcely used at all, it seemed. It had an inscription on the flyleaf, "To Mary, from Mother, December 25, 1922."

Joyce felt a pitiful joy in buying that particular Bible. It seemed so sorrowful that a Bible from a mother to her child should be lying out in the open on a bookstall like that, and only two years after it was given. What if it had been hers from her mother? What if it had been Aunt Mary's Bible! She fell to wandering about that other Mary. Was she dead, or didn't she care about the book? Were they both dead, mother and child, in those two brief years? How did a precious, intimate thing like a Bible get to be sold in a secondhand store? It seemed almost indecent. Surely some relative or even a trustee who had to sell things at auction would have had the decency to give a Bible to some friend who would care for it; or to some mission that would use it for the glory of God. So she brought the Bible and carried it tenderly with a thought for its unknown owner and donor.

Joyce had a great many bundles when she had finished her purchases. She looked at them in amazement when she finally settled herself in the train once more for her return trip to Silverdale. She really had spent very little money for all those big packages. She began to count up. The Bible had cost fifty cents, and she knew it was very cheap. The saw was a dollar and a half, but it was the best of steel. There was a big bundle of gray denim for upholstery. She had got it at a reduced rate by taking all that was left of the piece. Two or three yards of flowered cretonne to cover her box dressing table. Perhaps she could have waited for that, but it wasn't good policy for her to seem too poverty-stricken if she expected to get a position in school, and what she bought must be the right thing so that she would not have to renew it right away. She must make her little house look cozy if the minister and his wife dropped in to call, or any of those nice young people at the church should run in.

That big, bulky package with the handle contained a lot of

wire springs, some upholstery webbing, and twine, a long, double-pointed upholstery needle, and several pounds of curled hair and cheap cotton. This constituted Joyce's venture. With it she meant to make a bed and perhaps two chairs. Maybe it was foolish, and she ought to have bought a cot for five dollars and let it go at that, but she would have had to buy a mattress or something to put over it, and when it was done it would not be so comfortable as one that she could make. For Joyce had often watched an old neighbor of theirs in Meadow Brook who was an upholsterer. She knew all the little tricks. She knew how the webbing should be nailed on taut, how the springs must be sewed to the webbing, and then tied down level, and the padding of cotton and hair put on the top of that. She was sure she could do it, though she had never tried it. Joyce was not beyond trying anything if necessity drove her to it. She had once made a lovely feather fan out of chicken feathers and an old ivory frame. She felt she could make a bedstead if she tried hard enough. There was yet the frame to be dealt with, but she had her saw, and anyhow, the springs and webbing and hair had cost but very little, and it would surely be much more comfortable than a hard cot, besides looking a great deal better in her room, and costing no more than, nor as much as, a cot.

She had bought a few necessities for her wardrobe also, a couple of remnants to make more thin dresses, a pair of fifty-cent slippers from the bargain counter to save her shoes while she was working. In fact, most of her purchases were from the bargain counters, a hair brush and comb, a change of undergarments and nightwear, two pairs of stockings, and some towels. What a lot of things one needed to live! And when she counted up there was just twenty-four dollars and eighty-seven cents left of her small capital. It made her gasp as she thought of the weeks ahead before her engagement in the Bible school would commence, and how was she to live? She must be very, very economical. But yet she need not be afraid. The barrel of meal had not wasted so far. God would take care of her, and her heart began to sing as she remembered how He had brought her safely so far out of her difficulties.

Then when she got home she was hailed by Mrs. Bryant. Mrs. Ritter, down the street, wanted to know if Joyce would be willing to come in and sit with her sister for the evening. She had made an engagement to go to the city with her husband, and now her sister was sick and she didn't like to leave her

alone in the house. There was really nothing to do but give her
medicine every hour and answer the telephone and the doorbell. Mrs. Ritter would be glad to pay her for her time, fifty
cents an hour was what she thought would be fair. She
wouldn't be home till the midnight train, but Mr. Ritter would
walk down with her after they got back, so she needn't be
afraid to come home.

Joyce thanked Mrs. Bryant for speaking of her. She said of
course she would go, and went about her little house with
shining eyes, singing. The barrel of meal was filling up again.
How wonderful! There would be three more dollars! She had
taken a good dinner in the city at an automat restaurant which
Mrs. Bryant had recommended, and she did not feel the need
of an elaborate meal that night. So she drank some milk and
finished her crackers and cheese, rolled up one of the remnants with her scissors and thimble and thread, and started out
to Mrs. Ritter's. If all went well she might be able to get another dress started during the evening.

The next day she invested in some boards and went to work
sawing. It was rather rough work, and she got splinters in her
hands and sawed some of the joints a bit crookedly, but she
finally put some very creditable corners together, sawing off
parts of each and dovetailing them into one another as she had
seen carpenters do, until she had a good, strong framework a
little over six feet long and thirty inches wide, which was the
size of the space in which she could put her bed without running across the windows.

When she had satisfied herself that the framework was
strong she began nailing webbing across the bottom, interlac-
ing it rather closely, as she had seen old Mr. Carpenter do.
When it was finished she lifted the structure upon two boxes
and sewed the springs into place at regular distances.

It took two days to get those springs tied down satisfactorily
on a perfect level, and Joyce had several pricked fingers before
she was done, and was almost wishing she had bought a hard
little army cot and learned to enjoy it. But the third morning
she covered the springs with a layer of cheap cloth, then the
cotton, and lastly the hair, covering the whole with ticking.
Then, with her big needle, she tied this down at every three or
four inches, until she had a soft, firm mattress, fine enough for
a princess. The work really, though crude in some ways, was a
great success, and one to be proud of, and when it was done
she put it on the floor and threw herself down upon it with a

great sigh of relief. Now, at last, she had a spot where the tired would be taken out of her when she had worked to the limit of her strength, something to look forward to when she came to her lonely little house at night after a hard day.

By this time Mrs. Bryant had managed to do a good deal of talking in the neighborhood about the bright young teacher who had come there to live and was having a little spare time this summer to help people out in an emergency, and several calls had come for her.

Once she had had to drop her hammer and saw and go to help Mrs. Smith to finish canning cherries, and succeeded in being so satisfactory that she was engaged to help with the strawberry preserves, gooseberry jam, and currant jelly.

Mrs. Jennings, on the next block, heard of her and engaged an afternoon a week at fifty cents an hour to take care of her children while she went out to the club meeting, and sometimes an extra evening. During these evenings she got quite a lot of sewing done, gradually acquiring a complete little wardrobe of plain, simple clothing made all by hand, but quite serviceable and pretty.

She met the gray-haired librarian of the Silverdale Memorial Library, and was asked to come in and help with the new cataloging. This took several afternoons and evenings, and meanwhile the furnishings of her little home grew slowly.

Once she was called in for three days to take care of some children while their mother went to the hospital for an operation on her throat; and several times after that she went to help nurse someone in a slight illness, where training was not required. She began to be known as the "Emergency Girl," and thought about putting out a sign and getting a telephone.

Meantime, she had met a kindly old man who was on the school board, and had arranged to take examinations and put in her application for a position should any be vacant for the next winter. This necessitated the purchase of some books, and another trip to the secondhand bookstore.

She had been living most economically, getting one meal a day usually, at a little restaurant among the stores where the tradespeople ate, and good wholesome food could be had at most reasonable rates. This gave her always something hot once a day. For the rest, she was living on ready-to-eat cereals, fruit, bread and butter, and milk, or if it rained too hard to go out she would cook an egg on her little alcohol can and eat her dinner at home. It really cost very little to live when one was careful. As for heat and light, she did not need either at this time of year. A candle did for emergencies. The twilight was long, and the electric light in the street was quite enough to go to bed by. Often she was out at somebody's house for the evening, caring for a child or an old person while the family amused themselves in the city, and there was always plenty of time then to read or study or sew.

So her life had settled into a pleasant little groove with interesting prospects ahead, and still the "barrel of meal," as she called her worn little pocketbook, always contained enough to live upon and get the real necessities, and sometimes a fragment or two of luxury. Winter was coming sometime, of course, with need for heat and light, and she must prepare for it too, but it wasn't here yet. Still, she did not feel that she had arrived at the point where she cared to let the Meadow Brook people know where she was. Some of them might take it into their heads to hunt her up on a motor trip, and she wasn't just prepared yet to show off her little house. Besides, she wanted to be anchored firmly with a regular school job before she told anyone where she was. Well, she knew there were people in Meadow Brook who would gladly have offered her a home just for Aunt Mary's sake, and she was a proud little girl and didn't want to have anybody feel they must offer her help. Besides, it wasn't exactly loyal to the family to explain her position at present, and she was one who would be loyal to her family even if her family were not loyal to her.

So she went her various helpful ways, and eked out her small necessities, with always something in the little brown pocketbook. Day by day the little house grew more homelike and cozy.

The homemade bed was a wonderful success. Mounted on four solid little square boxes six inches high, and nailed firmly to them, with a valance and cover of gray denim, and cotton pillows covered with the same, it seemed a luxurious couch. At night when the cover was removed it made a wonderful bed. When Joyce finally attained a fluffy pink coverlet made of cotton batting and a remnant of pink cheesecloth tied with pink yarn, she felt that she slept in luxury. Sheets and pillowcases were not expensive when one bought remnants of coarse cloth and hemmed them; and washing was not hard to do with the outside faucet and drain so near. It might not be so easy in winter, but it was all right in summer. And presently Mrs. Bryant made it still easier for her by suggesting that she use the tubs and hot water in the laundry in return for helping her out by getting supper once in a while when she had company.

Gradually the little house in the side yard took on an atmosphere of home. The two barrels, sawed in the middle half around, fitted with four springs in the seats, and upholstered in gray denim with padded backs and valanced standards, became two easy chairs, really comfortable to sit in. Joyce was proud of them. She invited Mrs. Bryant to take a seat in one when it was finished, and that good lady was almost disposed to doubt the girl's word when she told her it was made out of a barrel.

"My grandmother made one," explained Joyce, "and we always kept it carefully. I often wanted to make one when I saw a nice clean barrel, and now I've done it."

"Well, I think you're a wonder," said Mrs. Bryant after she had lifted the valance and felt the sturdy barrel staves for herself. "Just a wonder! You get so much more out of life than those flapper girls do! I wonder they like to be such fools. I can't see what the boys see in them. My Jimmie don't like 'em. He says, 'Mother, you don't know what the girls are like nowadays,' and I believe him. I'm sure I hope he stays sensible and finds a girl someday that will be the right kind. I was most afraid there weren't any left, but now I've seen you I'm real encouraged."

The said Jimmie appeared at home one weekend from technical school, where he was learning to be an electrical engineer, and kindly offered to wire her little house for her, probably at his mother's suggestion. So, at last, she had light and a place to cook, and she saved enough from getting her own dinners to buy a tiny electric grill, which gave her great comfort.

One corner which she called her dining room blossomed out with shelves, on which little blue and white cups and plates, bought at the ten-cent store, made quite a display.

She found a table and two wooden kitchen chairs at a secondhand store one day and bought the lot for two dollars, painted them gray, and she had a dining room set. The box dressing table had long ago been decked out in pink-flowered cretonne and made commodious harbor for her meager wardrobe. By and by she would find a chest of drawers and paint that gray also and then she would be fixed.

The only thing that really troubled her when she stopped to think was how she was going to keep the place warm when winter came. And presently that problem, too, was solved, for Jimmie, hearing of the difficulty on one of his weekends at home, suggested that he would build her a chimney out of the big pile of stones on the back of his father's lot, with a fireplace of stone in the room. If that didn't give her heat enough in the middle of winter she could get a little coal stove and set it up in one corner with a pipe into the chimney. Thereafter ever Saturday when he came home he worked for several hours on the chimney, in return for which Joyce helped him with his mathematics for the next week, so that she did not feel he was making the chimney for nothing.

By the time the vacation Bible school opened Joyce felt quite at home in the church of her choice, and was growing shyly intimate with Mrs. Lyman, the minister's wife. They had given her the primary department, and when she arrived at the church on the opening morning of the Bible school, she found that there were forty-nine little midgets, not one of them over five years old, all ready and eager to study the Bible. Joyce, with reverent heart, set about her glorious task, praying that she might be allowed to lay the foundation of belief in Christ and the Holy Scriptures even while they were so young. She entered into her work with eagerness and was inclined to spend even more time than she was required in preparing for each day's work, it was all such a joy to her.

But, sometimes, when she lay on the soft couch alone in her little toy house at night, and the streets were still save for the night watchman's whistle now and again in the distance, and the electric light flickered softly over her white wall, and played tricks of design on her curtains and draperies, she thought of the days at home with Aunt Mary, and how different it all would be if her precious aunt could have been with her here. How she longed to tell her everything that had happened, and talk over each day's doings just as she used to do. The loneliness was inexpressible, and the tears would come. Then her heart would go back to the dear home where she had spent so many years, and familiar faces, would come back, and little happenings, till she felt as if she could not bear it, being away like this. And then she would remember Nan and Gene and how hard the days had been before she left, and knew that she had done the wisest thing in going, and that God had set His seal upon her choice by prospering her in her way.

But always, when she had one of these times of retrospect, she did not fail to remember the boy who had spent that happy day with her and Aunt Mary in the woods so long ago, and to feel again the pain of that night when she found him and knew that somehow he had been doing something unworthy. Then she would pray with all her heart, as indeed she prayed every night, for him, that he might be converted and get to know Jesus Christ. Indeed, this was the great prayer of her life, the one big desire that her heart had set above all other desires. And as the days went by and she prayed for it, she grew gradually to feel that somehow it would be accomplished. She might never see, might never even know on this earth that it had been done, but she had faith to believe it would be done because the Bible said:

"If ye ask anything in my name, I will do it," and because He also said, "The Lord is not willing that *any* should perish; but that *all* should come to repentance."

And so she came to feel that someday her friend would find the way, and that perhaps, sometime in a heavenlier sphere, she would see him again with the smile of a reconciled God reflected in his face. And her heart was comforted.

Chapter 21

Darcy Sherwood had dropped out of Meadow Brook life as completely, apparently, as if he had died.

His old friends and associates did not realize it at first, thought he was gone on one of his short trips, or had taken on a new operation of some sort. Nobody ever seemed to know just what Darcy's business was, only that nobody ever spoke of him as one who had no business. He was one who kept his mouth shut about his own affairs, and much as his friends would have liked to ask him questions, they seldom did. If they did they were surprised to find that, although he answered them pleasantly, they had gained very little real knowledge of what they had started out to investigate.

People talked about him, as people always will talk about those they do not understand, and they said a great many things about him that were not true, while things that they did not say or think about him, things that were, some of them, worse than those they did think, were very often true.

Darcy had a strange code of honor and of life.

He was the product of a naturally loving disposition left to come up without much training, left to experiment with life for himself, and to search out his own view of the universe and his own doctrines of right and wrong. There were certain things he would not do though heaven and hell were against him, because he had decided in his heart that they were not right—not "square," he called it. One was that he never would harm a woman or a child in any way, directly or indirectly, if he knew it; and another was that he must always help the downtrodden, sometimes without regard to whether their cause was right or wrong, according to law and public opinion.

With all this he had the unusual combination of being both extremely clever as a businessman, and entirely unselfish in his personal life. Strong beyond most, he could walk among pitch when he liked without being soiled, yet he often chose to play with that pitch and minded not if others saw it on his hands, or misunderstood his actions. Beautiful as the devil must have been before he fell, with dark eyes, bronze gold hair, inclined to curl, and a smile of more than ordinary beauty, yet sad, too, with the sadness of the lost sometimes. Nobody quite knew what it was about Darcy Sherwood that made them like him so, or just what they so utterly disapproved of. And he went his way without seeming to care which they did. Only little children and old women saw the real Darcy, and won his rare confidence.

Darcy had a brother-in-law after his own heart, who knew how to keep his mouth shut—not as clever as Darcy, not always so good, but much richer in respectability, and most kind to Darcy's sister, a good dull girl who loved Darcy devotedly, but who never understood him. Sharp little Lib was a product of this home and her uncle's training. Where she got her sharpness was always a problem to Darcy. Certainly not from her simpleminded mother, nor yet from her somewhat commonplace father. Yet Darcy was fond of them both, and respected their ability to keep their mouths shut. It was something that Darcy had always taught everybody, sooner or later, with whom he came in contact.

And now Darcy was gone.

"I'll be away for a while, I don't know how long. Business trip. All you know about it, Mase, see?"

Mason Knox nodded.

"I getcha!" he said, and went on cleaning the carburetor of his car.

After a while his brother-in-law raised his head and gave Darcy a keen glance.

"Anything gone wrong, Darcy?"

"No, Mase, nothing wrong. New line, that's all. Been working on the wrong dope, I guess. Going to try a new line. But first I've got something to do. May take a long time. May be only a few days. Don't let Ellen worry. I'll write if there's any need."

He went the next day. Mason Knox and Dan Peterson were the only two in Meadow Brook who knew anything about his going, and that was all they knew. When people began to make inquiries Mason Knox answered with: "I couldn't say. He might and he might not be back soon. That depends."

When Dan Peterson heard that Darcy had disappeared from his usual haunts, heard first through his own son, who was a devotee of the baseball field on afternoons, he looked thoughtful, and wise, and went and told his father.

And Darcy had a strange method of going. He did not take the train, nor buy a ticket. He waited until night—no one quite remembered when they saw Darcy Sherwood last, when it came right down to the question some months afterward. Even the sharp-eyed Tyke, who was vigilant night and day as soon as his eyes were open to the necessity, had somehow missed his movements.

Darcy went at night, alone, without baggage or any impedimenta whatever; first to the graveyard, where he took from a tangle of grass and weeds under the hedge on the outer edge of the next field a pick and shovel that came strangely to hand, and went silently and deftly to a spot that he seemed to know well.

Here he worked for half an hour or more, lifting sod and soil from the place and setting them aside, as if he had done it before, pausing now and again to listen to a stir in the hedge or to mark the scuttling of a wild rabbit. Then, after a longer pause than usual, there came the sound of soft clinking, crashing; the gurgle of liquid coming through a small aperture, yet muffled, as if it were flowing underground. For a long time this went on, while Darcy stood watching the darkness, listening to the distance, identifying each falling leaf and stir in the shadows among the weird shafts of marble, and sighing cedars of the cemetery.

After a time he put back the soil and the sods into place, laid the pick and the shovel in the bed of a little creek just over in the next field, where the water tinkled over it harmlessly and obliterated all finger marks from its handle; and then stole away down the road, leaving behind, in the place of the dead, a strange, penetrating, unmistakable odor, which by morning would be purged away and escape into the elements.

Down in the road he paused, where he had encountered Joyce, and for a moment let his soul feel all that he had felt then—the delicacy of her hallowed touch, the thrill of her presence so near him, followed by the scorching shame that she should find him here, and by her question, with its piercing meaning, its wise conclusion, its sorrowing rebuke. The deep, wonderful look in her eyes as the flashlight revealed his identity to her, of recognition and of hurt surprise—he felt it all again! The tone of that voice that from his childhood he had treasured like the beautiful song of a bird in the holiest place in his heart. It was almost as if he suddenly felt that for a moment God was looking at him through her eyes, and he too saw himself as God saw him, and did not like it.

There was more to it. There was a kind of recoiling in horror from himself as he suddenly saw that in what he had been doing he had been untrue to himself and to his code. He had respected himself for the way he had kept to his self-made laws, and now his self-respect was broken. He could not go on and anymore take satisfaction in what he had been doing.

He stood there in the darkness with bowed head and went over it all again, as he had gone over it a thousand times since that night when he had seen her go from him into the dark, and the thought of her had driven him forth on this quest. Then, still, with bowed head he went on down the road.

A strange thing happened to him. He seemed to think as she must have been thinking, to know at each turn of the road what she would have done, which way she would have turned.

He knew that she had slept in the hammock, for he had sent his colleagues away, and taking another way about to overtake her, had seen her enter the gate, and watched her through the night until she stole away in the gray of the morning. So far he knew her way and could follow the trail.

But when he reached the streets of the little town beyond

and must choose between houses and turning corners it was not so plain. Ye he had resolved to leave no clue unfollowed, no spot where she might have turned unsearched.

He had a plan to make his search complete. He would make a map of each day's wanderings, note each house and corner and way of egress, choose the most likely and search it to the end, then come back and choose the next. It seemed, perhaps, the work of a lifetime, yet he did not feel that he would be long in finding her. There was something in his soul that told him he would find her. He had to find her and tell her what he had been doing, and that he never would do it again. He had to absolve his soul from that before her eyes. He could not lift up his head and respect himself again unless he did. She had stood like a young saint within the shrine of his heart, and now he felt cast away from the presence of all that he held really holy in the world.

So he went step-by-step over the way that Joyce had gone, his clever judgment quickly deciding which corner she would have chosen, where she would have paused, and how gone on again. And Joyce would have been surprised to know how far he traced her very steps.

It was not until he reached the city that his way became bewildering. He had dropped into a number of homes on his way where people lived who often visited in Meadow Brook, and casually, as if he had an accident on the road and needed to borrow water or a tool for his car, which he had left out of sight down the road, he would put one or two keen questions that would make him sure she had not passed that way while these people were about. And so his little notebook became filled with tiny tracings of maps, with streets and corners noted, and each turning that he had not followed marked for returning someday in case his quest was not successful.

He thought much as he took his way on foot through the world, and began to feel himself a pilgrim on a holy quest, not a knight, for his self-confidence had been too badly shaken for that. He had not so much the feeling that she needed him and he could help her to her inheritance if he found her, as he had the need of her in his soul. It seemed sometimes that he could not live until he had unburdened his soul by confession to her and had told her he would sin that way no more. He wanted her restored confidence, her clear-eyed smile, the feeling that she was his friend, though ever so far away, that there was something sweet and true between them. He had never thought of her as his in any way except as a guiding star, but now that he had lost that star, his life seemed all awry, as if he could not go on without her, as if all was darkness and horror, that she should think of him as so unworthy.

As he thought out his pilgrimage before him it occurred to him that the churches should be his goal. He knew that she always went to service, to prayer meetings, and Sunday school, and morning and evening church gatherings. There was his key to the situation. If she were still in the land of the living, if nothing evil had befallen her, she would be at some place of worship at the time appointed. And so, when a bell from some steeple rang a call to worship, he would pause, and wait, and watch the worshipers till all were in, or if he passed an open church door he would enter, sit down and gaze about until he had searched every face, and was sure she was not there. Then he would quietly get up and leave. Seldom did he hear the service that went on about him, seldom pretended to listen. He was there but for one purpose, and he had no time to waste. Words indeed passed through his consciousness as they were spoken, in story or song, but they left no impression there. He was not a scoffer at religious things. They had simply never touched him. He stood on the outside of them. Except for that one afternoon in his life when he had sat in the dim aisles of the grove and listened to Mary Massey reading the story of the blind man, he had never really taken heed to the Bible. Oh, he had heard it read in school, of course, and now and then in a service that some strange fancy carried him to as a boy, never in Sunday school, for he had not been sent there, and it was not a place he would have chosen to go because it meant confinement in the house when one might be out-of-doors. He had always been a law unto himself and he was rather proud of the fact. Now a great depression was upon him because he felt he had not kept his own law. It was Joyce's clear eyes, her keen question, that made him see that in breaking the law of his land, he had broken also the law of that inner, finer self. It was in his thoughts of her that he came to see that there was always something behind a law, it was never just a law.

What was that in Mary Massey's prayer so long ago?

"Help us for Christ's sake to have our eyes open to sin, so that we shall always know when we are not pleasing Thee."

It had been long years since he had heard that first and only real prayer of his lifetime, for other prayers that he had happened to hear had meant nothing to him, but the words of this were so clear to him as if it had been heard only yesterday. He pondered on the words as he walked down the highways on his search. "To have one's eyes open to sin, so that one should always know—" That had been his trouble. Strange! He had prided himself on never making mistakes, on keeping his code in mind, and yet what he had been doing had not seemed to be hurting anyone, and it was not until that clear-eyed girl had been a witness of his deeds in the darkness that he had felt the conviction. There had been something like that in the story her aunt had read. He wished he had a Bible that he might find it and read it again.

The desire grew upon him as the days went by, till the next time he reached a city he searched out a bookstore.

It was a little dusty bookshop in a back street, with a kindly old gentleman in spectacles in charge, and when Darcy asked for a Bible he looked at him over his spectacles with a smile and asked what type of Bible he would like. Darcy didn't know. Did they have different types? He had supposed a Bible was a Bible.

"Aren't they all alike?" he said with a troubled frown. "I want one that has a story of a man that was born blind and was healed. Would that be in them all?"

"Oh, yes, oh yes," said the man happily, trotting away and returning with an armful of Bibles. "I'll find it for you. There's a concordance in the back of this one. This is a very good Bible— Scofield Bible, you know. Has notes and explanations. Good binding too, though it is a little expensive. Let's see, let's see, blind man, blind man—*born* blind—yes, here it is, one of the Gospels. I thought so. John nine, sir—" and he handed over the open page to Darcy.

Standing in the little dusty bookshop, with the daylight fading and the streetlights beginning to blink out here and there, the young man read the old story over again until he came to the last words of the chapter: "If ye were blind, ye should have no sin: but now ye say, We see; therefore your sin remaineth."

Like a spear it thrust conviction to his soul. Yes, he had not been blind. He had been proud of his ability to see, to be a law unto himself—and he had sinned against all that was best in himself.

He bought the book and went out into the dusk, pondering. He went to a hotel and read the story over again and turned the pages aimlessly to find more about it, but in his soul there grew that knowledge of himself that brought a sense of sin. So far it was only sin in the eyes of the girl who stood to him for all that was pure and holy in the world, but it was sin, and the weight of the knowledge of it lay like a burden upon him. His smile grew grave whenever it appeared, and his eyes took on their sad wistfulness. People looked after him sometimes and thought how strangely sad he looked for a young man as fine and strong as he seemed to be.

The next time he entered a church in his search the preacher was reading the Bible, and the words he read caught Darcy's attention.

They seemed to be stranger and sweeter than any words he had ever heard. It reminded him of the place where Jesus heard that the blind man had been cast out and He came to find him. These words were these:

"Behold, what manner of love the Father hath bestowed upon us, that we should be called the sons of God: therefore, the world knoweth us not because it knew him not. Beloved, now are we the sons of God, and it doth not yet appear what we shall be; but we know that, when he shall appear, we shall be like him; for we shall see him as he is. And every man that hath this hope in him purifieth himself, even as he is pure."

So far he had been listening with deep interest. It seemed like what would have been written for Mary Massey and her niece. They were pure. They lived their lives according to what would please God. That was the dominating principle of her existence. He listened wistfully. They were so far removed from his world. He had never counted himself in with them, never expected to be nearer to them, except that one bright day in his childhood; but they had always lingered like luminaries in his sky, and always he had felt that if he had been born into a different walk in life, among Christian people like them, he would have belonged to them, have chosen them for his lifelong companions if they had been willing. He had known even as a child that he did not belong with them— known that he could not fit, and kept away. Yet he had never been able to feel satisfied with other people; always there had been a silent aloofness in his manner, except with little children, among whom there was no such thing as class.

He had named this thing that separated them "class" in his thoughts. Now he began to see that it was something else. It was sin. It was right and wrong that had separated them all these years. They were not people who stopped at class. There were no social classes in their eyes, else they would not have companioned with him that glorious day so intimately. He had come to know, years back, that education had something to do with separations, and he had taken pains to study and read, and make himself acquainted with the best literature, and now he no longer felt that he would be separated from them in that way. But this thing that was back of it all was sin—had been sin all along. Perhaps if he had gone there, as that woman with the dear eyes had asked, he would have learned to know sin and not have been wise in his own conceit. Perhaps he might even have come to be in the same world with them.

But the words were going on and they struck him sharply: "Whosoever committeth sin transgresseth also the law: for sin is the transgression of the law."

Yes, he was a transgressor of the law. He had broken the law of the land. That had never seemed a sin before. It had been only a matter of getting away with it. The sin would have been in being discovered, to his mind. Everybody else was doing it, some doing it bunglingly, and not getting away with it. He despised them. He had gone into it more for the game than the money. He had known he could do it without discovery.

But he had not gotten away with it. He had been discovered. And by that girl! Not only that, but by the girl he most honored in all the earth!

If he had been asked at the start whether he would like to have her know what he was doing he might not have thought much about it, but when her eyes looked into his with their question it was to him as if the great God had asked him: "What are you doing?" It was like the question that the Lord God called in the garden in the cool of the evening: "Adam, where art thou?" only Darcy did not even know that story, knew Adam only as a hazy being of history or mythology, he could not have told which.

But he knew God's voice when he heard it, even though it spoke through the voice of a woman—the woman he loved.

Suddenly, he knew that too. He loved her. He had loved her all along. That was why he was going after her. She was lost and he was finding her. And somehow it was beginning to dawn upon his soul that he would not find her until he had found the God she loved, and set this thing right which was wrong with himself, if there was any such thing as setting it right in this crooked world.

And then, if Darcy Sherwood had not been bound to find

Joyce Radway and bring her safely home, he might have felt that life was not any longer worth living; for all the laws by which he had lived, and all the principles by which he had stood, were crumbling beneath him like the sands of the sea, and he felt himself stumbling in the darkness.

Chapter 22

About this time the school board in Silverton were sitting in solemn conclave, deciding who should take the vacant position in the primary department of the public school, left vacant by the sudden death of the woman who had taught that department for the last twenty-five years.

The position had been open since spring, and filled temporarily by pupils from the normal school, most of whom had not proved satisfactory to someone on the board, although three who had made formal application for the position were now under consideration.

"Well, I have a new name I'd like to present," said Mr. Powers, who had just entered late, and had not heard the wrangling over the three names by their various advocates. "She's a pippin, too, and I think you'd better take her."

"Oh, now, Powers, don't get in any more names. We're having trouble enough as it is," laughed a member who was in a hurry to get home. "Let's put these three to a vote and be done with it. make that as a motion—"

"I object," said Mr. Powers. "This young woman has fine recommendations. I took the trouble to look them up. She's teaching over in Lyman's church at that summer Bible school he's so crazy about, and he says she's the best teacher he ever had. Gets the kids and all that! Don't have a bit of trouble with discipline, and has 'em right with her from the word go!"

"Where does she come from?" growled one of the men, who was trying to get his candidate voted on.

"Why, she lives in the little land office down on Bryant's lot. Mrs. Bryant can't get done talking about her, how much go she has, and what she can do. She's bought that building and had it moved there. Has a lot of initiative and all that, and is right there in an emergency. It seems she saved their house from getting on fire just by keeping her head. I say that's the kind of girl we want in our school."

While he was speaking the new superintendent entered.

He had just been called to fill the vacancy caused by the old superintendent's being called to a city school. He was young and good-looking and they all stood somewhat in awe of him. He had a grave manner and seemed to know just what he wanted. They all rose to greet him.

"Professor Harrington, we've just been trying to get this primary teacher decided upon," said one man. "Powers here is holding us up by presenting a new name. Don't you think we'd better just stick to the three we've decided upon and tried, and pick one of them? At least we know what they are."

The young superintendent turned toward Powers.

"Who is the person in question?" he asked, looking straight at Powers and trying to find out whether he thought a recommendation from him would be worth the paper it was written upon.

"Why, her name is Radway. Miss Joyce Radway," said Powers. "I'd like to have you see her, professor. She certainly is intellectual-looking and all that. I had the pleasure of watching her teach this morning over in the Roberts Avenue Church. They have some kind of a religious summer school there to occupy the children during vacation, and the pastor tells me she is the best teacher they have."

"I shouldn't think a minister would be a very good judge of what was needed in the public schools," piped up the advocate of one of the other applicants.

"Well, this one is. He's making that school a success, I can tell you—has something over five hundred kiddies there regularly every day, and crazy about the school. He won't have anybody there that isn't a crackerjack teacher—"

But the attitude of the superintendent suddenly drew the attention of the speaker. Professor Harrington was sitting alert, all attention, interest in his eyes.

"Did you say her name was Radway? Joyce Radway? There could scarcely be two of that name, I should think. It is rather an unusual name. If it's the Miss Radway I know, I should say have her by all means. I've been hunting for her for the last two months, only gave it up because I was called here. Did she come from Meadow Brook, do you happen to know?"

"Why, I don't know, I'm sure. I didn't ask about that. But I can find out. Suppose I go and bring her!"

"Do," said the professor. "I'd like to see if she is the same one. She certainly gave promise of being a rare mind. I had the pleasure of looking over her examination papers—"

But Powers had already seized his hat and gone out the door. There was a special reason why he wanted to "put one over" on the men who were sponsoring the other candidates, and he didn't mean to lose a single chance. He went at once to the school telephone and called up Mrs. Bryant, asking her to ask Miss Radway to be ready to come back with him.

And so it was that Joyce, summoned from her preparation of the Bible-school lesson for the next day, hurried into a pretty little blue voile she had just finished and was ready when Mr. Powers arrived to go before the school board.

In a few minutes, she stood, at last, before Professor Harrington, who had wasted many precious hours of his time, to say nothing of telephone charges and letters, trying to locate this special teacher, and when she finally stood before him he looked into her clear blue eyes and said to himself, *That's the girl I want.* And aloud, to the school board, he said gravely:

"I feel sure, from what I know of Miss Radway's work, that she is eminently fitted to teach in our school."

Joyce lifted astonished eyes to the fine, scholarly face and didn't in the least recognize him. But she had sense enough left in spite of her perturbation not to say so, and in a few minutes she was dismissed from the room and the vote was carried in her favor.

The fact was, every man of them was prepossessed in her favor as soon as he looked into her eyes, and the three bobbed-haired candidates hadn't a chance, with her on the spot.

"But I thought she was a cook!" said one wife when her husband got home from the school board meeting and told her about the election of the new teacher. "Mrs. Powers told me she got dinner for her one night when she had company."

"I asked Powers about that," her husband answered. "It seems she just did it to help them out when she first came, while she was looking for a job. Powers said he never tasted such cooking. His wife offered her twenty-five dollars just to stay and cook dinner on Sunday for some guests and she wouldn't do it."

"Well, I don't blame her. Mrs. Powers is very unpleasant to

get along with, all the maids say. But it does seem strange to hire a cook to teach in the school. I think we'll send Genevieve to a private school this fall."

"No, we won't send Genevieve to any private school, not if I have anything to say about it, and I guess I'd have to pay the bills. Not while I'm on the school board either. How do you think that would make me look?"

"You could resign. You could say you didn't approve of having cooks teach our children."

"Well, I do approve. It's a pity Genevieve couldn't learn to cook too. I've seen this girl and I want my children under her. I count it a privilege to have them under her. I like her looks. She doesn't paint her face, nor bob her hair, nor wear clothes way up to her knees. And she doesn't wear dangle-dangles in her ears, nor pull out her eyebrows. She wears neat, sensible, pretty things and looks like a good girl, and that's the kind we want our little children under. That Miss Harlow you wanted me to vote for makes eyes at every man that comes near her, married or single. This girl tends to her business and knows what she's about. I voted for her, and I mean to stick by her. Now! I want it understood that she is *not a cook*. She may know *how* to cook, but that talk about her being a cook doesn't go another step from this house! Understand! If it does, there's going to be a big overhauling somewhere."

"Oh, of course, if you've taken her up," said her wife disagreeably. "It seems she has all the men on her side even if she doesn't make eyes at them."

"She doesn't need to. She's a good girl and she doesn't want 'em; and that's the kind the children ought to have."

So Joyce was established in the primary department of the Silverton School, under the very immediate supervision of the new superintendent, who paid her marked attention from the first, to her evident embarrassment.

Joyce was not averse to having friends, nor to going out and having good times like other girls, but it happened that the very first thing this luckless young man asked her to was a dance, and she had to tell him she didn't dance.

Joyce didn't like to go around flaunting her principles, and never talked about those things unless she had to, but he argued the question with her. He certainly wanted to take her to that dance. But when it came to arguing, Joyce just smiled and said she was sorry to seem ungracious, but she didn't care to learn to dance. Well, would she go to an orchestra concert in the city with him then? Yes, she said she would enjoy that. So they went. But he, poor soul, felt himself called upon to bring Joyce into a better way of thinking about the dancing, "a more modern view," he called it, and they certainly did not get on very well.

Then he told her how he had hunted for her in Meadow Brook, and how he had admired her from seeing her just once; how she was different from other girls, that was what he admired about her; and Joyce looked up with a smile and said:

"Then why are you trying to make me over just like all the rest?" He looked at her a moment embarrassedly, and then began to laugh.

"No," he said after a moment. "I don't believe I do want to. I like you just as you are." After that they talked about books, and summer, and the beautiful meadows about Meadow Brook, and they seemed quite good friends. He asked her why she ran away, and she said evasively, that it was hard for her to stay where she and her aunt had been happy so many years, and she felt it would be better for everybody if she went, and went quietly, without waiting to bid all her dear friends good-bye. She saw he had not been intimate with any of her intimate friends, and rightly surmised that he had not heard anything peculiar about her going.

It did occur to her that he might write back sometime and speak about her to someone, but it seemed rather unlikely; and she was going to write home pretty soon anyway, so she thought no more of the matter.

A very pleasant friendship sprang up between Joyce and John Harrington. Not that there was anything sentimental about it, as yet. John Harrington might express his admiration of a girl, but that was all until he was quite sure of himself; also quite sure of her. It was one thing to run after a new teacher with all his heart. It was quite another thing to commit himself personally. Harrington was a most judicious young man. He would not have been called to take charge of the Silverton School if he had not been. He was well satisfied in his mind as to his own feelings toward Joyce, but it was not yet time to commit himself. Joyce needed molding and modifying. She needed modernizing somewhat before she would be fitted to become the wife of a superintendent. So he set himself to mold and modernize her.

Joyce was simple-hearted and happy. She loved her work, and she was having a good time. The superintendent did not

pick her out to focus his entire attention upon her and make her
an object of jealousy, therefore she enjoyed the occasional trips to
the city to hear some fine music, and the constantly kindly help-
fulness of the young man as her head in the school. Things were
going well with her, and she thanked God every night.

Somehow, however, with Harrington's advent there had
come so many new things that her time was more than filled.
The letters she had planned to write to Meadow Brook were
still unwritten, and the more she thought about them (usually
at night, after she had got to bed, and was reviewing the day),
the harder they seemed to write. How to explain her going,
what to say about Nan and Gene. It would be so disagreeable if
Nan should take it into her head to come after her and coax her
to come back and live with them. Nan hated housework, and
she could not help knowing that she was valuable to her in that
way. No, she was not yet ready to write home.

So the days drifted by, full of hard work, and pleasantness.
She loved her young pupils and they loved her. Often they
invited her to their homes, and here she met many pleasant
people who showed themselves as more than friendly. She
could have spent every evening in a merry round if she had
chosen. But, here again, the fact that she was a very old-fashioned girl and neither danced nor played bridge nor mah jong,
nor could be persuaded to learn, set her apart, and saved many
evenings for reading and study and necessary sewing. People
tried to persuade her at first, laughed at her, and teased her,
but she remained sweetly firm, yet without preaching to them,
and they finally, good-naturedly, let her alone.

Sometimes she had little gatherings of two or three people
in her wee house, and served them chocolate and delectable
little cakes, or Welsh rarebit or hot pancakes made on her little
electric grill. Harrington was occasionally included in these
gatherings. No, she never received young men alone. She told
them they could not come without some woman friend with
them. They laughed at her old-fashioned ideas, but they went
away and found some quiet elderly friend and came again.
Joyce's home began to have a reputation all its own, showing a
girl could live alone and yet keep free from all the unconven-
tions of the modern world. If anyone grew troublesome there
was always Mrs. Bryant to whom she might call, and Mrs.
Bryant understood and always happened in whenever she
knew Joyce had a caller who might want to stay alone.

So the fall passed and the winter entered in.

Jim had finished the chimney and fireplace, and the little room was warm and cozy, even on a bitter November evening with the wind howling outside.

It had not taken Harrington long to find out which was the most influential and intellectual church in the community and to connect himself with it. Thereafter, he set about bringing Joyce to go with him sometimes. He felt if she could but listen to the wise and modern thoughts of this most learned divine, who preached at his chosen church, it would be easier to win her from some of her narrow views. But when he asked her to go to church with him, one evening, she told him she could not leave her own, that she had asked her Sunday school class to go with her that night. When he said, then they would go the next Sunday night, she looked at him with her clear eyes and said:

"I'm sorry to have to say no again, but I cannot go to that church at all. That minister dishonors my Lord, and I do not feel I can ever listen to him again."

He told her it sounded pharisaical for a young girl like herself to set up to criticize a man of the minister's years and standing. Didn't she know that the great denomination for which he stood was back of him, and that they knew better than she did, a young girl with little experience? Besides, what about that Bible verse that said you mustn't speak evil of dignitaries? She had been taught by dear old-fashioned people, and it was beautiful to look back on such an upbringing, but, of course, it wasn't progress to stay just where her forefathers had stood. She ought to go on to higher realms of thought. It wasn't Christian to stand still. Things were not as they used to be. Science and art and everything else had progressed and grown, why should not religion? Men had learned more of God, and grown wiser. They had learned that He was not the same God their fathers had supposed.

Her answer was to look at him steadily with rising color, and repeat:

"'Jesus Christ, the same yesterday, and today, and forever.' And I'm not speaking evil of dignitaries. I'm telling you he dishonored my Lord. The Bible says, 'From such turn away.'"

"Oh, now, don't you think you are pressing a point too far?" he said. "Of course Christ is the same, it's our views of Him that have changed. We have grown, and are able to see Him in a bigger, broader sense, as a grand example for the whole world; not just a little personal God who attends to each detail of our life."

"I'm afraid I wouldn't care much about Him if He wasn't personal, and didn't care for the details of my life," she said. "I take great pleasure in that verse: 'He knoweth the way that I take,' and 'The very hairs of your head are all numbered,' and 'Fear ye not therefore, ye are of more value than many sparrows.' And my God isn't a little one, either, because He attends to all the details. He wouldn't be a God at all if He didn't."

"I certainly wish I had your memory," said the young man with a look of admiration. "You have a fine mind. You would have made a good lawyer. But I hate to see you so narrow. It isn't like you in other things to be narrow."

"Enter ye in the strait gate," began Joyce thoughtfully, "for wide is the gate, and broad is the way that leadeth to destruction, and many there be that go in thereat: Because strait is the gate and narrow is the way which leadeth unto life, and few there be that find it."

"And so you are actually priding yourself on being narrow!" He spoke almost angrily. It was annoying to have her so stubborn, so ignorant of modern ideas, so bound by these old traditions.

"No," she said sadly. "Those are not my words. They are my Lord's. I didn't make them. I'm only telling you why I'm narrow, as you say."

"Well, if you'd only go to a respectable church, and hear some really good teaching along intellectual lines I feel sure you are bright enough and open-minded enough to give up these silly, pharisaical ideas. They are really too egotistical for a sweet young girl like you."

Joyce lifted her eyes sadly to his.

"You don't understand because you can't," she said. "Your eyes are blinded. There are a great many people like that nowadays. I didn't know it till I came away from Meadow Brook. I didn't understand what the verse meant when it said that the natural man could not understand the things of the Spirit. Now I know. You can't understand because you haven't been born again."

The young man made an impatient movement.

"Oh, I dislike that phrase. Please don't use it. It's so ridiculous to talk that way in this age of the world."

"Jesus Christ used it," said Joyce quietly.

"Well, it isn't a thing to be talked about," he said crossly.

"How should you set up to say I'm not 'born again' as you say it?"

"Because you don't understand. Because you can listen to a minister who doesn't believe that Jesus died to shed His blood to wash away our sins. Because you can listen to a man who can dare to say that they called Jesus divine because they couldn't think of any other word to use, and who said the blind man only thought he was blind, and Jesus just waked him up to open his eyes and use them. I heard him say all those things, and I can't go and listen to him anymore. It is dishonoring my Lord to hear him."

"Well, I think the person that brought you up was awfully to blame," he said with contempt in his voice. "To saddle anybody with as many hidebound doctrines as you seem to have is a sin. Whoever it was will have to answer for it someday. You have an unusually fine mind, and if you would once give up these foolish legends and prejudices with which your mind is filled you would be a brilliant woman with a great future before you."

Joyce stood up and looked at him gravely, her eyes brilliant, her cheeks flushed.

"I may not be a brilliant woman," she said sweetly, "but I certainly have a great future before me. I'm going to live and reign with Jesus Christ someday, and I don't really think it matters so very much whether I'm brilliant down here or not with that in view. But you'll have to excuse me from any further talk on this subject. You have cast a slur on my faith, and we really haven't anything in common when you do that. I *know* my Christ, and you don't seem to. I must go now."

She swept out of his office, whither he had summoned her on pretext of consulting her about some of her scholars who were to be promoted. There was something so final about her going that it quite depressed him, and after a night's wakefulness he went to see her, and had the good grace to apologize to her, and to say he would like her to try and show him what she meant by her faith.

"If you will come to the church where I go you will find out much better than I can teach you," she said, for she did not more than half believe that he wanted to know.

So he agreed to go with her the following Sunday evening, and she began to mention his name in her prayers as she knelt in the moonlight of her little room. "Dear Father, show me how to make him understand," she prayed. But always her prayer ended with: "Find Darcy please, and don't let him lose the way home, for Christ's sake."

Chapter 23

Matters had come to such a pass in the Massey home that Eugene and his wife scarcely had a pleasant word to say to one another, and Nan spent much time in weeping.

She had ransacked the house to find some papers of her mother-in-law's that would prove that the house was theirs, but had found nothing. On the contrary, there were letters and papers that showed that both Gene's mother and his aunt had always known that the house belonged to Joyce. There were also references to "money" and Nan began to fear that Gene and she would have nothing. Gene's business wasn't very good, and it had been growing worse of late, because he was so distracted by this matter of the will that he scarcely gave any attention at all to it; and Nan was running up terrible bills which she dared not tell him about, hoping every day that Joyce would turn up and matters would straighten out. But Joyce did not return, and every day the bills grew.

At first, when she found them, Nan considered burning these letters that said so much about the property, but after reading them carefully over again, she was afraid to do so, lest somehow that would be only making a bad matter worse. What if Joyce knew of these letters and should return some day and demand them? So she purchased a strong metal box, locked them therein and hid them among her own private possessions. If they were ever demanded she could say she had put them away for safekeeping. If they were not, and it came out that the house was theirs after all, she could easily burn them sometime.

But things were going from bad to worse, and after two of the tradesmen whom she owed had visited her, demanding their money when she had none to give them, she decided that something radical must be done.

So she dressed herself in deep mourning one day and went to call on the minister.

There were dark circles under her eyes and a sad droop to her lips. She carried a black-bordered handkerchief and asked to see Doctor Ballantine privately.

Mrs. Ballantine took her into the study, and Nan addressed herself to him with instant tears.

"Oh, Dr. Ballantine," she said, stanching the flood with her handkerchief and sinking into the offered chair, "I'm so miserable and unhappy! I simply had to come and see you!"

Doctor Ballantine put up his pen, and slipped a blotter over the sermon he was just finishing for the morrow, and expressed himself sympathetically, wondering anxiously what had happened. Had this woman come to tell him of some great tragedy or to confess her sins? Alarm filled his heart, and instant premonitions of danger to Joyce. Somehow Nan was not the kind of woman that one would ever think of in connection with any religious convictions. It never even entered the good man's heart that she had come to inquire about her soul. Afterward he thought of this with some wonder and self-reproach.

But Nan recovered from her brief emotion and began to talk.

"It's about my husband's cousin, Joyce Radway," she stated, and the good doctor was instant attention. "You see, we haven't heard from her since she went away."

"Is that so?" said Doctor Ballantine with startled tone. "Where is she? Perhaps you would like to have me write, or telegraph to the minister there to learn of her safety. Are you afraid she is ill?"

"Oh, we don't know—" wailed Nan, breaking down again. "We don't even know where she is. She hadn't told us!"

"You don't know? She hasn't told you? Why," said the minister, half rising from his seat, "that's not at all like Joyce to leave you in anxiety. Didn't she tell you where she was going?"

"No," sobbed Nan. "No, she didn't tell us. She just walked out of the house without saying a word, and never came back. We thought of course she would come back pretty soon. She always did before when she got upset or angry—"

"Upset? Angry?" said the puzzled minister. "What, may I ask, what do you think she was angry at?"

"Oh, nothing at all, just a little thing. You know Joyce has a fearful temper. Or perhaps you don't know it. Those quiet, mild people never do show up what they are till you come to live with them. Of course I don't blame poor Joyce. She had to be on such a strain all the time poor Mother was ill. She wouldn't let a person but Joyce come near her, and it was almost more than the girl could bear. I sometimes used to be afraid she would go out of her mind before the end came, there were so many demands made upon her. And a young girl like that wants to have a good time, you know—"

"That doesn't sound like Joyce—" The minister spoke gravely. "She was devoted to Mrs. Massey. You haven't known her as long as I have. She was only a tiny child when I came here, you know, and Mother and I—we loved her. She was like our little one that was taken away."

"Yes, I know, she was attractive," Nan hastened to say, mopping her eyes daintily. "And she liked to pose as a dutiful daughter. Still, you know, Doctor Ballantine, a girl likes a good time. I knew you thought a good deal of her and were interested in her welfare and all, and that's why I came to you. I haven't told my husband I was coming. I don't know what he would say if he knew. He's very proud and independent, and he feels this thing keenly. But I just thought I would come to you to see if you couldn't help find Joyce. You know her friends and know her so well. I thought you might know some place to look for her that hasn't occurred to us. We have been here so short a time. But you mustn't tell my husband. You must promise me that before we begin."

"It's never a good thing for a woman to hide a thing from her husband," said the minister, still gravely. "Mrs. Massey, my advice to you is to go home and tell your husband you have spoken to me before you tell me anything more about it. Then if he wishes me to be in your confidence further we can go on from there."

"Oh, Doctor Ballantine!" broke out Nan afresh with frightened tears. "I couldn't possibly do that. You see he is so sensitive about it because it was his words that made Joyce angry. He told her, very kindly—he always speaks gently in his family—and I was right in the room when he did it. I heard every word. There wasn't the least reason in the world for her to get angry, only she was just in the mood for it. She's very temperamental, you know. He asked her to please not let her electric light burn all night, that the bill had just come in and was pretty large, and we must all try to remember and turn the lights out whenever they were not needed. Now you know there wasn't anything in that to make a girl get furious and stamp her foot and fling herself out of the kitchen in a pet. I was just putting on dinner when she went, and I thought of course she would come back pretty soon. She always did before. But this time she didn't. I suppose she must have been waiting for us to come out and coax her back, but we thought it wisest for her not to run after her, for we had noticed ever since Mother's death that she showed a tendency to get into a huff and stay there, and we thought if we just went quietly about and ignored her temper she would come out of it sooner. That's the way we always do with the children."

She paused for encouragement, but the doctor, with set lips and stern eyes, was watching her, saying nothing. Nan began to catch her breath again in a trembling sob, and went on:

"When it began to get dark I got worried and told Gene he simply must go out to the barn and bring her in. It was too damp and chilly for her to stay out there after dark. That was where she always went when she got in a pet, and we expected, of course, to find her in her usual place. But when Gene went out with his flashlight there wasn't a trace of her anywhere, and he came back all upset."

She paused to observe the impression she was making, but the minister's face wore a mask of dignity and she hurried on.

"I wouldn't tell you these things, of course, for it is terrible to me to reveal the little weaknesses of my husband's family, but I must tell someone and get some help, for I am nearly crazy. I sometimes think my husband will lose his mind. He is naturally very fond of Joyce, for she was brought up like his own sister, you know, and he is almost breaking under the anxiety—"

The minister said nothing to help her.

"We have searched the world over, every place we can think of, and no trace whatever of her. It is almost like the case of Charlie Ross, and now Gene can't sleep at night, he is so anxious—"

She paused and wiped her eyes.

"I want my husband to get the detectives at work after her, but he keeps hoping we shall hear. He simply can't bear the publicity of it all, and for my sake especially. So I decided this afternoon to just come and confide in you. You're so wise and kind—"

The minister arose with that compelling look that makes a caller arise also.

"Mrs. Massey," he said. "I wish there were some comfort I could give you. I will think this matter over, and will talk it over with my wife. I never keep anything from my wife, but be assured it will go no further. Meantime, I advise you to go home and tell your husband what you have done. There is nothing to be gained by keeping it from him, and I most certainly cannot enter into any plan whatever to help without his full knowledge and sanction. Meantime, of course, Mrs. Ballantine and I will consult, and if there is anyone that we think might help in this matter we will let you and Mr. Massey know. I don't mind telling you that we have been anxious about our young friend even before you came. It seemed so utterly unlike Joyce to go off in that way without a word to us. She—is not like that. There must have been—some reason—something more than you have stated—perhaps more than you understood—perhaps some misunderstanding on her part. Really, Mrs. Massey, Joyce *is not* like that. I have known her a long time—"

"That's what I say, Doctor Ballantine. That's what I'm afraid of. I'm just afraid to mention it to my husband, it would be so perfectly terrible to him to think of such a thing in connection with his family, but sometimes—sometimes—I've really been afraid—now, of course, I wouldn't want you to mention this even to Mrs. Ballantine—unless you simply have to—but sometimes I've been afraid that Joyce was—losing her mind."

"Now I know you're shocked, but I simply *had* to tell you, and I thought if you could just kind of quietly inquire around among the insane asylums in this neighborhood, and see if any young person has been brought in like that. You, being a minister, can get entrance into these places—"

"Mrs. Massey!"

The minister's voice was stern. Nan hardly knew him.

"Mrs. Massey, nothing like that has happened! Joyce Radway has never lost her mind! She is too filled with the spirit of Christ for that. She is too much God's child. There is nothing like Jesus Christ to keep a mind sane and steady. Don't ever utter that thought to any living being again!"

Nan cringed as she stood by the study door. His voice was almost like the command of one who had authority over her.

"Oh, are you *sure*?" she managed to say weepily. "That's such a comfort. That thought has tormented me night and day, perhaps Joyce was shut up in some awful insane asylum—"

"Hush!" said the doctor sternly. "That could never be. She may have fallen into some danger, or be sick in some hospital, but never that! She is God's own child."

Nan slid out of the door like a serpent, rebuked, murmuring:

"Well, I'm glad I came, you've given me so much comfort!" but she walked down the street with angry eyes and set mouth. Her mission had been a failure so far as winning over that old dolt was concerned. What a fool he was over Joyce! What a fool everybody was over her! What did they see in her anyway to be so crazy about? She couldn't understand.

Nevertheless, as she drew toward her own home, meditating on her recent interview, something in her heart told her exultantly that she had not failed entirely, for she had managed to give a different coloring to the situation, much as the old minister had hated to accept it. He would think it over, and he would presently come to be uncertain, and perhaps to half believe what she had told him. And when later, other developments occurred, he might give credence to the thoughts which she had put into his mind. Nan was not extremely clever, but, somehow, the devil in her shallow heart comforted her with this, and the hope that someday, if trouble really broke, Gene would thank her and be proud of her for having prepared the way for a creditable story that would not reflect upon them.

By the time she had got supper ready she was quite pleased with her afternoon's work. She had planted the seed in Doctor Ballantine's subconscious mind and it would grow. By the time he told his wife it would even so soon have begun to grow. She need not worry about developments. Perhaps even Gene would never have to know that she had had anything to do with it.

Chapter 24

So far Lib Knox had resisted all attempts to be friendly with Tyke. He had tried candy, a little white kitten, and a fox terrier poodle, but Lib only turned a cold shoulder.

Even the day when he arrived in a motorcycle with a sidecar and offered her a ride he almost failed, although he could see that it went hard with her to refuse. It was when at last he told her that she was afraid, and dared her to come with him for a five-mile spin, that she finally yielded. Lib never could take a dare.

Seated in the chariot, she surveyed her comrades with superior arrogance and enjoyed to the full her triumphal departure from the district where she lived. But once out on the highway, Tyke let out all the power and shot through space as if he had suddenly taken leave of his senses. Lib gripped the sides of her car and sat erect, her eyes bulging, her white lips set in a frightened smile. She was badly scared, but she was game.

For several miles he tore away at this mad pace, seeming to graze telephone poles, and almost telescope automobiles, and just escaped killing men and dogs. Then he slowed down and turned into a side road where there was comparatively little traffice, a crossroad leading to another highway.

Lib, breathless, still gripped the car, obviously speechless.

"Now, look here, kid," said her captor, bending toward her insinuatingly, "you thought that was fast, didn't you? But that ain't a continental to what I kin do with this here brig. Why, I kin go so fast it'll take the hair right off'n yer head and leave yer bald like a old man. It'll take yer breath outen ya, so't'ya can't speak right fer a week, an' it'll maybe sweep ya right out in the field and leave ya fer the crows ta pick. An' that's what I'm agonta do'ith ya kid, ef ya don't tell me where that doggone uncle of yourn is hanging up. See? I'm givin' ya time till I get ta that highway out there t'consider. Ef ya don't come across with what I want y'll be slung like an arrow through the air, an' ya won't know yerself. Y'll wonder where's yer daddy an' yer ma, and yell like a little baby, but it won't do no good, fer nobody can't hear ye when your goin' like a wild cat. Now, what say? Are ye giving me the necessary information, ur shall I let 'er go?"

Lib was gripping the sides of her car with small, wiry fingers that were white and tense. Her little freckled face was white beneath its tan, and the bronze-gold of her bobbed curls ruffled above eyes that were wide with fear. She swallowed to get her voice, and suddenly her sharp little lips trembled into an impish grin and she trembled out tauntingly:

"The devil you do!" roared Tyke angrily. "I'll give ye enough then, you little runt you," and they shot into the highway into the midst of the worst traffic they had yet seen. Tyke was so angry he could scarcely see where he went, and he let out the power till they seemed to be but a streak in the air as they flew along to what seemed like destruction. It seemed to little Lib of the fiery heart that she was aging as she went, that if she ever stopped she would be old and tottering, that her hands were numb and her face stung with the wind, and she was cold to her soul through the thin little clothing she wore. But she gave no sign, as the car went on and on, and miles of trees and meadows and houses and towns shot by in the flash of an eye. Lib wondered if it would go on forever. And then, just as she thought she could not hold on another minute, as she wished she might drop from the back and be crushed into insensibility by the fall, and never come to life again anymore, because her heart hurt so in her breast, and her eyes were going to cry (which to Lib was the worst thing that could ever happen to her, that she should be weak enough to cry)—just then, when things could not have gone on any longer and she exist, they came to a road leading into the woods and the motorcycle slowed down and bumped into the rough road and up a hill into dense woods, suddenly coming to a standstill.

Tyke turned upon her with an evil look.

"You little devil, you!" he said, glaring at her with the glare of one who had been baffled.

Lib was too frightened to speak, and her teeth were chattering with the cold, but she lifted her game little face toward his evil one and suddenly stuck out her tongue and made an impish face at him, expressing all the hate and loathing of her little courageous soul. The man looked down at her astonished, blinking, scarcely believing that such daring could come from a baby.

"I c'd kill you, you young 'un—" he muttered.

"I don't see what good that would do," said Lib unexpectedly, her quick mind intrigued by the situtation. "You couldn't find out where my uncle lived by killing me, could you? It isn't written inside my head anywhere," and she laughed a ghoulish little laugh made all the more weird by the tremble of her voice.

"Well, I'll be—"

But Lib was gathering her strength with her breath as it returned.

"I never said I wouldn't tell you where my uncle was, did I?"

The man was speechless. Could it be that this mere infant was kidding him? Not scared at all, but just putting one over on him? He stared at her in bewilderment. Lib, eyeing him, knew that she had gained a point. She summoned voice again.

"But I ain't going to tell you till I get back home again. If you had asked me polite like a gentleman when you first took me, I might uv; but now I shan't tell ya a thing till I'm back home.

Come on, get a move on. I've gotta get back and study my spelling fer tomorrow. Can't you get through this road or do ya have to turn around?"

The nonchalance of her! Tyke couldn't help but admire it while yet his anger smoldered. It was for all the world like her cool, collected uncle, white and calm under fire. He was amazed, but somehow, he was conquered.

"You swear you give it to me straight 'f I take you home?"

"I don't swear," said Lib coolly. "It's naughty. My mother doesn't like me to."

Tyke grew black and swore under his breath.

"I ain't takin' no nonsense!" he lowered. "You gimme that address ur I'll kill ya yet, I swear I will."

Lib was getting her second wind. She eyed him furtively. She was not nearly so frightened now. She was trying to think what to do.

"Well, it's up in Canada somewhere," she said, "a name that begins with a Q. If you'd start the car home I could mebbe think. Quebec. That's it. I never can remember that name. But I can't think of the street until we get back home. There's a street there by the same name. You run back and I'll show you where to find it. It's seven hundred thirty-seven that street. Now, will you take me back?"

The motor began to rumble again.

"You tellin' me straight, you little devil?"

"Sure!" said Lib, settling back and trying to still her teeth from chattering and her weak little knees from trembling. "Let's go fast again like we did. I'm getting hungry, and my mother won't like you if you keep me away so long."

Tyke glared at her, but he put on his goggles and started toward home. When they reached the edge of the town Lib sat up straight and directed his movements.

"You go up that street and down the first turn to the right," she said. "No, it was the next street I meant, I guess." She studied the street markers thoughtfully, the while she made him go past the houses of her most intimate friends, and enemies, casually greeting them as she passed by in this her triumphal procession through her own domain.

And so when she had traversed them all, the streets of those she wished to impress, she exclaimed, "Oh, yes, there 'tis! State Street. That's it. Seven hundred thirty-seven State Street. Now, you c'n let me out here, if you please. My mother don't like me to be out with strangers and she mightn't be nice to you." And Tyke wisely let her out and went on his way wondering, saying over to himself.:

"She's a little devil but she's a tough one. She's a tough little nut, that's what she is. I wonder now if she's makin' a monkey out o' me! Guess I'll get some gas and take a try at Canada. Better to tend to such business myself. Taint safe to trust ta ennybody these days. Wonder now ef I could get a warrant. Guess not, seein' it's Canada. He's a sharper all right. He lit out to a safe place all right with his dame. Guess I'll have to go up. No other way. Have to put one over on him somehow and get him back where we can do something under the law of the United States." He swelled himself proudly at that as if he himself were a worthy citizen. Then he went to one of his haunts to prepare for the journey.

In her little nightgown beside her bed little Lib Knox knelt down for perhaps the first time in her life to pray. She had not wanted her supper though there were griddlecakes, and Lib dearly loved griddlecakes. But she had something on her mind, and her primitive soul took the old, old way to the only Power she knew for help.

"Oh, God," she prayed, "that's a bad man after my uncle, please, and I don't know where he is. Won't you just please take care of him? I don't know what he wants, but Uncle Darcy ought to be told he's coming, and I don't know how to do it. Won't You please try. I s'pose You can see in the dark and know where he is, and if You'll just please hide him when that man comes I'll be glad, and I'll try to do something for You."

She half rose in the darkness, shivering in her little thin gown that was too short for her growing length. Then she slid down on one knee again and spoke in a whisper:

"And say, God, You knew that was a lie I told, didn't You? That about Quebec? I just got it outta my geography lesson we had today, You know. I thought I oughtta tell You, seeing You're going to help. You won't mind a lie for once, will You? You see I had to or he mightta killed me. You wouldn't a wanted me killed, would You, God? Or else why did You make me? Besides, what would Mother 'uv done? So please won't You kill that naughty man if You can. If not, keep him away from me anyway. Good night."

Having paused a moment with a crown of moonlight on her little rebel curls, she crept into bed and was soon asleep.

The next morning Lib awoke very early, and, procuring a

paper and pencil from her geography, which she had placed under her bed the night before, she wrote in crooked little handwriting:

Dere Unkle Darcie:

Ther is a bad man cums here to find out whar you ar. He tuk me a rid on a motrsikle, I didunt lik it but I didunt let hym no. He thretend to kyl me if I didunt give hym yor adres, so I maid upp one and he brot me hom. I wisht that yoo wud cum home so I cud tak ker of yoo. It is offul hard takan ker when I don't no wher yoo ar.

I wish yoo wer hear. It is lonesum. From Lib.

P.S. I was skard, but he didunt no it.

Lib had found an envelope in the table downstairs, and she sealed the letter and took it to her father to address, but her father shook his head.

"I don't know, Lib. Uncle Darcy didn't leave his address. He's traveling, I reckon. But we'll send it where he goes sometimes."

And so the letter started on its warning way to Darcy.

Chapter 25

The winter had come on, introduced by a long and brilliant autumn, and Joyce was so engrossed in her work that she scarcely realized how long it was since she had left Meadow Brook.

In addition to her work she had become deeply engrossed in Bible study.

In one of her trips to the city she had discovered a Bible school of national renown, and found that she could so arrange her schedule as to make one or two evening classes a week possible. Thereafter when she was not actually busy with her schoolwork, or doing some little helpful thing for somebody else, she could be found studying her Bible. It had become a fascination, this searching for new riches in the Book. She had always enjoyed studying it, but never before with such a hunger for it as came now. Day by day gave her new wonders, a new opening up of the revelation of God to His children.

When Professor Harrington asked her to go somewhere with him he frequently found that she had another engagement in the city. Becoming curious, she finally took him to one of her classes, with the result that he entered into a lengthy argument with her all the way home, trying to persuade her to give it up. He informed her that it was ridiculous for her to waste her fine mind being led by men who ignored the simplest principles of science, and pinned their faith to a book that was so old that no one could be sure who wrote it, or where it came from. He told her that a person was a fool to swallow whole the teachings of men who denied geology, zoology, science in every branch; who taught that the legends of Scripture were actual truths; and who dared to enter into the occult and profess to have spiritual relations with the Maker of the Universe; who even descended to the ridiculous and marked out the future from the mystical writings of the men they chose to call prophets.

When he reached this point Joyce sat up straight in the train, her cheeks glowing, her eyes bright, so that those sitting near must have noticed her, and said:

"Stop! I cannot listen to any more of your talk. You and I simply have nothing in common!"

He saw that he had offended her, and sought to make his peace. He apologized and said they would speak of something else, and for the remainder of the half hour that the late train took in dragging from station to station till it reached Silverton, he made himself most fascinating, telling in his best style of a trip he took to Switzerland the summer before.

Ordinarily Joyce would have enjoyed this with all her eager young mind, visualizing the beautiful descriptions and putting herself there almost as if she had experienced it herself. But now she only sat quietly, looking straight ahead, a withdrawal in her manner, a look in her eyes as if she saw something that others could not see; an air that showed she was thinking deeply about something, and her thoughts were not following his words.

He was piqued and mortified. He could not believe that she would not yield to the things that she had often enjoyed before in his conversation. In fact, it had been a source of much pleasure to him to tell her of rare experiences he had had in travel and watch the flush of her cheek and the glow in her eye as she enjoyed it with him. It cut him that he could not reach her, that she had withdrawn her friendliness. It mortified his pride and his sense of superiority. And most of all it hurt him in his self-love. Perhaps he would have named it love for her, for he had come during the winter to recognize that that was what he felt for this girl; and seeing that was the case, he was the more determined to mold and make her as she should be to fit his walk and station in life. Albeit, his love for anyone was merely another name for self-love. He wanted her and her love merely to make himself more complete for himself, and so he was really in love with himself all the time.

For the rest of the ride Joyce was absolutely silent, and when they alighted at the station and started toward her home she said nothing, and she walked a trifle apart from him and ignored the arm he offered.

In a sudden yearning for his heart's desire, he took her hand and drew it within his arm, holding her hand in a firm warm grasp and speaking with a new tenderness.

"Joyce, don't you know why I have spoken to you as I have? Don't you know that it is because I love you, because I cannot bear to see your brilliant mind filled with such twaddle, such nonsense, such rot—!"

"Stop!" she cried, wrenching her hand away from his clasp. "Don't you ever dare to speak such words to me again! Don't dare to talk about the wonderful words of inspiration in that way. It is blasphemy!"

"Now, my dear child—" he began, trying to get possession of her hand once more, "you have wholly misunderstood me. The words of Scripture are just as beautiful to me, and just as sacred in their way as they are to you. It is a mere difference in the way of looking at them. Now I—"

"Mr. Harrington, I am not interested in how you look at the Bible. I would rather not hear you tell about it. You have filled me with horror."

"Are you not interested that I am telling you that I love you?" he asked in deep impassioned tones. "I am asking you now to be my wife? Cannot we put these trivial things away and be one in spirit now?" He leaned toward her gently and tried to capture the little gloved hand once more.

But Joyce quickly put her Bible in it and drew away from him.

"No!" she said. "No. We could never be one in spirit or in

anything else while you deny the inspiration of the Scriptures and call those wonderful expositions that we heard tonight rot and twaddle and nonsense. You are one of those people that it warns against in the Bible: 'Beware lest any man spoil you through philosophy and vain deceit, after the tradition of men, after the rudiments of the world, and not after Christ.' It also says: 'Avoiding profane and vain babblings, and oppositions of science, falsely so called.'"

"Now, Joyce, please don't quote Scripture at me. Let us drop that. If we love each other those things will settle themselves by and by. Let us talk a little while about ourselves. Tell me, you love me, Joyce, don't you? I'm sure I've seen it in your eyes."

"No," said Joyce frankly, "I don't think I do. I don't think it would be possible for me to love anyone who thought of the things that are the most precious to me in the way you do."

"But, those things aside, you really in your heart love me? Tell me you do, Joyce. I long to hear you say the words. Just speak out your own true heart. Once that question is settled, the other things will all fall in line."

"I can't put those things aside, Professor Harrington. They are a part of my soul. Nothing counts without them."

There was a long silence. They had almost reached Joyce's little home. He suddenly turned her about.

"Let us walk back down this next street. It is not late, and if you will not let me come into your house, at least we can walk a little longer. I must have this question settled tonight. I cannot let this separation go on between us any longer."

"The question so far as I am concerned is settled now," she said firmly.

"But, Joyce, if it were not for this difference? Suppose I thought as you do, would you say yes?"

Joyce hesitated. Theirs had been a pleasant companionship in a way.

"I cannot tell," she said thoughtfully. "It would have made so much difference, I cannot tell how I would have felt."

"There!" he said triumphantly. "You see, I was right. You do love me, only you are so filled with this fanaticism that you won't let yourself see it."

"You are mistaken," said Joyce gravely. "I have never even considered it, because from the first of my acquaintance I have known that you were this way."

"This way? *What way?*" he asked sharply. It hurt him to have her criticize him now, when he had declared his love for her. Joyce thought a moment.

"You do not believe. You do not understand the things of the Spirit. You base whatever faith you have on the wisdom of men, not in the power of God. Haven't you ever heard that the wisdom of this world is foolishness with God?"

"We are talking around in a circle," said Harrington crossly. "I was speaking of loving one another. From the moment I laid eyes upon you I knew that you were mine. Does it mean nothing to you that I came after you when I did not even know who you were? Does it mean nothing that the vision of your face stayed in my heart—"

"From the moment I laid eyes on you I knew that you were not mine," said Joyce suddenly. "It is getting very late. Hear! The clocks are striking twelve. I must go home this minute!" Her heart had suddenly gone into a panic. She wanted to get away by herself and think. Life was a strange thing. Was this man going to insist on being in her life?

Harrington, deeply offended, led her to her home in silence. She bade him good night and received a stiff good night in answer. He stalked away in the moonlight, a handsome picture of a man with a rising future, and much that was good and beautiful for a maiden to think upon. Yet she turned into her little warm room as to a haven, and knelt down by her couch.

"Oh, my dear heavenly Father! Keep me. Don't let me get bewildered by things. I don't want to love anyone now, please. And I know he isn't a right one to love."

From that night forth she unconsciously ceased to pray for him. It seemed somehow as if her duty were done there, and it was not for her to further seek his salvation. It seemed almost to her as if he desired her soul's destruction, so determined had he been to drag her away into his world. It almost frightened her when she thought about it. For several days thereafter she kept to herself as much as possible when at school.

For several days Harrington maintained a grave aloofness toward her, did not come to her room, nor appear in the hall when she would be likely to be about. When he needed to give a message to her he sent it through one of the seniors, or wrote a stiff note signing himself J. S. Harrington.

Joyce felt that she was being punished, and managed not to have to go to the office at all that week. She never had been a

frequenter of his office at any time, however, so that was
scarcely noticeable.

But one morning he happened to pass her room quite early,
before scarcely anybody had entered the building, and he
heard her singing softly to herself as she put the arithmetic
problems on the blackboard for the day.

> And He walks with me, and He talks with me,
>   And He tells me I am His own;
> Oh the joy we share as we tarry there
>   None other has ever known.

The words were the words of a hymn, he knew, one of those
he had once criticized as being "emotional twaddle," yet there
was something exquisitely lovely and dear in the way she sang
it, the perfect confidence of her soul in that One in whom she
trusted expressed in those simple words. He glanced at her
wistfully as he passed the door and took in all the slender grace
of her pose, as the white fingers, holding the chalk, made rapid
lines of figures on the board. The sun made a bright background of beaten gold, outlining the lovely head, and he
glanced back wistfully. Here was a rare girl indeed. Why, in
this age of progress, should it be that such a choice flower of
womanhood should be tainted with a primitive fanaticism? It
was as if she were a flower left over from the Victorian age, out
of place in a world that had grown beyond her—exquisite, yet
impractical. How could she possibly hope to get on in the
world with such notions?

In the calm reflections of the night—of several nights—in
which he had lain awake and gone over their last conversation,
he had chided himself severely for going so far. He simply must
not let himself go again, not until he was sure that he could
make her over. Never would it do for him to hamper his future
with one who was so utterly unadaptable to life as he found her
up to date. It simply would ruin his career.

Yet that afternoon he made a special trip to town to find a
certain book, one written in the vague modern shibboleth,
sweet and mystical, with the emphasis on loving one another,
and being able to see the good in everybody, and the next
morning, with a perfect rose just coming out of bud, she found
it lying on her desk. No name, just the rose and the book. Of
course she knew who put them there, but if she had not, his

smile and greeting as he passed her in the hall would have told her. And that day she prayed:

"Now, Father, help me. Keep me."

When Tyke came back from Canada there was vengeance in his eye. It had not taken him long to find out that there was no such street and number as Lib had given him, but he did not turn about and flee home without first examining every inch of the city where there might be a possible clue to Darcy. He went to the general delivery and asked for letters for Darcy Sherwood. He even stood for hours behind a pillar in the post office and watched the comers and goers, hoping to find Darcy among them. He walked over the city in daytime and at night, examined its haunts and amusements, looked over the hotel registries, and searched in a number of places where it seemed likely to him he might find his former partner, but no trace did he find of Darcy.

The first meeting with his three friends after his return was not very satisfactory. They chided him for his absence, derided him for going to Canada at all at the instigation of a sharp child, and charged him with trying to serve his own ends by the delay. They even went so far as to suggest that perhaps he was in with Darcy himself and this was all a big bluff. Tyke drew off and fairly bellowed at them in his wrath, and finally settled down to a plan which he said would bring things to a climax within a week. The four heads were bent together long over a paper on which Cottar was jotting down suggestions for Tyke to act upon. It was Tyke, after all, who was made to play the part out in the open. And once, while they were talking in a little shanty far away from the town, with a bit of a candle in an old lantern for light, and their paper spread out on a rough box, there came a face at the window, a long, white, thin old face with only two teeth, one above and one below; a long heavy wisp of snow-white hair straggling over a high yellow forehead, and watery, faded eyes, yet keen, watching them. It ducked down when Tyke lifted his head once and looked nervously that way as a twig rubbed up and down on the roof in the wind from the old apple tree outside, but the eyes peered up again and watched long and silently, listening; and crouched when the men put out the lantern and stole away into the night. It was only old Noah Casey, harmless and wandering about again, escaped from the poor farm, and traveling some of the old roads of his youth. Nobody minded old Noah, though he gave them a start now and then.

He was following a voice now, the voice he had heard loudest inside the shanty, the voice of the one with the red hair. Crouching low, he stole from tuft to tuft of the marshy grass, a thing of the night, old, flighty, his worn garment colorless like weathered wood, his wisps of hair blowing like gray clouds about his mild, anxious face from under the tattered felt hat. A bent old gnome in the dark, with something on his mind.

Chapter 26

Along in the early spring one night just as Eugene and Nan were about to retire, the telephone bell rang and a man's voice asked if Mr. Massey was at home, and if he could see someone on important business connected with his cousin Miss Radway.

Eugene was immediately excited, and fairly shouted into the telephone, demanding to know who was speaking.

"That's all right, pard. I ain't tellin' all I know over the wire. Alone now? I'll drop around. This is absolutely Q.T., you know."

Nan stood trembling in the doorway, white-faced, frightened.

"You go to bed!" ordered Eugene, trying to still the excitement of his own voice, and getting up to pace the room nervously. "Go to bed, I say!" he roared as Nan still stood in the doorway watching him.

There was a wild look in his eye that made her afraid of him sometimes. He had been hard toward her ever since she falteringly told him of her visit to the minister, and he had looked at her as if she had been a viper and answered her only:

"You FOOL! If you could only learn to keep your mouth shut! Yes, weep. WEEP! That's your line! Oh, why did I marry a fool?"

Since that day Nan had kept much to herself, and not ventured to take any part in the frantic search for Joyce that was still going on in a stealthy way. Now, at the look in her husband's eye, she vanished, sobbing softly to herself, went hurriedly up the stairs and flung herself noisily on the bed. A moment later she rose stealthily, removed her shoes and prepared to listen to whatever went on downstairs. Her heart was beating so wildly that she had put her hand on it, it almost hurt.

Eugene forestalled any attempt on her part to listen by closing the doors of the sitting room, and her only possibility of finding out anything lay in the back staircase or in watching out the window.

The night was dark and a ghoulish wind was roaring about the house, a real March night with dark clouds driven across a starless sky. She could not even see the stealthy figure like a flat shadow that slid across the open space before the door and flattened against the side of the house some minutes before the knock that echoed so slightly she almost thought she was mistaken. She heard the door open and blow shut with a gust of wind, and there were voices, low murmurs, that was all. She strained her ears to hear, for she felt sure Gene would not tell her anything. He said she was a fool and he could not trust her.

Downstairs, in the sitting room, Tyke stood flat against the wall by the door and ordered Gene to pull down the shades. This done, he selected a seat in the darkest corner of the room and motioned Gene to a seat in front of him.

"You plumb sure thar ain't no one lis'nen in on us?" he asked, eyeing the various doors.

"Positive," said Gene, eyeing his caller suspiciously. This man of course wanted money, and he wasn't a very pleasant looking customer. Perhaps he ought to have sent for a policeman and had him in hiding. Yet there might be something he would not have wanted a policeman to know. No, rather take the chances himself. He glanced nervously toward the telephone to make sure he could reach it from where he sat in case he needed it. Nan, of course, would be worse than useless in an emergency. Still, perhaps he had made a mistake in sending her to bed. However, he felt pretty sure she would manage to find a cranny to listen, and when he heard a soft creaking on the back stairs and saw Tyke start nervously, he made no move.

"It's only a mouse in the wall," he said. "Go on."

'Well, I came here purely out o' kin'ness," began Tyke ingratiatingly, his eyes roving from door to window and back again. "I'm 'war I'm doin' a dangerous thing; an' I'm riskin' m'life. The man we gotta deal with is a desp'rate feller, an' he wouldn't stop at nothin'. We gotta work still as death ur we won't get nowheres. Now, to begin, 'bout how long uv you ben sure your young woman relative was kidnapped?"

"Kidnapped!" said Gene with a start. "Kidnapped. Yes. Why—" Then it was money the man wanted. "Why—I've been coming slowly to that conclusion for some time. Haven't been able to prove it yet of course—That is—" Here, he was telling too much himself. He oughtn't to tell this man anything. He ought to let the man do all the talking.

"Well, I kin," said Tyke, unconsciously raising his voice a trifle. "Got four good witnesses 'sides myse'f to prove it in court. Know the very day an' hour when it happened. We all seen the body, and one of us seen him buryin' her."

"Body!" exclaimed Gene, jumping up, white to the lips. "Burying!"

"Sit still, man! Keep yer shirt on! We don't get nowheres carryin' on with them highstrikes. Somebody might be round an' hear ya. You can't never tell. You gotta learn to keep quiet ef you wantta hear what I got ta say."

"Go on," said Gene with dry lips and stiff articulation. The horror of it froze his senses. In spite of him his mother's face came reproachfully between him and the stranger. What had he done to Joyce? How had he been responsible for all this that had happened to her? He was not a bad man. He did not want her inheritance at the expense of her life. He was merely a selfish man. This girl was his own blood and kin, and he was responsible for her safety. Fear sat upon his face. What might not come to him when the town heard this?

But the stranger was asking him a question.

With an effort he pulled himself back to attend.

"Just when did you say you seen her last? April? Twenty-four? Yep. That's the day. Long toward evenin' wasn't it? She went down acrost lots to her yants grave, didn't she? What say? You didn't know that? Oh, I thought—well, it don't matter. That's where she went, and he met her thar. Must uv had a date. He was waitin' there for her. You see we was doin' some work there round a lot, in the cem'try, me an' a couppla others, an' when we got back home we found we hadta go 'nother place next day so we walks back t'get our tools we'd lef' hid. Seein' there was somebody there seemin' to be feelin' bad— she was cryin' real hard, an' he was coaxin' her—we didn't like to intrude, so we set awhile under the hedge thinkin' he'd get away. We knowed him, ya know, a great one with the dames.

They always fall fer him, no matter what they are! Pretty soon we see 'em walk away down a piece to the road jes' as we thought they would, only she was talkin' fast, an' cryin'. Still we didn't think nothin' of it, knowin' him an' all, till suddenly we seen him pick her up strugglin' and chuck her into a notymobile he had standin' there, an' fore we could sense what was goin' on they was off down the road.

"We talked it over an' we come to the conclusion it was just a little quarrel they was havin' an' none o' our business. But two days after that Billy he missed one o' his wedges, an' he reckoned he musta lef' it up to the cem'try, so we all decides to walk up, bein' a pleasant evenin', jus' fer the walk. On the way we talked about the girl we'd seen an' decided to look at the headstone an' see if we could make out if she was a relative of ennybody we knowed. I ain't from Meadow Brook myself but I got frien's buried up there. But when we come in sight o' the cem'try we seen that there car thar again, jus' in the same place, kinda hid like behind the alders, backed down off the road, an' we listened, an' heard the ring of a spade. We thought that was queer, an' we clum the bank an' stole round to the back of the cem'try where we could see. We hadta go awful still, cause he stopped every now an' agen to listen, but we fin'lly got where we could see, an' he was diggin' a grave!"

Gene caught his breath and Tyke sat watching him cautiously to see just how far he could go with his tale.

"Thur was a long bundle did up in a carridge robe layin' on the ground, and bime bye when he'd dug a long time he turns around and he listens, an' then he snaps on his flashlight, an' turns back the cloth an' there was 'er face, jes' as plain, same girl as we'd seen settin' on the grave, only dead as a doornail. Her face shone bright in his light an' we couldn't make no mistake. Then he covers up her face an' snaps off the light and rolls her into the hole, an' we could hear the dirt bein' shovelled down in again, an' me an' my pards were weak as little babies. We couldn't do nothin', jes' lay in the grass there an' never moved till we heard his autymobile chugging' down the road. We was most too scared to speak then. An' we got away acrost the fields an' never come home till mornin' we was so plumb scared.

"We was tryin' to figger out what to do, but next thing we heard the girl had went away visitin', an' we figgered it out that what you didn't know wouldn't never make you all feel bad, so we kep' our mouths shet. But here lately, I ain't ben sleepin' well. Keep a dreamin' I see that there girl with her purty white face a cryin' out to me fer justice to be done on that there feller, an' I made up my mind I wouldn't hold back no longer, I'd tell you the truth, an' you kin do what you like about it. My han's is washed clean, enyhow. But if you all want ter prosecute him it's a clear case of murder in the first degree, an' we'll all stan' by ya."

"But you haven't told me who the man is," said Gene, his breath coming fast and his eyes taking on a wild look. "Murder! Think of it! To one of our family!"

"Why, I 'sposed you knowed a course. Ain't he ben comin' here to see her? I knowed he was here the night after he took her away 'cause I seen him myself, follered him to the gate. Fact, there ain't been much happened to him sence that I ain't knowed 'bout. Had him watched, ya know. Can't take no chances with a feller like that. Why, his name is Sherwood. Darcy Sherwood. Great baseball pitcher. Often had his name in the paper. That kind takes the girls ya know."

"Darcy Sherwood! Of course!" said Gene. "Where is he now? I'll get out a warrant for arrest tonight."

"Well, that's the rub," said Tyke uneasily. "You see he got away a few days back. He's ben keepin' close, and been away a lot, but he musta got onto it that we had him spotted fer he made tracks fer Canada. I follered him up there, but found he'd left, given a wrong address an' all that. But he's back somewheres in this neighborhood. I'm sure o' that. You jes' wantta put it in the han's of the p'lice an' you'll get yer party all right, all right! Better not tell who yer witnesses are till ya get him safe an' sound in jail, though. He mighta got onto the fact of who we are an' cleared out."

Gene's mind had run rapidly ahead of the visitor's words. He was thinking fast what he had to do.

"We must dig up the grave and find the body," he said, speaking rapidly. "You can locate it, of course."

"Sure. We can locate her all right; but it ain't no use diggin' it up. Didn't I tell ya that part? This other party, this fourth man I was speakin' of fer a witness, he ain't one of my bunch at all. He was just goin' through the medder adjoinin' next night after the burryin' an' he heard a sound of a spade and he steps to the hedge curious like to see who was diggin' a grave that time o' night, it was still kinda light, an' he sees this feller diggin' her up, an' presently he takes up the big roll an' carries it away in a car. Got scared likely. Thought somebody was onto

him, an' didn't dast leave her there. My man went an' looked
in the hole after he was gone an' there wasn't nothing there but
broken glass. After that we went too, an' it's all true just as he
sez. So he's got away with it all good an' slick. He's an awful
slick feller. I knowed him back in France. I got an idea where
he may have hid her though. There's more'n one graveyard
round these diggin's."

Late that night Eugene let Tyke out the back door, and he
stole away into the mists like some creeping thing to hide. But
Eugene walked the floor all night, his white face drawn and
pinched, his eyes bloodshot and looking like hidden fires.
There was something more than revenge working in Eugene
Massey's heart. There was conscience. One cannot have a
mother like Mary Massey without having to suffer for it sometime or other, if one has wandered away from her teachings.

And all night long Nan lay in her bed with wide-open eyes
and tried to piece together the few words she had overheard
from her perch on the back stairs, and make sense out of
them—lay and dreaded the coming of the morning.

Chapter 27

One evening late in March Joyce was coming out from the Bible school on the way to her train. She had omitted the second
class that evening because she had papers to correct when she
got home and it would keep her up very late if she waited until
the late train.

As she came into the street a gust of wind caught her hat and
flung it along the pavement. She darted out after it, and after
quite a race captured it, but not till several large drops of rain
had fallen in her face. She turned to hurry toward the station.
It was not a long walk, and she usually preferred to do it on foot
rather than to wait for trolleys, which were few and far between on that side street. But it was all too evident that a storm
was upon her. Dust and papers and litter were being blown
along in the gutter, and the wind lifted in wild swoops and
banged signs and shutters and any loose object in sight. People
hurried to cover, umbrellas were raised and lowered quickly, or

the wind seized them and turned them inside out. People in automobiles hurriedly fastened on side curtains, and the street was almost deserted in a trice.

Joyce turned to see if a car was coming, but none was in sight. She held her hat, and ducking her head, hurried on as fast as she could fly, but at the second corner the wind took her and almost tore her from the sidewalk. It was with difficulty she regained her footing and huddled by some steps with her hand on a building to steady her. Then the rain fell in torrents, and she turned and scurried blindly into an open doorway a few feet away.

Other people had taken refuge there also, they were crowding in and Joyce was pushed with the throng inside the door, not knowing what kind of a place she was entering. But there were other women in the company, caught in the storm as was she, so she was not frightened. Before she had opportunity to look around and know where she was a burst of song broke about her:

> Free from the law! O happy condition!
> Jesus hath bled and there is remission!
> Cursed by the law, and bruised by the fall.
> Christ hath redeemed us once for all.
>
> Once for all, O sinner, receive it!
> Once for all, O brother, believe it!
> Cling to the cross, the burden will fall,
> Christ hath redeemed us once for all.

It was a religious meeting of some sort, right there in the heart of the city!

She pressed in at last where she could stand behind the last row of chairs next to the aisle and see the platform. A piano was there and a girl playing the hymn. A young man was playing on a cornet, and there were singers and some men seated in chairs behind a low desk table.

She forgot that she was missing her train in her deep interest in the meeting, and her own voice joined eagerly in the old hymn she had known ever since she could remember:

> Now we are free—there's no condemnation,
> Jesus provides a perfect salvation:
> 'Come unto me,' oh, hear His sweet call,
> Come, and He saves us, once for all.

Her eyes swept over the congregation. Men and women and children were there, people of plain dress, mostly, some young giddy children of the street, some old men in worn garments, a few tired-looking women, not many mighty. Back by the door, caught as herself in the storm were a few better-dressed people, in luxurious furs and velvets, people obviously amused at their surroundings, as they would have been equally amused if they had dropped into an opium joint for the moment, or a traveling circus, or a Hindu temple, or any other alien environment.

But Joyce felt that she had dropped in on home and her heart went out in the song:

> 'Children of God,' oh, glorious calling,
> Surely His grace will keep us from falling:
> Passing from death to life at His call,
> Blessed salvation once for all.

The congregation rustled into their seats with the closing chorus and gave Joyce a full view of the people on the platform. A man with a good voice that could be heard out in the street was speaking now. He said:

"Before you go home I want you to listen to somebody else a moment. A dear brother came to me tonight wanting to tell me what Christ had done for him, and I have asked him if he will tell you what he told me. He says he is not a public speaker, but when I put it to him that he might help somebody else he consented."

Someone stepped to the front of the platform and began to speak. A man just in front of Joyce rose up at that instant and put on his overcoat, and she could not see the platform for a moment, but the voice rang into her soul like a song of long ago.

"I don't like to talk about myself," said the speaker, "never did, but when your leader showed me a verse in my new Bible that said: 'If thou shalt confess with thy mouth the Lord Jesus, and shalt believe in thine heart that God hath raised him from the dead, thou shalt be saved!' I had to do what he asked, because I *believe*, and I want to *confess*."

Joyce's heart stood still with wonder and then went flying on in great glad leaps and bounds. There could not be two voices like that one. She stretched her neck to see, and when the man ahead of her sat down, there was Darcy Sherwood standing on the platform, with a new grave look upon his face, and he was saying the most wonderful thing:

"I've been a sinner all my life, but I never knew it until one day God sent a woman to look into my eyes and ask me what I was doing. I was in the bootlegging business then and doing pretty well. It had never occurred to me that there was anything like what you'd call sin about it. But it began to seem as if somehow God had got into the woman's eyes and was looking at me. I saw that the breaking of the law of the land that had been made for the good of the land was a sin. I was a lawbreaker and I was a sinner. And somehow that sin grew until it was the heaviest thing I had to carry around.

"I gave up bootlegging right away that night, but somehow that didn't seem to make any difference. The sin was there just the same and it grew heavier and heavier on my soul. I never knew I had a soul before that.

"I heard a Bible story read long ago about a blind man, and there was one verse I always remembered. It said: 'If ye were blind, ye should have no sin: but now ye say, We see; therefore your sin remaineth.'

"I began to see that was just like me. I had always prided myself on seeing what was right and doing it. I had been a law to myself. But now I saw that was all wrong. I had no right to make my own laws. There had to be somebody wiser than I who could make the laws for everybody.

"I bought a Bible and began to read, and presently I began to see that there was something else back of it all that I hadn't got at all yet. There was something bigger than federal laws. I had broken the law of the land and I could go and pay the penalty of that and wipe it out, but there was a higher law, a law of the universe, that my spirit had been breaking, and I didn't see any way to wipe out that debt, pay that penalty. In fact, I didn't know that higher law, and how was I to keep from breaking it?

"Then one day I came on a verse that said: 'And this is his commandment, that we should believe on the name of his son Jesus Christ.'

"There it was! I hadn't been doing that, and I was a sinner. I could see how God would be very angry with me about that. God, to be a God, holy and good and all that a real God would be, and I a little creature setting up myself to not believe on Him! It really seemed a reasonable offense. As I thought about it, it seemed greater than killing anybody, or robbing a bank, or forging, or any of the things we count sins in the world. It seemed—well—so contemptible in me. And the more I felt it, the more I didn't like the feeling, and I kept on reading my Bible.

"My Bible is a pretty nice kind of a Bible. I suppose you all know about it. It is called a Scofield Bible and it has little explanations and notes here and there that lead you on and that let you in on the meaning of a word in the original Hebrew or Greek, and make it a lot plainer to a beginner like me. By and by, after I had worried about my sin a lot, I found that I didn't need to worry at all—that my sin had all been prepared for, and the penalty paid; that Jesus Christ had set me free from the law of sin and death, and all I had to do was accept my pardon and go out unburdened.

"Well, there isn't much more to tell. I took it. You better believe I did! If you had been as unhappy as I was you wouldn't have wasted a minute in taking a pardon like that. Why don't you, by the way, if you never have? It pays. I'm here to tell you it pays *above everything else I've ever tried.* If you don't see it, just try it anyway, and you'll find out."

The audience rose to join in the closing hymn, and during that and the benediction Joyce's heart was in a tumult of joy. She could not see the platform because the two men who stood in front of her were unusually tall, and some people had come in and were standing in the aisle beside her, crowding her from her position, but the instant the benediction was over she set herself to get up that aisle somehow. However, she might as well have attempted to throw herself out to sea when the tide was coming in. It was impossible to make any progress, and finally she slipped into the backseat and decided to wait. She must see Darcy at any risk, no matter if she lost the next train. She must tell him how glad she was!

There was a crowd around the platform. Likely people had come up to speak to him. His words rang over again in her heart as she waited, her eyes lighted with a great joy. At last the crowd thinned and she managed to work her way through and get to the front, but as she did so she saw several men going out a door back of the platform, and when she arrived there was but one man left up there, seemingly a janitor, picking up the books. Her heart sank.

"Oh, can you tell me where the speakers have gone? I must see one of them a minute, that last man, Mr. Sherwood!" she cried eagerly.

"Him? Oh, he went while they was singin', lady, he'd to ketch a train. I showed him the way to the station. Good, wa'n't he? Beats all what the Lord does when He gets a chance at a soul—"

But Joyce had gone, down the aisle with swift steps, out into the street where it was still raining briskly, and the water pouring along the gutter in deep angry tides. She paid no heed. She fled along on winged feet, across the water, down another block; wet and breathless, she arrived at last at the station.

She did not glance at the clock to see if she had missed her train; she hurried out to the gates, and scanned every entrance to a train, but the man was just closing the gate and slipping down the sign for the New York express, which was moving away in the distance, and there was no other train sign up except her own, the last one out to Silverton that night. She glanced at the clock. There were three minutes before it left. She cast a despairing glance around. He was probably gone on that train to New York and she had missed her chance of telling him how glad she was. She must go home of course. She would be in a terrible predicament if she missed that train, and had to stay in the station all night, for she had no money for lodging and would not have known where to go if she had. And there were her examination papers.

The guard had his hand on the gate and his eye on the clock. She hurried through the gates and onto the train, sinking into a seat just as the train began to move, and feeling a rush of bitter disappointment so deep she could hardly restrain the tears.

Yet beneath it all, as she put her head down on her hand and tried to control her feelings, there was a deep gladness. Her prayers had been answered. Darcy had found the way home. The horror of that night in the cemetery was all cleared away. She had her friend once more, whether he ever knew it or not.

Afterward, while the wheels were turning in a drowsy tune, and the sleepy passengers, with closed eyes, were trying to snatch a bit of rest on the way, her heart woke up and began to tell over to her every word that he had spoken, every precious look that showed his heart was changed, every intonation of the voice she had known so long. And to think the Lord had used her to make him listen to God's voice! Oh, it was too dear, too wonderful!

The look of glory stayed on her face the next morning as she came blithely through the hall at school and met the young professor.

"You look as though you had fallen heir to a fortune," he said sourly, as though he begrudged her her happy heart.

"Why, I have," she said brightly and smiled.

"Can't you share it?" he said wistfully.

"I'm afraid not," she said gently. "It wouldn't share. You wouldn't understand."

"How do you know I wouldn't?" he said crossly.

"Oh," she tried to explain. "It's just—that I've heard from home." Her eyes were all alight.

"Oh!" he said rudely, and turned away.

"There's another man in Meadow Brook," he told himself gloomily. "I must do something about this right away. I'm a fool, but I can't help it."

At recess time he entered Joyce's classroom with a smile and handed her a newspaper still in its wrapper.

"Here's a paper from Meadow Brook that just came in the mail. I thought perhaps it might interest you. There's a boy in high school there who persists in thinking that I'm interested in their baseball team, and every time they win a game I get a sheaf of papers. Of course they don't interest me. I hardly remember the names of people there anymore. I was there so short a time."

Joyce thanked him and put the paper in her desk for a leisure moment, going on with the blackboard exercise she was writing. Harrington was disappointed. He had hoped she would open the paper in his presence, and he might perhaps get some clue to her interest in Meadow Brook, but she was as cool and disinterested as a lily. Well, he must find a way to keep her in his company, there was no other way. It was against all his principles to be too attentive until he felt she was worthy of his position, but there seemed to be no other way, with her. It was perhaps, after all, a proof that she was really worthwhile that she held herself aloof. Or could it possibly be subtlety? No, he decided not. Her religion was genuine, and that would preclude subtlety. Well, at least her method had shown him his own heart, and now he must find a way to win out, for it was getting toward spring and he must have this matter settled before he went away on his vacation. He had an eye to another larger school with better pay. It would be an advantage to him to have it known that he was engaged to a personable young woman. It was a wealthy community, where he was hoping to be called, and Joyce would shine in such society with a little tutoring from him, always providing of course that he could rid her of her ridiculous fanaticism.

Chapter 28

That morning Darcy received Lib Knox's letter.

He was passing through a city where he had been in the habit of receiving mail, and he stopped to see if anything was in the box for him, and to pay his box rent and give it up. There he found the letter.

His face grew tender and stern as he read. Dear little brave Lib. Well he knew who the bad man with red hair must be, but how did Tyke ever find out Lib? Some deviltry somewhere. But one thing was certain, he must abandon his plans and go home to protect her. He would take Tyke out in the open somewhere and give him a lesson if necessary.

He glanced at the date on the letter and frowned. Already he had been in ignorance too long. There was time enough for any number of things to have happened to Lib, and well he knew that Tyke was a bad man. To the warning concerning his own welfare he paid no heed whatever, passing over Lib's solicitude for him with a tender smile.

More alarmed than he cared to own even to himself, he studied up timetables and took the first train that would make connections for Meadow Brook. He must tell Mason to look after Lib better. They were too careless with that child. As soon as his quest was over he must try and do something about Lib. She wasn't being brought up in the right way. She wasn't being taught right and wrong. She was too much on her own, just as he had been. That must all be changed.

So he boarded the train for home, and on the way he closed his eyes and tried to exercise his new power of prayer. What he was praying for was that he might find Joyce Radway, and as the train rumbled along he began to think to himself that perhaps, after all, he had been a fool. He had got interested in his quest as a quest and had not remembered that it might by this time be unnecessary. For aught he knew she might have reached home.

Still, there was Dan Peterson. Dan always knew about where to find him within a few days, and there had been no word from Dan all along the line.

He closed his eyes and tried to pray. He was just learning to pray, and since he had read the promises to those who prayed and believed, he had spent much time upon this one petition: "Oh, God, help me to find Joyce and keep her safely."

It was dark when Darcy reached Meadow Brook. He had come by a way of his own and had not seen anyone he knew. He took the shortcut across by the railroad and in at the back gate, and so entered the house from the kitchen door.

His sister was sitting by the dining room table with her head upon her arms, crying in the dark. Lib was standing with her face flattened against the windowpane, the slow tears coursing down her cheeks. Darcy reached up and turned the light on, blinking at them wonderingly. His first startled thought was that Mase must be dead. He put out a hand gently and laid it on Ellen's bowed head. Good, simple Ellen!

Ellen lifted her head and saw him and screamed, dropping her face down again upon her folded arms and breaking into renewed sobs. But Lib ran to him and threw her arms around his neck, burying her wet little face on his shoulder.

It was so he learned what had come to him, sitting in a dining room chair beside his sister with his hand upon her bowed head and little Lib in his lap, her face against his breast, sobbing as her mother told the story brokenly. Mase, she said, was out trying to see a lawyer and find out what to do. But there wasn't anything to do. Everybody said there wasn't anything to do. The case was all against him.

Darcy took the blow straight with white, stern face and steady eyes. The hand that held little Lib's did not tremble and his voice did not shake. The thing he was thinking was:

"Now I shall have to stop hunting for Joyce. Oh, God, take care of Joyce!"

But he opened his lips and said: "Well, Ellen, don't take it so hard! It's all in the day's work, and it'll all come out in the wash. Anyhow, Ellen, I've found a new line. God isn't forgetting any of us and you just put that away and think about it."

Ellen sat up and wiped her eyes and stared at him. This was strange talk from Darcy, and yet it was like him. She broke out afresh with indignant tears that they should fasten a crime so heinous on this beloved brother. She was engulfed, overwhelmed by the shame and disgrace that had befallen them. She was old enough to have remembered their gentle mother who always tried to keep them "respectable."

"Never mind, Ellen, don't cry anymore. Give me a bite to eat and I'll go out and see what can be done."

"Oh, but you mustn't go out!" cried Ellen, and little Lib gripped him fiercely. "You mustn't! They'll get you. They're looking everywhere for you."

"That's all right," said Darcy cheerfully. "I'll help them. I'll go and give myself up."

And go he would in spite of all their efforts. He went away whistling down the street, just as he always did when he was at home. Whistling!

So first he went to the police headquarters and walked in as he had done many a time before, and they stared at him:

"I understand you're looking for me?" he said gravely with a new dignity about him they scarcely understood.

"Yes," said the chief, embarrassedly, almost deferentially, for Darcy had been almost like one of themselves. "Yes."

"Well. Here I am."

They scarcely knew what to say to him. They treated him like a gentleman, a stranger. It cut him the way they went about it. They were not his friends anymore. It seemed that they were afraid of him, as if they did not know how to take him. They had been prepared for rebellion, subterfuge. He gave none. He was his old grave self, with the old winning smile as he met them, his eyes upon them with the old question in them, the wistfulness. It disarmed them. They would have rather had to fight with him.

And by and by he asked to see Dan Peterson. He would find out if he had any friends left.

Joyce did not remember the Meadow Brook newspaper again after she had put it into her desk, for almost two weeks. It lay under a pile of copy books that were awaiting marks and she had been too busy to get at them. But one morning during study period she found time and drew them out and there was the newspaper. She took it out and was about to throw it in the wastebasket, realizing how much out of date it must be. Then a longing overcame her to see some of the old familiar names again, and she slipped off the wrapper and decided to take just a moment to look it over before throwing it away.

It was well that the top of her desk was raised and that the eyes of her young pupils were occupied with their work, for the letters that met her gaze flaring across the top of the paper in the blackest of type made her gasp and turn white. They almost shouted at her as she read:

BASEBALL IDOL IN TROUBLE!

DARCY SHERWOOD WANTED ON CHARGE OF ABDUCTION AND MURDER OF JOYCE RADWAY

Who left her home in Meadow Brook one year ago and has not been heard from since.

The article went on to state that there were eyewitnesses to the murder and burial of the girl who were willing to testify in the case. It was also rumored that Eugene Massey, the cousin of the murdered girl, had located the grave and exhumed the body which had been identified by portions of clothing worn when Miss Radway left her home. Meantime, Darcy Sherwood had also mysteriously disappeared, some said to Canada, and a reward was offered for any knowledge of him; although it was also stated that the detectives had been right on his track for months, and could easily locate and produce him when he was needed.

For a moment Joyce thought she was going to faint. It went through her mind to wonder if Harrington had known what was in the paper when he gave it to her and took this way to let her know it. But she rejected the idea instantly. His manner had been too pleasant and altogether intimate for that. He was one who could never brook a thing like this publicity in an intimate friend. His life was too well ordered and conventional to make it possible to treat a girl just the same as ever if he knew anything like this had been connected with her name. Her next impulse was to hide the paper where no eye could ever see it. She folded it quickly into a thick square and stuffed it into her handbag. As she did so its date caught her eye, and her heart froze within her. It was more than two weeks back. What might not have happened in that time? Darcy in such awful trouble and she, the only one who could help him, chained to these children.

Chapter 29

Joyce cast a helpless look around at the busy little figures behind their desks. She glanced at the clock. It was only half past nine. There was a train to the city in three quarters of an hour. She must make it. She would have to go home for money, too, and to change some of her things. She must get someone to take her place, and she must manage it so that no one would ask her any questions. Her brain seemed fairly burning up with the rapidity of her thoughts.

Miss Beatty was a retired teacher who lived not far away and who sometimes substituted when a teacher was ill. Would she be at home now, and free? And how could she get out to telephone her?

With fingers that trembled so that she could hardly move her pencil she wrote a little note to the teacher of the senior high school class and sent it by one of the children. It read:

"Dear Miss Clayton: Can you let me have Mary Grover to keep order for a little while? I am obliged to be out of the room."

Mary Grover appeared in three or four minutes. Meantime Joyce had summoned her senses and picked up everything she did not want to leave in her desk, and slipped out to the telephone booth in the hall. She dared not take the time to run across the street to the drugstore for more privacy. While she waited for her number she prayed that the Lord would arrange the way before her. Her head was throbbing so that she could scarcely see, and her heart beating wildly. She did not dare to think except just about getting to the train. It seemed if she did, that she would have to cry out and shout the horror of her soul at what had happened.

Queer that at such a time our breathless minds will pick out trivialities and dwell upon them. During that tense moment while she waited for her answer it came to Joyce how Professor Harrington would smile in his cynical way if he knew what she was doing, and ask her, didn't she think Miss Beatty would be home just the same if she didn't pray? Then Miss Beatty's precise voice echoed reassuringly over the wire. "Yes? Ellen

Beatty at the phone!" and Joyce, with a thrill of triumph, spoke in her trembling voice:

"Oh, Miss Beatty, I'm so glad you are there! I hope you aren't busy. This is Miss Radway at the school. I've had bad news from home and I must catch this next train. *Could* you take my place?"

"Why, yes, I think so," answered the kindly voice. "I'm very sorry—"

But Joyce cut her off quickly:

"Oh, thank you, then. Will you come over at once? I'm leaving directions on the desk, and Mary Grover is with the class till you get here. I haven't a minute. Good-bye."

She wrote a hurried note to Harrington there in the telephone booth:

> I have had bad news from home and must go at once.
> Miss Beatty is taking my place. Did not want to disturb
> your class, and had not a minute to wait. Will telegraph if
> I cannot get back tomorrow. Sincerely, Joyce Radway.

She slipped back to her own room and dispatched this note by another delighted child, got her hat from the dressing room and got away before Harrington had had time to even open her note. She ran all the way home, hastily changed her dress, put a few things into her little briefcase that she had bought at a bargain counter to carry her papers in back and forth to school, and arrived at the station with three or four minutes to spare and a tumult in her heart that demanded an opportunity to cry.

Those three or four minutes seemed longer than the whole preceding three-quarters of an hour, and she walked to the far end of the platform and kept her eye out toward the street. She somehow had a feeling that Harrington would not like it that she had not consulted him before going, and she was almost sure if he could make it that he would come down to the train. But it had happened that Harrington was busy with three guests from another school, committeemen sent out to size him up, and Joyce's note lay harmlessly on his desk for half an hour before he even had an opportunity to read it. Even then his mind was so filled with wondering if he had made the right impression that he scarcely took it in except to be annoyed, for he had purposed taking the guests in to Joyce's room to show it off, intending later, if matters developed sufficiently to whisper a suggestion that she might be the future Mrs. Harrington. It was very annoying of Joyce not to consult him. He would punish her for that by coldness for a few days. She was altogether too prone to take matters into her own hands. That's what came of having an independent religion that taught one to think in unconventional lines. He had no thought of her trouble. He didn't take that in. But Joyce was riding away into the morning and facing the awful facts that had called her from her work. Facing the possibilities that might be ahead of her.

Suppose they had found Darcy and had the trial! There had been time enough for that she supposed. Supposing they had convicted him! But how could they when it was all false? Still, if such things could be published in the paper when they were not true, what might not happen? Law was a strange thing. Would they have hung him? Or electrocuted him? Did they do those things so soon after the trial? The paper had spoken of eyewitnesses. False witnesses of course. How could they be true since the thing never happened? And what was Gene doing in it all? The paper had spoken of Gene. She hardly dared to get it out again and read it over lest someone should read it over her shoulder. It seemed so terrible to see Darcy's name in such connection. Darcy who had just given himself to Christ, who had made over his life. And this to meet him at the outset. It was enough to make some lose their faith. Not Darcy. Oh, not Darcy! She cradled the thought of him like a child in her prayers as the miles crept by and the morning went on.

By and by the train stopped suddenly with a jerk and a groan and after one or two attempts to creep a few steps, lay there for a long time. She remembered dimly that some such thing had happened on her way up. She wondered idly if it were a part of every day's journey? Her impatience leaped ahead anxiously. Oh, if she were only there!

At last the train started on again and suddenly she realized that she must plan what she would do when she got there. Should she go home and send for the police, or should she go and try to find Darcy? She had no idea where he lived now, and if he were at home he would probably be in jail unless he had been able to prove that he was innocent. Then suddenly she thought of Judge Peterson. He would know what to do. He was a judge. She would go straight to his house. Afterward she would have to go home and explain her absence and what she was doing, she supposed, but that could take care of itself. She had Darcy now to think about.

She had hoped to get the noon train from the city out to
Meadow Brook, but when she reached her home city her train
was so late that there was no Meadow Brook train till quarter of
two. Then her impatience could wait no longer and she called
up Judge Peterson's house.

At first she could get no answer, but just as she was about to
give up in despair a gruff voice said: "Hello! Dan Peterson at
the phone."

"Oh," said Joyce in a relieved little voice. "Then is the judge
there? I would I like to speak to him a moment please."

"No. He isn't here. He's over at the courthouse. Everybody's
over there. I just happened to run home for some papers. Who
is this?"

"This is Joyce Radway." Joyce's voice was all of a tremble.
What if she should be too late after all. What if the trial was
days ago?

"What! Joyce! Oh, *Glory!* Is that really you, Joyce? Where
are you? In town? Say, take the 'L' and I'll meet you at Sixty-
third Street with the car. You're wanted here, you certainly
are. And say, you there yet? Say, don't talk to anybody on the
way out! Mind that! What's that? In time? Oh, sure the nick of
time. Couldn't be better. All right. Get a hustle on. I'll meet
you."

Joyce hung up the receiver and hurried out to the elevated
train, her heart beating high with hope.

Dan dashed out to his car and rattled over to the courthouse,
sent a note up to the judge's desk and waited by the door. The
message came up.

> Say, Dad: The dead has come to life. Have her here in
> half an hour. Where do you want me to bring her? Here or
> over home?
>
> Dan

The message came back with one word written across the
back:

"Here."

But a light flashed from the eye of father to son as Dan
turned to dash out again.

Dan almost upset a small, forlorn figure pressed close to the
swinging, leathern doors, with woebegone look and white,
tearstained cheeks.

"Hello there, kid, did I hurt you?" He paused in his wild

rush to set her on her feet again. "Why, little Lib Knox, is this you?" he said tenderly, discovering her identity and the tear streaks on her cheeks. "This is no place for you, child. Come on, take a ride with me."

But Lib drew a sigh of sobbing and held back.

"No, I gotta stay here," she said. "I gotta stay here an' help my Uncle Darcy."

"Come on, then, an' we'll help him." He swept her under one arm and marched away, she wearily resisting. "Listen, kid, I've got glad news. Wait till we sail an' I'll tell you who we're goin' after."

Lib suddenly relaxed and looked in his face. There was no mistaking the light in Dan's eye. He had really some glad news. Lib climbed into the machine and sat back wearily, a poor little sinner with all her spirit gone, and allowed herself to be led away from the scene of her sorrow. Things had been going hard in there where Uncle Darcy was with the bad red-haired man. She knew it by the stern look on his face when the door swung back and she got a glimpse. She knew it by the leer on Tyke's evil face, and by the smug exclamations of the ladies who sat in the backseat and the knowing winks of rough men near the door. She knew it by the hard set of the old judge's mouth as he eyed the witnessess, and by the way he worried them with questions now and then like a cat with a mouse. If anything could be glad now, Lib was ready to believe it.

When they had swung the second corner beyond the courthouse Dan leaned down and whispered:

"Now, Lib, do you know who we're going after? Guess?"

"God, I guess," said Lib drearily. "I guess that's all's could help my Uncle Darcy any. I heard the men say he was as good as hung now!" She caught a sob with a gulp and let the big tears roll down her worried little face.

"Well, I guess God had something to do with it," allowed Dan comfortably. "He generally does. Cut out that weeping, Lib. That's not like you!"

"But it's all my fault!" she sobbed out, utterly broken at last. "It's 'cause I went and took that ride with that nasty red-haired man in his motorcycle. He-he-he made me tell where Uncle Darcy was."

"Why, how did you know where he was?"

"I-I-I *didunt!*" wept Lib. "I made it up. I told a *lie*. I said he was in Canada. And I told God it was a lie, huh-huh-huh!" she sobbed. "But it didunt do any good. God didn't like it." Dan put one arm around her gently.

"There now, Lib, that's all nonsense. You did a brave thing and it didn't have a thing to do with your uncle's trouble. It probably only held the man off a little longer. Besides, there's no need for you to worry anymore. Listen. Who do you think we're going after? Joyce Radway. She's down at Sixty-third Street station waiting for us now. I just talked to her over the phone."

Lib Knox sat up as straight as a pipe stem and her eyes got round and great behind their tears:

"Then He *did* hear!" she said in an awestruck tone.

"Who heard?"

"God heard, away up in heaven like they said in Sunday school. I didn't believe it but now I do. But I tried it anyway, and He heard. I ast Him would He please bring her back to life again and He's done it!"

Dan pressed the little hand he held and said huskily:

"Yes, kid, He's done it. I guess there was more than one asking for that same thing. Well, here we are, and—There she is!"

Chapter 30

The trial had been going hard with Darcy, as little Lib had surmised. Even the old judge had been crabbed in some of his orders, and thrown anxious glances among the witnesses searching in vain for some ray of hope. He loved Darcy and things seemed to be going against him.

Not for one minute in his heart of hearts did Judge Peterson believe that Darcy Sherwood was guilty of such things as he was being charged with, and when he stood up straight and handsome in the prisoner's box to answer to the question: "Guilty or not guilty?" he had admired the straight, clear look with which he faced the roomful of curious enemies and anxious friends. Slowly Darcy had swept the room with his glance as if searching for one on whom he could rely. Anxiously his eyes rested on his sister Ellen, sitting huddled behind her handkerchief, and on the little shrinking Lib, looking so fierce beside her, surprisedly on the minister and his wife, taking in their kindly faces, something true and real about them. He knew they were Joyce's friends and he liked their being there. There was nothing hostile about them. Then his gaze wandered to the four men huddled together in a corner with Tyke spreading himself as their leader, making loud-mouthed remarks and casting furtive, sidelong glances, keeping his eyes away from the prisoner. Darcy took them in half amusedly, wholly comprehending, almost a smile of contempt flitting across his face, before he turned deliberately and faced his enemy, Gene, and looked him keenly down with a cold, righteous glance. Then he turned back to the judge and said quietly, "Not Guilty, Your Honor," as if there had been no pause between the question and the answer. The judge found himself watching the boy and wondering where he got his poise, his cool calm look, that might almost be described as that of peace.

From the start Darcy sat in his place and watched each actor in the little scene before him as if he were somehow outside of it all, detached from the whole thing, as if the outcome were of little moment to him, only the persons.

Darcy had not asked for a lawyer. In fact, he had refused one. He would not ask anybody to help him, nor tell anything that would give a clue to where he had been or what he had been doing. He had told them he would plead his own cause when the time came.

So the evidence went on. Witnesses were sworn in and testified to the most unpleasant details in a well constructed tale of horror. Tyke was clever, but Bill was sharp, and what the two of them could not think out the canny Cottar did. They had left no question unprepared for, no weak places in their line of evidence. They even had an old flashlight of Darcy's they had found where he had left it last at one of their meeting places, and most carefully had they preserved it without handling that the fingerprints might be observed. Obligingly Darcy put out his fingers for the impression, that smile of half amusement on his lips. So well he understood the revenge that was working all this elaborate network of lies to catch him.

Yet as the evidence went on he began to realize how cleverly it had been done, and how only a miracle of some kind could save him. He sat gravely watching it all, listening. Now and then jotting down a note for his own reply when his time came, but for the most part, gravely listening, and the day went on and blacker grew the evidence against him. The excitement in the courtroom was great. There were not wanting gruesome details and Darcy's face grew stern and his soul sick within him. To think that Joyce should, through him, be mixed up in a loathsome mess like this! He would rather have died a thousand deaths than to have had her name connected in such wise.

The spectators were strained to the highest point. Nan, heavily veiled and weeping, was most affected. When it came her turn to testify she told of the beautiful relation between herself and Joyce, but said that Joyce was very secretive and went out a good deal evenings, staying late. Once during Bill's blunt testimony she screamed and fainted and had to be taken out, but insisted on coming back again. And hourly the look of suffering grew on Darcy's face, as if the ordeal were actual physical pain. But once, there was a little relaxing of the strain, when old Noah Casey took the stand, and was asked to swear that he would tell the truth, the whole truth and nothing but the truth.

He climbed into his place and laid a trembling, knotted hand upon the Book, but when they asked him to swear he smiled about upon them and shook his head.

"My mother taught me not to swear," he said serenely, while the four who were sponsoring him frowned and cursed beneath their breath.

He stood there looking about on the throng, his quick bright eyes traveling from one face to another, half suspicious of them all, half frightened like a wild thing of the woods. And when the people laughed he laughed with them at himself. The difficulty about the oath over, he told his story, eagerly, somewhat like a child, in short hurried sentences, his bright eyes still hurrying over the audience, his long nervous fingers fingering the brim of his old felt hat. "I was going acrost the medder—" he began, "ahint of the graveyard—" and Gene's lawyer helped him out with questions. "You saw a bundle on the ground like a human body—" The bright eyes focused on the lawyer an instant.

"No, it was broken glass. Leastways that's what I thought I saw. They tell me—" The lawyer hurried into another question, and the judge interrupted:

"Suppose you look around, Noah, and tell me if you can see the man you saw that night digging in the graveyard?"

The bright eyes focused on the judge, and then turned quickly toward Tyke. The lawyer hastened with his assistance.

"Was it this man, Noah?" he pointed to the prisoner.

Noah Casey turned around toward the box where Darcy sat and saw Darcy for the first time:

"What! *Him?*" he asked, pointing with a long finger at Darcy who regarded him with a grin of friendliness. "Why, no, that's Darcy Sherwood. I know *him*. I've knowed him since he was little tad. Oh, no, it wa'n't Darcy. *He's* a good boy. He wouldn't do such a thing. The man I saw had red ha—"

But Gene's lawyer raised his voice:

"Your Honor, I am disappointed in this witness. Mentally he does not seem to be quite all that I supposed—"

"Undoubtedly," said the judge under his breath, and Noah was hustled off the scene.

But the afternoon came on and somehow the false witnesses were making a pretty good case of it against Darcy. The judge's eyebrows were drawn in a heavy frown and his breath came quick and deep. Those who knew him well knew that he was troubled, and it was just then that Dan's note was handed up.

No one but Darcy noticed the twinkle that came in the judge's eyes, and he wondered and tried to puzzle it out. The judge was his friend he knew, and wanted to see him cleared, but surely all hope was gone. The evidence was all on one side. Why prolong the agony? It almost seemed as if the judge were trying to keep the case going, trying to make time. He asked the most trivial questions and tripped up the lawyer again and again, holding a witness far beyond necessity.

All at once the judge drew a long breath and a light came in his eye. He sat back as if he were done, and ordered that the prisoner be allowed to speak for himself.

The leather door at the back of the courtroom had swung noiselessly but that moment, and little Lib had entered, straight and beaming, and behind her walked a lady, and Dan Peterson. Darcy gave one glance and then arose, and there was a new light in his face. It was almost as if he had come to a triumphant moment, instead of being about to plead for his life in the face of indubitable evidence against him. Those who were watching noticed with a shock that he actually had a kind of smile on his face, and a look of something—could it be peace? What utter nonsense! Perhaps he was going out of his mind. Anyone might, having to listen to such a list of his own horrible crimes!

But Darcy was speaking in his quiet tone:

"It almost seems a pity to add anything after such well established evidence as you all have heard. If I didn't know I wasn't guilty I would almost think I was after listening to what has been said. So I won't try to argue in my own favor. I see Miss Joyce Radway herself has just come in, and I'm going to ask if she may come up here and tell you whether I ever abducted her, or murdered her, or buried her."

Then indeed there was a great stir in the courtroom. People stretched their necks to see, and rose up in their seats, but the judge commanded silence. Under cover of the confusion Tyke attempted to escape, but was stopped by order of the watchful judge.

Joyce came to the front of the room, proudly escorted by Lib who held her hand to the very witness stand and then stood by with glad eyes to watch her.

Joyce turned and faced the excited throng, then looking toward her old friend, Judge Peterson, she spoke in clear, ringing tones that everybody could hear:

"Your Honor, I haven't seen Mr. Sherwood but once since I left home a year ago to go to Silverton and teach. Mr. Sherwood does not know I saw him then. He was making a speech in a religious service in the city where I happened to be one evening, and it was a good speech too. I wish you could have heard it. I tried to get up to speak to him but the crowd was so great that he was gone before I got to the platform."

She turned her face toward the courtroom a little more, looking down at the seats where the witnesses sat, and noticing with startled eyes the man of the loud voice who had addressed her as "girlie" on that memorable morning one year ago.

"I don't know what you have been trying to do to my old friend, Mr. Sherwood, or where you got such utter lies. I went away from Meadow Brook because I wanted to teach and I knew my relatives were opposed to my doing it. I did not realize that I could be misunderstood or make trouble for anybody by doing so, but my going certainly had nothing whatever to do with Darcy Sherwood. We have seldom seen each other since we were schoolchildren together, and he has always been most kind and gentlemanly to me whenever I have met him.

"I happened to see an old copy of the *Meadow Brook News* this morning and read to my horror what you were saying about him and me. It made me sick that my old friends and my relatives could allow such an awful charge to be made on such a man as Darcy Sherwood. I had to get somebody to take my place in school while I came here, and I was afraid I wouldn't get here in time before you did something dreadful you could never be forgiven for. But I'm glad I came, and I'm—*ashamed* of you all."

If anyone had been looking at Darcy then they would have seen a wonderful look in his eyes, but everybody's attention was centered on Joyce. There had not been such a sensation in Meadow Brook in years as the dead coming to life just in time to save a tragedy.

The judge stood up and addressed Darcy. His voice was trembling. He was very unjudgelike in his manner.

"My boy, you are free from the charge and the court dismisses the case." He was smiling and there was something like a mist in his eyes.

Darcy inclined his head slightly.

"Your Honor, I thank you. I am glad to be exonerated from a crime that I did not commit; but I want to ask your permission now to confess to one that I did. I want to take the penalty, whatever it is, and be cleared in the eyes of the law forever."

The courtroom grew suddenly hushed. People who had risen and begun to adjust wraps and pick up their gloves sat down again. All ears were strained to hear every word.

"You have my permission," said the judge looking instantly grave and anxious. "Is the attorney here to take down the confession? Mr. Robinson—"

There was a little stir in the room while the attorney came forward, and then Darcy went on:

"For several months prior to the time last spring when I left town I had been in the bootlegging business."

"Oh! Ah!" were whispered here and there with nods of previous conviction from people who had been half disappointed to have the trial turn out so well.

"I gave it up because I had come to feel that it was wrong. I confess it now because I want to pay the penalty of what I have done. Judge, I will be glad if you will put this through as soon as possible. I am ready to take what is coming to me."

The judge bowed gravely. There was no denying that he looked relieved.

"This will have to go through the regular routine of course," he said, "but it can be run through quickly. Mr. Robinson, you get the items, numbers of cases sold, and so on; prepare the indictment, and we'll try to get it through tomorrow."

The judge straightened up and looked about him, his eyes resting on the four witnesses, holding their hats ready for a speedy departure, and at that moment the district attorney jumped up briskly.

"Your Honor," he said. "I ask that these four witnesses be held for perjury."

A murmur of satisfaction went rippling over the courtroom as people rose to go out.

People were rushing around Joyce as she came out, still escorted by little Lib, proud as a small peacock. Nan was the first to envelope her in a smothering embrace, weeping copiously upon her neck with a loud show of affection. Many old friends lingered, waiting just to watch her dear face alight with the relief and triumph of the moment. The minister and his wife were close behind Nan and eagerly asked her to come home with them.

"No," put in Nan decidedly, "she's coming to her *own* home of course. Everything in your room is just as you left it, *darling—*"

Joyce couldn't help smiling at the affectionate appellative.

"For pity's sake get rid of that awful child, and come on," whispered Nan loudly. "Don't let her hang on you like that. Let's get out of this terrible crowd! How curious people are! Come on home!"

Poor little Lib dropped Joyce's arm as if she had been shot, but Joyce quickly caught the little cold hand and drew it back close with her arm, her own warm fingers keeping the little hand clasped tight.

"I want her here, Nan. She is my dear little friend," said Joyce pleasantly.

"For mercy's sake! You always had such queer friends, Joyce," she laughed disagreeably. "Well, never mind, bring her along, only come on!"

But Dan Peterson's hand was on Joyce's shoulder.

"No, Mrs. Massey, Joyce is coming with us. Father wants to see her right away at home," and off he carried Joyce and Lib in his own big shiny car, while Nan tried to hide her chagrin by taking to herself reflected glory, and trying to make a little social hay while the sun shone.

Joyce went home with the Petersons and was presently sitting in Judge Peterson's library, learning about her inheritance, and being prepared for the reading of the will which was to come after supper as soon as the Masseys could be summoned to the hearing.

But all the time her mind was on the listen, and she was hoping that Darcy would come. Surely, surely he would come and speak to her, just thank her or something. He had been busy with the attorney when she left the courtroom, and had flashed her just one gorgeous smile as she looked back at him. Had she been mistaken? Surely there was a promise in that glance, that he would see her again. She wondered why everything seemed to have suddenly gone so flat. She ought to go back of course on the night train and be ready to teach on the morrow, but her heart was not willing to go—not yet—and Judge Peterson presently settled the matter by saying that she would be needed the next day for the technicalities of the settlement of the estate.

So she sent a telegram to Harrington:

Will be back to teach Monday morning. Cannot possibly come sooner. (Signed)

J. Radway

Chapter 31

The will was read at last.

Gene and Nan, glowering in the corner of Judge Peterson's comfortable library, learned with dismay that their part was only a small patrimony which Mary Massey had in her own right. The rest, house, and meadowlands, and money enough to keep her comfortably were all Joyce's left her by her mother from her own father's estate.

It had been her mother's wish that Joyce should not know that she had anything but herself to depend upon until she grew up. She felt that so she would the better come up unspoiled and independent. So she had placed the property in her sister's hands in such a way that unless Mary Massey died Joyce would not know that she had anything until she came of age. Judge Peterson was the other trustee of the property and

was to use his own discretion about telling Joyce in case of her
aunt's death before her majority. But during the interval of
Joyce's absence from Meadow Brook Joyce had come to her
majority, so there was no longer any hindrance to her entering
into her inheritance at once.

Mary Massey had not told her son the whole thing for rea-
sons of her own, but she had left a letter explaining the matter
to him, and reminding him of what she had always told him,
that she had very little to leave him, but commending Joyce to
his tender care, and saying she had little fear but that Joyce
would always be generous with him.

Gene and Nan arose silently when the business of the will
was concluded. They had a look of withdrawing. A hurt,
stricken look.

Joyce sprang up and went over to them, saying eagerly:

"Of course, Gene, you'll stay in the house."

"It's your house," said Gene. "Of course we'll get right out."

"Please don't," said Joyce earnestly. "At least not unless you
don't want to stay, of course. The house was your mother's
home. All these technicalities of law don't change the matter a
mite to me. I know Aunt Mary expected us all to live there,
and she knew I would say so. Even though it is mine it's just
the same as yours. Besides, I've another little house of my own
in Silverton and I presume I shall go back there and go on
teaching. I should not be happy doing nothing. The house may
have been bought by my father's money, but it was made into a
home by your mother's loving care, and it's yours as much as it
is mine. As long as you live I want you to feel you can live in it
if you want to."

"You could sell it," said Gene, still independently, "or rent
it. I will pay you rent," stiffly.

Joyce laughed.

"No, indeed. You won't pay me rent. If you try to I'll pay you
for your mother's love and care. How would that be? And I
don't want to sell the house. I love it. I like to think it's there
for me to come home to now and then. And, Nan, you don't
need to feel hampered there. You can arrange things just as
you like, just as if it were your own. Just treat me like a sister,
that's all, and share with me in what there is."

"I'm sure that's very generous in you, Joyce," said Gene,
feeling a sense of shame over the way he had always treated
her. "We'll think about it. Aren't you coming home with us
now?"

"Why, I'll be down tomorrow, I guess," she said pleasantly. "I want to get all these papers signed and everything fixed. I must be back on my job Monday, you know."

"I shouldn't think you'd have to teach now," said Nan, an envious note in her voice. "Why don't you just telegraph them you aren't coming back and quit?"

"Why, that wouldn't be honorable," laughed Joyce. "And besides I like it. I wouldn't leave the kiddies for anything till the term is up."

"You're a queer girl," said Nan speculatively. "I don't see why you don't just want to have a good time."

"Why, I'm having a beautiful time," said Joyce, wide-eyed. "I'm doing what I've always wanted to do."

They went home, and the evening passed and still Darcy did not come. Joyce began to wonder if he were not coming at all. If, perhaps, she might be going to have to write him a note or call him up or something; for she did not mean to go back to Silverton without telling him in so many words how glad she was that he had found her Lord.

Joyce spent Friday in going over her things in the old home and packing up what she wanted to take back with her to Silverton, but she went back at night to Judge Peterson's. The minister and his wife came in to call that evening and they had a beautiful talk, but all the time Joyce was listening for a step that did not come, and wondering. Was Darcy still shy? Surely he would come just once after all that had happened, after she had come home to make things straight and set him free.

She thought she heard the minister speak his name as they were about to leave, talking to Dan Peterson over by the door, and Dan said, "Yes, tomorrow," that was all. She wanted to ask, but something held her back, and no one mentioned Darcy. Was it his second trial that was coming off tomorrow she wondered?

She did not sleep well that night. She kept waking and thinking of Darcy. Was he going to have to go to prison after all for bootlegging? It seemed so hard now that he had begun his new life. She wished she dared ask about the law.

The next morning at the breakfast table she followed a sudden impulse and told the judge and his wife all about Darcy's speech in the meeting on the night of the rain. Dan had gone into the hall to answer the telephone and when he came back he tiptoed in and stood by the door quietly, as if someone were praying. His eyes were down and his face looked strangely

tender as if he were hearing a miracle. Neither the judge nor
Dan were much on religion, but Mrs. Peterson was a saint if
there was one, and her face glowed with joy over the story. The
old judge cleared his throat three times before he growled out
the words:

"Yes, Darcy's all right, Darcy's all right." His glasses seemed
to be blurred and he had to take them off and polish them
before he could see right again. "He needn't have confessed
that at all. It was all over and forgot. But still, I like him better
for it. Great stuff in him!"

Then Joyce summoned courage.

"Will he have trouble again, with this other trial? What will
be the penalty? Will he have to go to prison?"

"Oh, no, oh, no! Nothing like that," said the judge hastily.
"Oh, no, he'll just have to pay a penalty. Probably about five
hundred dollars or something like that, according to the
amount of stuff handled. Know how much it was, Dan?"

"About," said Dan gruffly.

"Great boy, Darcy!" said the judge emphatically. "He'll be all
right this morning. Case comes off before noon, doesn't it,
Dan? Where's my notebook?"

"Yes, before noon," said Dan, and then they both went out
and Joyce, with relieved heart, went to singing and playing on
the old tinpanny, yellow-keyed square piano, singing with all
her heart, the song they sang that night in the meeting:

> Free from the law, O sinner, receive it,
> Free from the law, O brother, believe it—!

and Mrs. Peterson, up in her room making her bed and
plumping up the pillows, said to herself happily:

"Bless her dear little heart. I wish we could keep her here."

Darcy came home with Judge Peterson at noon to lunch. He
seemed a new Darcy. His face was alight, and his smile was
joyous.

He did not talk much during the meal, but what he said
rippled with humor, and kept them all in gales of laughter. The
new gravity that was upon him when he was silent sat well
there, and gave him an air of one who had found a solid foundation.

As they arose from the table he looked at Joyce and said in a
tone that everyone could hear:

"Miss Joyce, it's a gorgeous afternoon and I thought perhaps you'd like to take a walk through some of the old paths. I have something I'd like to tell you, and if you don't mind being seen in the company with a lawbreaker like me we might stroll down to the old woods."

Joyce looked up with her face flooded with glory: "Oh, but you're not under the law now, you know," she said brightly.

"No, not in any sense, thank the Lord," said Darcy reverently. "Not even under the law of the land."

They walked down the long, smooth road together past the bridge and around the turn, and there on the hill before them lay the woods in all the beauty of the springtime verdure. They had been talking of the trial, Darcy telling her all that had gone on before she arrived, and also of the second trial where he had paid the fine and been set free. But now, at the turn of the road, they stopped and looked. The scene was so lovely, one could but exclaim at the beauty of the hillside. The fields were green and dotted with violets where they walked, and all about were spicy odors of the spring, with exquisite perfumes in the making. Before them rose the woods, pale greens stippled with red buds on their tips, and a background of darker pines. And now they spoke of Aunt Mary and the day they had spent together.

As they entered the woods frail anemones scattered their pathways, and hepaticas, blue and white, met them in groups where maidenhair hid, and little curled fern fronds stuck up through the black mold. As they walked down that pine-strewn path, flower-broidered and dim, each was conscious of the last time they had passed that way. They had gone out from that arched silence a boy and girl, they were reentering man and woman.

For a few moments neither spoke. Then Darcy, as if he were treading holy ground:

"It was here you sat when I first saw you."

Joyce flashed him a golden look.

"And you there?" she pointed. "I have always wanted to go there and sit myself," she said, "with my feet hanging over that rock."

"Let's go!" he said, and caught her hand.

He helped her down to a comfortable spot, where the mossy rock shelved over the water, and the little brook babbled over bright stones in a quiet, musical way.

Sitting there he told her of the deep experience of his heart.

Of how that day and the story of the blind man had lingered with him all those years, until he came to understand that he was blind, and he was a sinner and needed a Saviour. He told her how her eyes had pierced his soul, like the thought of God searching him, and how he had finally surrendered. He spoke of the peace and joy that were his now, and of his Bible.

And then Joyce told him how she had come in out of the rain and heard him talking, and tried to reach him and failed.

The sun dropped lower in the west and the long shadows came within their sweet retreat. Finally, they sat in silence, just listening to the birds, and the tinkle of the water, feeling how good it was to be here after the years.

Suddenly Darcy began to speak again:

"Joyce, I'm going to tell you something. You may think perhaps I oughtn't to tell you, that I have no right to speak of such things—that I am unworthy. But somehow I think you ought to know. After I've told you I'm not going to presume upon it. I know as well as you do that I'm unworthy. But I've loved you all my life, and it's kept me from a great deal that I might have done if I hadn't. I never dreamed of you as mine, not in any material sense of the word. I always knew I wasn't big enough and good enough for you, but I've kept you like a shrine in a temple, a place to worship at. You can't know what it's meant to me. I'm telling you this because it's the only way I can thank you for what you did for me. You saved my life, and I want you to know that all that a man has to give a woman, that I have given to you. There will never be any other girl for me!"

Joyce's head was turned away. She was trying to keep the blinding joy of her heart from leaping to her eyes.

"And you refuse to let me give anything back to you?" she asked in a little faltering voice.

"What do you mean, Joyce?" He lifted his eyes and looked at her anxiously.

"I mean, does it mean nothing to you that I have loved you too, ever since the day we were here last?"

He caught her hand.

"Joyce! Do you mean that? You loved me all that time? But of course you did not know me, did not know that I was—"

"I loved *you*," said Joyce firmly. "And I love you now. I didn't know it was that when I came home to save you, but I guess it was there all the time only I hadn't told myself about it—yet—"

"Oh, Joyce, my darling!"

He gathered her close to his heart and closed his eyes in an ecstasy of joy.

"It makes me feel so humble!" he said at last looking into her eyes. "To think that I, a sinner, a lawbreaker—"

She laid her fingers on his lips.

"'For ye are not under the law,'" she quoted softly, "'but under grace.' Have you forgotten that He puts His righteousness upon us?"

They came back from their walk in the twilight with the stars looking down upon them and a new moon shining in a clear sky, but they did not see it. They were walking hand in hand and talking of many precious things.

The Petersons had been waiting dinner for them almost an hour, but they were serenely unconscious of the fact.

They went to church the next day and sat in the old Peterson pew, side by side, with the judge and Mrs. Peterson and Dan, for the delectation of all eyes, but they didn't know that either. They were as happy as any two people could be in this world.

Monday morning, with the first ray of light, Darcy was up and at his car, and before the people of Meadow Brook had begun to think about waking up he and Joyce were on their way to Silverton. Joyce had around her shoulders her gray fox neckpiece. Nan had ostentatiously thrown it out the window in the gray of the morning when they stopped there for Joyce's trunk saying: "Here, Joyce, you'll need this. It's chilly. I had it put carefully away for you in camphor all winter."

They had the road to themselves for the first two hours and Darcy's racing engine flew out along the road as smoothly as perfect steel and well-oiled bearings could make it. They drove into Silverton at ten minutes to eight, and went straight to Joyce's little house to leave her trunk, much to the wonder and delight of Mrs. Bryant who hadn't known what to make of Joyce's absence.

Joyce was wearing on her finger a splendid diamond. Darcy had routed a jeweler friend out of bed late Saturday night to get it, and paid for it with a check that almost cleaned his bank account out entirely, but he wore a look on his face of utter happiness.

They drove up to the schoolhouse five minutes before the bell rang, and Professor Harrington stood on the steps talking to a teacher. Joyce was still in her new spring suit and pretty, becoming little hat, with the gray fox around her neck, and Harrington felt his resolve slowly melting away from him. How could one be cold to a girl who looked like that? She certainly was stunning in those clothes. He had thought all along that clothes would make a big difference. But who the deuce was the big, good-looking giant who brought her.

And then the giant stooped and kissed Joyce, and he frowned.

"Was that your brother?" he asked as Joyce came flying up the walk afraid that she was going to be late.

Joyce lifted a saucy face and smiled:

"No, Mr. Harrington," she said sweetly. "That is the man I am going to marry. Have you time to come down and meet him?"

Novels of Enduring Romance and Inspiration by

GRACE LIVINGSTON HILL

BANTAM
SHOP·AT·HOME
C·A·T·A·L·O·G

Special Offer
Buy a Bantam Book
for only 50¢.

Now you can have an up-to-date listing of Bantam's hundreds of titles plus take advantage of our unique and exciting bonus book offer. A special offer which gives you the opportunity to purchase a Bantam book for only 50¢. Here's how!

By ordering any five books at the regular price per order, you can also choose any other single book listed (up to a $4.95 value) for just 50¢. Some restrictions do apply, but for further details why not send for Bantam's listing of titles today!

Just send us your name and address and we will send you a catalog!